P9-DYE-080

THE
SECOND
BOOK
OF
ORE

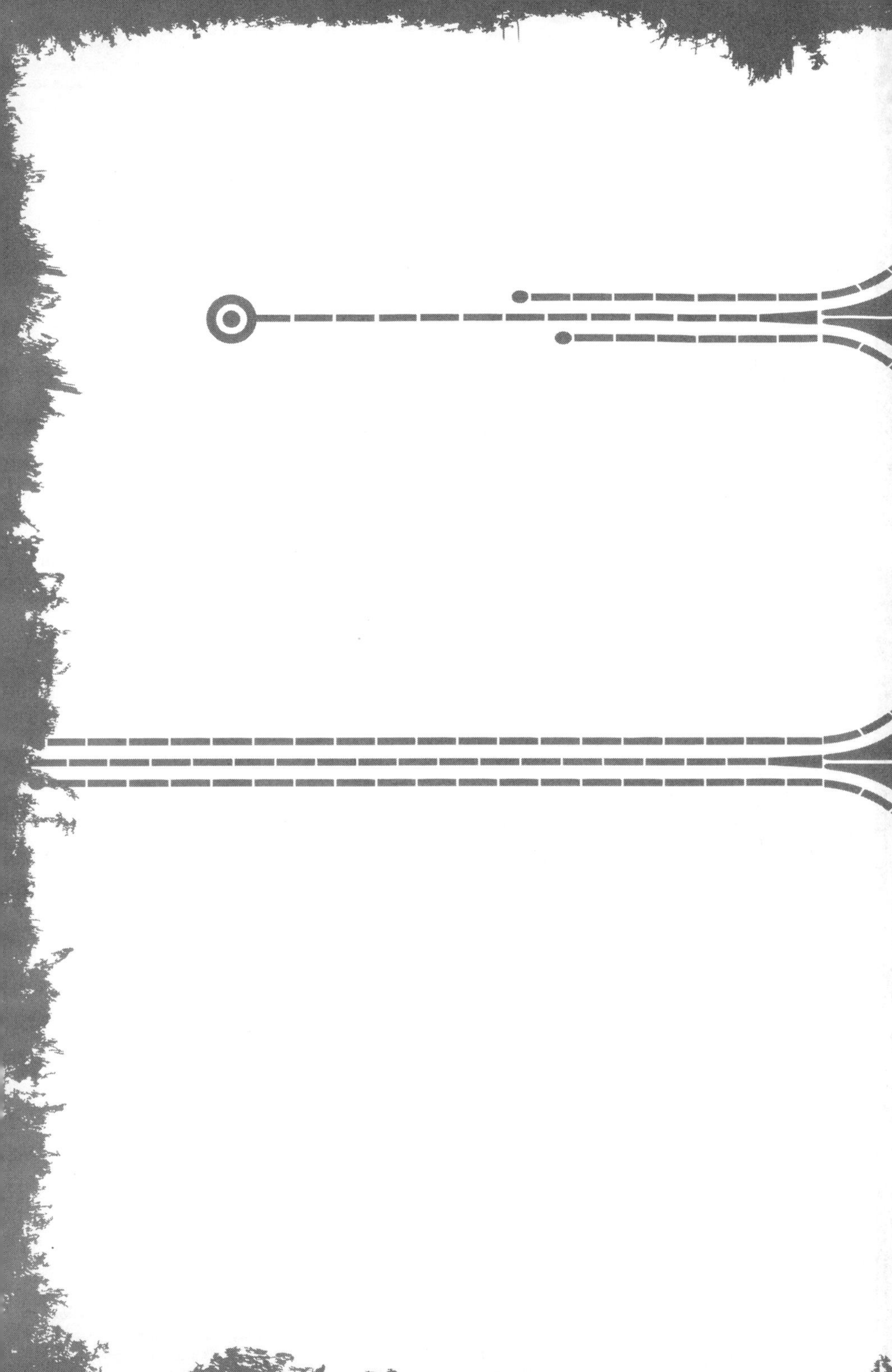

CAM BAITY & BENNY ZELKOWICZ

THE SECOND BOOK OF ORE

WAYBOUND

DISNEY • HYPERION
Los Angeles New York

Printed in the United States of America
First Edition, April 2016
1 3 5 7 9 10 8 6 4 2
FAC-020093-16015

Library of Congress Cataloging-in-Publication Data
Names: Baity, Cameron, author. | Zelkowicz, Benny, author.
Title: Waybound / Cameron Baity ; Benny Zelkowicz.
Description: First edition. | Los Angeles ; New York : Disney * HYPERION, 2016. | Series: The second book of ore | Summary: As the war between the Foundry and Mehk intensifies, Phoebe Plumm and Micah Tanner struggle to decipher a message the Ona—a speaker for the God, Makina—has given them.
Identifiers: LCCN 2015019320 | ISBN 9781423162391 (hardcover)
Subjects: | CYAC: Science fiction. | Adventure and adventurers—Fiction. | Metals—Fiction.
Classification: LCC PZ7.B1677 Way 2016 | DDC [Fic]—dc23
LC record available at http://lccn.loc.gov/2015019320

Map illustration on pp. 172–173 by Kayley LeFaiver

Reinforced binding

Visit www.DisneyBooks.com

THIS LABEL APPLIES TO TEXT STOCK

For Minky and Binky
—CB

For my parents, who have always blazed the way
—BZ

PROLOGUE

THE SPARK

In the time before, nothing was all.

It stretched vast and fathomless, a den of infinity.

Alone in the void dreamed Makina. Everseer was She, Divine Dynamo brooding in the dark of absence. Yet lo—within the Forge of Her mind flickered a spark of life. The first light of the Way.

The Everseer looked upon this nothingness and was not content. Thus She spake, calling into the void the first word.

"BE."

And Makina set about Her work.

She laid out Her infinite and infallible plan as a foundation for all things, seen and unseen, known and unknown. Across this, She stretched the Expanse, which was the course of all-time. And to drive existence forward, Makina crafted the gears of fate. Then smiled the Great Engineer upon this, Her sacred machine.

Yet Her creation had no function. And She was not content.

So Makina did take of Her own flesh, tearing out a piece of Her heart of Ore. And from this did She form Mehk, from its grandest peak to its lowest crevasse. And from the rent in Her body poured forth Her lifeblood, glistening silver flux, and it pooled upon the world to become the mighty seas.

Lo, the Everseer did weep, for She loved Her creation.

And Her tears were embers, scattering across the world. From Her mouth a sweet breath did blow, stoking the embers with life. And from the living Ore did sprout the first mehkans, embers bright, and they went forth to see Her work.

Thus, with a spark of life, Her sacred machine engaged.

Praise be to Makina, Divine Dynamo, beloved Mother of Ore.

Accord I: Edicts 01–09

1

WANTED

Hieromylous T.R. Pynch was snoring on the patchwork floor, puddled like a deflated tire, when the building around him shifted with a weary groan. He snorted awake and found himself surrounded by gray, decomposing walls. It took him a groggy moment to remember where he was.

Right. He and the Marquis were in Sen Ta'rine. Imprisoned.

Mr. Pynch scratched at his bushel of spiny hair, which matched the scraggly mess of his muttonchops and brows. The fat nozzle in the middle of his lumpy face rotated like the cylinder of a revolver, and his mouth crumpled into a scowl.

The lanky Marquis was still bustling about on his telescoping limbs, just as he had been when Mr. Pynch passed out. The Marquis scrubbed with a tattered hanky at the array of lenses wreathing his signal lamp head and plucked at his metal-threaded tuxedo. Damnable busybody lumilows barely ever slept, Mr. Pynch noted. No wonder they were so uptight.

A wash of early light bled through the tattered skin of the walls, exposing its shadowy, bat-wing scaffolding. The suns were already up? That would mean they had been confined in this blasted, dilapidated tower for nearly fourteen clicks.

"If yer gonna tromple about like that," grumbled Mr. Pynch, "at least try and peep us out an escapement."

The Marquis narrowed the shutters on his opticle eye and flared back an illuminated message: *Flick-flick-flash.*

"Don't you go scapegoatin' me, ya puffed up muteling!" Mr. Pynch blustered. "I forewarned ya. 'Best lay low after our little transaction with the bleeders,' I said. And what do you do? Jaunt over to the nearest Sliverytik parlor, lose our hard-won gauge in a single toss, and then make a grandiose spectacle of it!" Mr. Pynch rose and puffed up his belly, causing his spines to nudge out from the flaps of his overcoat. "If it wasn't for you, we never would have gotten ambushed and incarcified."

The Marquis pointed at Mr. Pynch with a tainted white glove and blasted back a glaring argument.

"Oh, puddlemudge!" Mr. Pynch retorted. "I didn't encourage you one smidgeon!"

Flickery-flash. The opticle blasted an even brighter message.

"Well, if I did, it was just the viscollia talking!"

Blinkety-flash-flash!

"Look now, I've had just about enough o' yer—"

FLASHY-FLASH!

"ME? You be the one that's yelling!"

The partners threw up their hands and stalked away from each other. Mr. Pynch grumbled to himself, irritated.

He thought back to their abduction. At first, he had assumed it was the Foundry, but then his nozzle had detected the distinctive musk of their captors. There was no doubt—they were in the custody of mehkies.

But who? And why?

All they could tell was that they were still somewhere in the slums of the Heap. Mr. Pynch and the Marquis had been blindfolded in transit, but left alone in their cell, they had peeled up the shriveled skin of a wall to find themselves looking down on the city, teetering at the top of a skeletal sendrite skyscraper.

Only two ways out—a barricaded door or a long drop down.

A click came from the nearby hatch, then a dull grind like an axe being sharpened as the door swung open.

Five figures entered. The first was a volmerid, his tremendously oversized right arm barely fitting through the door.

Even though they knew his imposing bulk was mostly shaggy brown steel wool, Mr. Pynch and the Marquis couldn't help but backpedal. His fist of a face was hard and curled, glaring out from behind his matted coat. Like most simpleminded volmerids, this one was probably nothing more than a grunt and a thug. They would find no ally in him.

Spilling in behind the vol was a trio of identical shapes that melted into the shadows like liquid jets of black. Aios. Mr. Pynch didn't mind untrustworthy types—in fact, they made up the majority of his clientele—but the aios' inscrutability and cultish secrecy was something else altogether. Glimpsing an aio's cloaklike form or its gnarls of stabby limbs usually meant someone had hired the spook to kill you. *Three* aios, well, that was an unheard of kind of bad.

Then Mr. Pynch saw the last figure enter the room and breathed a hearty sigh of relief. "Jubilations and salutations," he beamed. "Immoderately pleased to make yer acquaintance."

The newcomer glided across the floor, the supple belt of her lower half humming through a glinting framework of rollers. Her body was draped in flexible metal bands that wound through her sprocketed figure like a helical gown. A pair of keen coppery eyes perched high on the long mask of her face.

The thiaphysi were regarded for their intellect and eloquence, but Mr. Pynch's sudden enthusiasm was due to their reputation for sentimentality (and gullibility). As the ribbons of her body whirled through her rollers, the mehkan's slender fingers danced across the belts, emitting a singsong voice from her hands.

"I apologize for your undignified treatment," the thiaphysi said, "but immediate action was required, and secrecy is our priority. We know what you have done."

"Pardon?" Mr. Pynch's mouth was suddenly dry. The Marquis's shutters fluttered anxiously.

"The conflict in the Vo-Pykarons," she continued. "The part you two played in hindering the capture of liodim."

Mr. Pynch's nozzle ticked, trying to sniff out a mood on the thiaphysi. He detected the bitter tang of irritation. Was she angry about the Vo-Pyks? Perhaps these mehkies were bleeder collaborators, planning on selling him and the Marquis out.

"We had no intention of tampering with the Foundry's operations. Me associate and I endeavored to avoid engaging—"

"It was a noble deed," she interrupted, the words emanating from her hands. "You have our deepest gratitude."

"—until we could strategize the most effective means of disrupting the cull," continued Mr. Pynch without missing a beat. "If there be one thing we cannot abide, it be injustice. We felt the urgent need to rescue the liodim posthaste."

Blinkety-blink-flash, the Marquis strobed with excitement.

The thiaphysi glanced at the Marquis but gave no indication that she understood. Prompted by his partner's urgent words, Mr. Pynch looked again at the thiaphysi and her cohorts and gasped as he saw the familiar symbol adorning their chests.

Well, rust take him! How could he have missed that?

"To be downright frankly with you," Mr. Pynch confessed with a grimy golden smile, "we had little choice in the matter. It felt to be our duty. Our function, you might say."

Their captors exchanged a brief look.

"You are Waybound?" she asked, clutching a delicate fist over her blood-red dynamo.

"Praise the gears!" Mr. Pynch proclaimed. The Marquis emitted a burst of joyous light. "Here we were, cogitating that we were the only pilgrims left in the Lateral Provinces still adhering to the edicts. Well, that be that. I suppose we'll be on our way then. Gettin' on with doing Her good work."

"Of course," came the thyaphysi's gestured words. "Perhaps you intend to bring Her message back to the Gauge Pit?"

The Marquis's opticle faded. The pungent stab of pure loathing curdled in Mr. Pynch's nozzle.

"Now it not be . . ." he began, then stopped to collect his racing thoughts. "What precisely did you hear? The facts be obscure, but I most suredly assure you, they do exonerate us."

"Silence," snarled the volmerid, shaking his matted mane of steel wool. He retracted the chain-link digits of his grotesquely swollen fist with a snap.

Mr. Pynch and the Marquis saw a ripple of movement in the corner. They turned to face the aios—the ghastly mehkies were closer, now within striking distance, frozen like statues of black ice. They hadn't made a sound.

"We know all about you," the thiaphysi said, the movements of her speaking hands choppy across her spiraling ribbons. "Informants and parasites. You vowed to protect the children, then betrayed them." Her fingers were an agitated blur.

Unconsciously, Mr. Pynch's hands fluttered to the rough stitches that Phoebe had made on his green silk necktie. "The bleeders?" he asked, confused. "What they be to you?"

"That is not your concern," she stated harshly. "You are prisoners. Fugitives of the Foundry for your actions in the Vo-Pykarons, reviled by us for deceiving the children." She lowered her singsong voice. "Your embers are forfeit."

Mr. Pynch braced himself, tensing his legs to evade the attack he knew must be coming. The Marquis tightened his grip on his dingy umbrella.

"And yet . . ." she said, the silken belts slowing through her hands. "There is another way. Makina shapes a path even for those who are lost. You must make amends."

"What way?" queried Mr. Pynch. "What you be wanting?"

"Not what we want. What She wants. We will spare you. In exchange, you will serve Her."

Flicker-flash-blink.

Mr. Pynch agreed with the Marquis. This did not bode well.

"Aid us in our strike against the Foundry." The thiaphysi leaned in very close, and her potent hate made Mr. Pynch want to cap his nozzle. "Or we, the Covenant, will send you to meet Her beyond the Shroud."

DOWNPOUR

James Goodwin adjusted his broad frame in the absurdly ornate armchair to keep its stony cushion from cutting off his circulation. It never failed to amaze him how gaudy and outmoded these people's taste was, with none of the Foundry's modern, streamlined elegance. Through a circular window trimmed with brocaded curtains, he saw ponderous clouds enveloping the embassy, while the yellow and indigo flag of Trelaine snapped fiercely in the winds from the bay.

Normally, it was good to return to Albright City. Not today.

He had been alone in this oppressive office for an hour, taking care not to glance at the Omnicams, lest it convey impatience. Premier Lavaraud was undoubtedly taking pleasure in keeping him waiting, but Goodwin would not acknowledge the insult. He sat inert, gazing placidly at the patriotic busts and tedious porcelain knickknacks vainly adorning every shelf.

"Be submissive and present the offer as we instructed."

"You will not return until he agrees to the new terms."

The voices of the enigmatic Board in Foundry Central were like drips of poison in his mind. As part of Goodwin's punishment, a silver bud had been grafted to his inner ear, and it was still sore where the device had been affixed. Now there was no way to evade their pestilent words.

In all his years working for the Foundry, he had only met the five representatives, or directors, as they were known. Of course, their faces had changed on occasion as one was demoted or replaced, but their purpose was always the same: to speak for the Board. No one knew a thing about the Foundry's true masters—not their number, their identities, or their ultimate intentions. Until receiving this detestable earpiece, Goodwin had never even heard their voices. Now he was never free of them. It was just one of many humiliations he had suffered in the long hours since the fall of the Citadel.

"Address him at all times as 'Your Excellency.'"

"Assume all responsibility."

One line was repeated over and over, as if he could forget: *"We are listening."*

At last, Lavaraud entered, brushing past Goodwin without a word of greeting. He was dressed in a long, traditional Trelainian topcoat of dark blue silk, secured by ivory fastenings.

Though the Premier was a small man, he was whip lean and imposing with a sepulchral face capped in a helmet of salt-and-pepper hair. Lavaraud's eyes were dark, hooded by heavy lids that seemed to blink in slow motion.

"Your Excellency," Goodwin intoned, forcing a kindly smile. "You have my thanks for meeting on such short notice."

"I detest your city," Lavaraud stated, his heavily accented voice hard and inexpressive, as he sat behind a vast mahogany desk. "I arrive in ungodly heat and now this?" He gestured to the overcast sky outside. "I detest all things . . . unpredictable."

"Yet we are honored by your presence," Goodwin replied.

"Your Excellency," instructed a voice in Goodwin's earpiece.

"Your Excellency," he added.

"Praise him for allowing diplomatic relations to resume."

"Allow me to express our gratitude that Trelaine has chosen to ally with Meridian, Your Excellency. We are fortunate to have such a committed partner for peace. Needless to say, the day your nation leaves the Quorum will be a momentous occasion."

"Let us be clear," the Premier declared. "You are buying our conditional loyalty, and we have accepted. Conditionally. A bribe, nothing more. Now come to the point. You are not here to merely ooze flattery."

Goodwin ran a hand through his snow-white hair, brushing his tender ear where the bud was implanted. "Of course, Your Excellency. As you recall, your shipment of metal substrates, ultra-high-tensile ingots, beams, and components was to arrive in full by the week's end. Unfortunately, we are experiencing a series of production setbacks that has led to key raw materials being contaminated, thus—"

"You take me for a fool?" bellowed Lavaraud as he sprang to his feet. "You would toy with Trelaine at such a time? How dare you try and scheme your way out of this!"

"Remain contrite."

"Mollify him. This is the crucial moment."

"Your Excellency," pleaded Goodwin, clutching his hands together. "I share your frustration. Which is precisely why I have come to you with a more favorable offer."

"He will acquiesce. Trelaine's economy needs this."

"Favorable for whom?" seethed Lavaraud.

"Trelaine, of course," Goodwin softly explained. "I believe you will be quite pleased with the generous compensation. All we ask is your continued patience and understanding."

"Patience! All your promises, all your puffery and rhetoric. Pah!" he spat. "Admiral Imaro is right to lobby for the Quorum to cease peace talks with Meridian. Perhaps war is the only option."

"Submit, James."

"This is your doing. Assume all responsibility."

"Your failure at the Citadel has caused this predicament."

"Your Excellency. I know you are a prudent and honorable man. I know that you seek only what is best for your people. Please, hear me out."

"And why would I trust a word of what you have to say?

You break one vow, then offer another." Lavaraud sneered. "What kind of man are you?"

Goodwin lowered his head, sighed heavily, and began to weave his story. "A man disgraced, I confess. In my haste to expedite the process, I issued an order to bypass the Foundry's usual inspection regimen. That is how your shipment came to be contaminated. Rather than send you an inferior product, I have elected to personally beg your forgiveness. And as a sign of good faith, I am prepared to improve upon my initial offer."

Lavaraud's stare bored into him. Goodwin withdrew a document from his coat pocket.

"One half of the agreed-upon shipment, delivered as scheduled by the end of the week, prior to the Council of Nations conference," Goodwin said. "The remaining half, plus an additional ten percent in raw materials, will be delivered no more than two weeks later."

Lavaraud scoured the document as he dropped into his seat.

For the first time since the earpiece had been implanted, Goodwin savored a moment of silence as the Board awaited the Premier's response.

"Twenty percent," Lavaraud uttered through clenched teeth.

Goodwin furrowed his heavy white brows.

"And because of your failure," Lavaraud added, "I must delay Trelaine's exit from the Quorum."

"But Your Excellency, I—"

"Let him speak, James."

"Until I see this payment in full, how can there be trust? The Foundry must prove its dedication to our alliance before I can make such a bold declaration and abandon my comrades."

"Let him have this small victory."

"But ensure that he doesn't jeopardize our deal in the interim."

"I understand your concerns," Goodwin said. "The Foundry, of course, will need your assurance that Trelaine will remain neutral and make no further commitments to the Quorum."

Lavaraud gave a slight nod. "For the time being."

"Accept."

"Then it is done." Goodwin returned the document to his breast pocket. "Our team will revise the amendment as discussed and return it for your signature within the hour. I assure you. There will be nothing else . . . unpredictable."

Goodwin chuckled, but the Premier was not amused. He pushed a button on his desk, and a security escort appeared.

"My profound thanks for your understanding, Your Excellency," Goodwin said with a hand pressed over his heart, "and again my most humble apologies."

He bowed to Lavaraud and followed the escort out of the room, maintaining his expression of heartfelt repentance until his back was to the Premier.

"We approve."

"An acceptable performance."

Never had Goodwin groveled so. He was a worn-out old lion, tormented and tamed, forced to perform tricks for invisible ringmasters. It sickened him to the core.

He was escorted out the embassy's front doors and into the sinking sauna of the day's foul weather. His suit clung to him like a wet bandage as he was led down a hedge-lined walkway, through lofty wrought-iron gates, and off the premises.

"Where is my driver?" Goodwin muttered as the embassy doors clanged shut behind him.

"Ten minutes."

His lips curled in a knot—the insults were never ending.

"A taxi then," he muttered.

Despite the humid drizzle, Goodwin straightened his lapels and held his head high as he marched down the sidewalk. The florid stonework walls of the embassy, weatherworn and spattered in years of pigeon filth, were an eyesore. They diminished the swooping grace of Albright City's iconic bronze streetlights. Goodwin's resentment grew with every step.

A convoy of black Autos approached with predatory speed. Three vehicles squealed to a stop by the curb while another two hurtled into position, cutting off any retreat.

"What is this?" he demanded.

"Be patient, James. Your Auto is in transit."

A door flashed open. Agents in black suits and sunglasses emerged to scan the streets—not Watchmen.

"We have a problem," Goodwin muttered.

"What is it?"

"Here, Mr. Goodwin," said an agent, opening the back

door of one of the Autos. A group of familiar faces stared out at him.

"James. Report."

He ducked inside the Auto and settled onto its luxurious leather seat as the door slammed shut. Goodwin nodded pleasantly to the five scowling officials that surrounded him. The gentleman in the middle was remarkably handsome, tanned and fit, with meadow-green eyes and sculpted chestnut hair dusted with just enough gray to warrant the word "distinguished." At the moment, his famous face was devoid of its trademark smile.

"Hello, Mr. President," Goodwin said, nodding to the others. "Ladies and gentlemen of the Cabinet. What a pleasant surprise."

"Saltern?"

"Find out what he wants."

"We have no time for his petty grievances."

"The hell it is," Saltern snapped. "Where have you been hiding, James? We've been trying to track you down for a week."

The sunken face of Dr. Jules Plumm flashed across Goodwin's mind—the two of them sharing that precious bottle of Chequoisie on the now-fallen Citadel's balcony.

"Abroad," Goodwin lied. "Attending to operations overseas." Not even the President of Meridian was permitted to know about the existence of Mehk and the Foundry's secret dealings there.

"No more evasions," cut Saltern. "Explain yourself."

"Pardon me?" Goodwin replied. He was not accustomed to being addressed in such a way, much less by this petulant man.

"You're negotiating with the Trels," Saltern interrupted. "Behind my back!"

Goodwin considered the members of the Cabinet.

"That's right," Saltern continued. "I know all about your little deal with Lavaraud. What are you up to?"

It took tremendous effort for Goodwin to keep his tone cordial. "Time was of the essence, Mr. President. You know that under normal circumstances, I much prefer to consult with you directly. But the Foundry saw an opportunity to undercut the Quorum's hold, and we acted. Of course, we did so knowing it was your intent to seek a peaceful settlement to—"

"Not by selling out to the enemy!" snarled the President.

"We are not selling," Goodwin corrected. "We are buying."

"If you think that silkbelly will be won over by your bribes, James, then you are a bona fide idiot."

"Do not presume to—" Goodwin began, his words sharp.

"Keep your temper! We cannot afford to antagonize him."

"Tell him whatever you have to. Just be rid of him."

"If this gets out, there will be a feeding frenzy," Saltern growled. "Prime Minister Kura of Moalao called my administration 'a mob of sniveling piglets.' I have an election in less than a year, James. The last thing I need is the Foundry undermining my authority with backroom deals!"

Goodwin took a deep breath. "Mr. President, I was only—"

"And just what do you think happens when the rats suspect

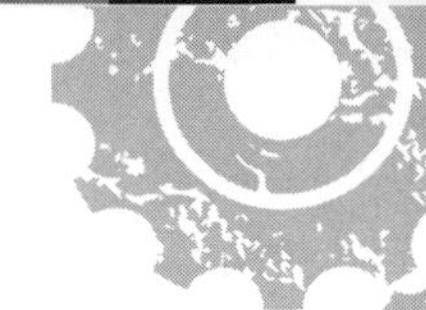

we are weak? They come in a swarm. Well, it is my job to protect the people of Meridian."

"Sir, I was pursuing a diplomatic solution on your behalf."

"You'll do nothing without my involvement, understand? Nothing. I am not, I repeat, NOT the Foundry's puppet!"

"Defuse the situation and leave."

Goodwin had suffered enough of little men shouting at him. But he resigned himself, relaxed the growing tension in his shoulders, and swallowed down his pride.

"On behalf of the Foundry, I apologize for circumventing your command, Mr. President," said Goodwin, the epitome of calm. "The error was mine alone, and it will not happen again."

"Let's hope not," Saltern huffed, and his Cabinet looked on in approval. "Now is not the time to cozy up to these thugs. We need to put our foot down and stand tall, or this great nation will never be secure." An advisor whispered something into the President's ear. "Cancel your deal with Lavaraud."

It took all Goodwin's willpower to not strike the man.

"And put everything you promised him directly into Meridian's defenses."

"I . . ." Goodwin assumed his friendliest expression. "Of course, Mr. President. I will submit it to the Board for approval."

"No," ordered Saltern. "If you can find the resources for those conniving Trels, then you can do the same for your own country. Do it now. You're the Chairman of the Foundry, are you not?"

It hit him like a sucker punch. There was no way Saltern could have known, but still the words wounded. Goodwin hid his fury behind a professional smile.

"I will begin the transfer process this very day."

"That's more like it." Saltern knocked on the window, and an agent opened the door. Goodwin was abruptly dismissed.

"Oh, and James," the President called. "Step out of line again and there will be real consequences."

The door shut, and the convoy sped away.

"Return to Mehk."

"Chairman Obwilé has a new assignment for you."

Goodwin's icy eyes stared after the Autos.

Chairman Obwilé. He was not ready to accept those words. That conniving little worm had seized the opportunity and stolen his title. This was not how things were supposed to be. Not at all.

The bruised sky growled, and a warm rain fell. He huddled his shoulders and pulled up his collar against the downpour.

Deputy Manager Goodwin waited for his driver, who was nowhere in sight.

RUSTING RITES

The Covenant camp was submerged in a canyon overgrown with bulbous, branching growths that looked like a network of pitch-black neurons. A few beams of sunlight and the ghostly glow of cocoon lanterns painted everything in mournful shadows. Hundreds of mehkans were assembled in silent reverence, crowded into the temple courtyard. They dotted niches in the walls and perched on cast-iron vegetation that filled the canyon.

Movement caught Phoebe's attention, and she turned her bloodshot eyes upward. The camp was hidden at the base of a primeval jungle, concealed by a camouflaged roof that mimicked the surrounding undergrowth. She watched the silhouette of a beast lumber across the canopy and envied the wandering creature. All she wanted was to be free from this place, from this moment—to vanish into the jungle without a trace.

Phoebe was a husk. She hadn't slept or eaten since they had arrived the previous day. She hardly knew anything anymore.

All she knew was agony. And that this was her dad's funeral.

A platform of dark, polished ore had been erected atop a fresh grave, one among many gently sloping mounds. Micah and Dollop stood on either side of her in solemn vigil, surrounded by the Covenant. Dollop whispered translations of the prayers and proceedings, but his hazy words washed over her. Micah was silent and stoic, his jaw set firmly and her father's Dervish rifle slung over his shoulder.

He hadn't moved more than an arm's length from her since their encounter with the Ona's likeness at the Hearth. She knew he must have been drowning in grief too, aching to spill it out, but she was glad he kept it to himself. Or maybe the relentless knife of loss had carved away his words.

On the platform before them, three axials in shiny robes shuffled about, reciting prayers in Rattletrap to which the crowd responded in unison. Phoebe was fixated on the raised bier behind them, the altar where her father had been laid. All she wanted was to see his face, but her view was obscured. The voices of the Covenant gathered into a rumbling vibration that she could feel in her belly. Their prayer shifted like snow banks, harmonies melting into one another in dreamy patterns. Then Axial Phy stepped forward.

"Come, Loaii," she croaked, reaching a hand out to Phoebe.

Her gut twisted. She could feel hundreds of expectant eyes.

"No," Phoebe whimpered. "Tell them to do it without me."

Dollop gently took her arm to guide her forward.

"Hey, she don't want to," Micah hissed, grabbing her other arm to hold her back.

"Sh-she must!" Dollop insisted. "Phoebe is-is his only cl-clan. Only she c-can bear the rust for him."

"But she said . . ."

Micah's words crumbled as Phoebe pulled from his grip.

She mounted the steps as if in a trance. The collective moan of the crowd grew louder. Axial Phy, her face half-hidden by the twinkling chains that dangled from her headpiece, clutched Phoebe's hand firmly. Her arthritic claws were warm, the skin loose and crinkled like a dried leaf. The axial turned Phoebe around to face the crowd, and she hadn't the strength to resist.

The Covenant camp stared. Phoebe kept her head down, not brave enough to face the chanting sea, the penetrating eyes. It was all she could do to pretend that none of this was real.

The crowd parted and five figures stepped forth. Phoebe recognized Orei, her shifting body of midnight-blue rings glinting. With her was the hulking crane-claw mehkan known as Treth and three others who must have also been Covenant Overguards. They carried an ancient hunk of metal that came up to Phoebe's belly, and with a gritty clunk, they set it at her feet.

Wide at the base and tapered at the top, the artifact was layered in carvings and bored through with an arrangement of holes. There was a circular window encrusted in years of green patina that displayed its gleaming heart—a column of interlocking golden teeth like the markings of a dynamo.

"Turn the gears, Loaii," spoke Axial Phy as she motioned to a handle jutting from the side of the device.

Hands pressed on Phoebe's shoulders, and she obeyed their command to kneel. She tugged weakly at the crank, but the mechanism was rusted and its teeth wouldn't budge. Out of the corner of her eye, she saw Micah move to help, but Dollop held him back.

Phoebe tried again, throwing her weight against the handle. Reluctantly, the gears groaned and began to inch forward. The artifact released a shriek like an animal in pain, and the Covenant's collective prayer rose in pitch to match it. Phoebe strained her entire body. The screech clawed through her, as piercing and wretched as her own suffering. She poured herself into the effort, focusing every ounce of pain into the exertion.

The raucous scream of the device reached a crescendo, as did the mehkan chant. Just when she thought she might collapse, Axial Phy pulled her back. The grating mechanism continued to steadily churn, caught up in the momentum she had created. Then the crowd went quiet, and Phoebe heard something new as the noise molted its harshness like dead skin.

It was a strange musical tone quite unlike anything she had ever heard. The resonance was eerie, wavering and multiplying, wrought with an aching sadness beyond words.

It was a dirge, like a choir of iron angels.

A warm sensation spread across the back of her head, then trickled down her neck. She looked up with a start—the axials were emptying a decanter on top of her, anointing Phoebe in a pearlescent substance that was thick as glue. They manipulated the stuff with great care as it flowed over her.

She gasped, too stunned to protest.

The axials eased Phoebe to her feet as the viscous liquid seeped down her shoulders and arms, all the way to the ground. The priestesses worked their hands in darting movements, sculpting the fluid into billowing sheets, contoured to her slender frame. It oozed over her head to form a cowl, and a veil of rivulets gelled into swaying beads before her face. The material dried and darkened to a lifeless orange-brown, congealing into a smooth film like the membrane of an egg.

The world went quiet.

At first, Phoebe assumed the mournful tone had stopped, but she could see that the gears continued to churn. The axials' mouths were moving in a chant, yet she heard nothing. The absence of noise was absolute. Whatever this supple garment was, it embraced her in merciful silence.

Axial Phy bent down and gathered up a pile of rust that

had flaked off the artifact's gears. She parted Phoebe's veil and smudged red runes onto her forehead. The old mehkan trickled the rest of the rust into Phoebe's cupped hands.

Then Phoebe was led to the raised bier where her father lay. As she approached, all warmth drained away.

Her father had been laid out on a dark slab framed in decorative coils of burnished copper vine. His body had been rubbed from head to toe in flaking gold leaf so that he glowed like a setting sun. He looked blissful, an ancient idol, a remnant from some vanished civilization. Through her smear of tears, Phoebe could still see a cruel splotch of red marring the gold—the fatal wound on his chest where Kaspar had struck him.

An uncontrollable seizure of grief shook her.

Axial Phy guided Phoebe's hands to sprinkle the rust over her father's body. Her tears fell with the flakes. The five Covenant Overguards held the copper vines and unwound them from wide, flat seed casings. The growths were natural pulleys, and as the mehkans fed out the vines, hand over hand, the slab shifted and descended like an elevator.

She was not ready for this. She would never be ready.

Because of the soundproof shawl, all she could hear was her own rasping breath as her father sank to his final resting place.

Phoebe watched the glimmer of her father's golden form fade into the ore, the splotch of blood going black—her one and only dying light. Her mind plunged with him into darkness.

RAW

creeeeee. Screee.

Pain is all that's left of me. All that I am.

Greencoats found me at the Citadel. Brought me here, to their lab at the Depot. So close to the tunnel home. Yet they keep me in Mehk. Keep me on this slab. My prison.

They used to come in, with starched collars and flaking dry skin. Stank of antiseptic, masking my spoiled blood on their hands. I tried to fight. Tried to scream. Could only gurgle and splatter.

So they don't come in anymore.

Blinding lights. The white was too much, erupting in my eyes. I closed them. Didn't help. Lids too thin, transparent as insect wings.

So they took the light away.

Screeeeeeeee.

And the sound. A wall of noise that made my brain curdle. Crashing machines, hurricane fans on Computators, voices shrieking at me.

So they took the sound away. Quiet as death.

Except that squeak.

What is that? Why are they making that noise? They're doing it on purpose, trying to torture me. Bet they can read my thoughts with their machines. Know what I will do to them.

That's why they're afraid of me.

Their needles plug my arteries, long glass ones like icicles. Are they taking poison out or pumping it in? Straps on the gurney sink in deep. I feel my skin trying to grab them, to hold on.

Not skin. No skin anymore.

Nothing contains me. No boundary between in and out. I'm a heap of nerves and jellied bones plugged into their machines.

Screeeeee. Screee.

Thundering footsteps. I dare to open my eyes. Try to focus in the dark. I hear the rattling scratch of a paper suit and respirator. Gear to protect them from me. It crashes in my ears.

A figure approaches.

It's him! I knew he'd come. Feel a new acid burning my eyes.

Mr. Goodwin.

He can change this. Will fix me. Put me back together.

Something in his hands. A clipboard with a light. Scorches. Can't look. But he's walking slowly. Carefully. He knows the sound hurts. The only one who doesn't want to give me pain.

He will make me better again.

Mr. Goodwin sits in a chair next to me. I try to turn, but the tendons in my neck are pulled too tight, ready to pop. He angles his little light to see me. Mucus breath rattles my deflated lungs. I squirm on the gurney, and his paper suit rustles.

He's afraid too. Fear of this raw and dripping thing. He thought he could manage the sight of me, but how could he?

How could anyone?

Screeeeeeeee.

Still that sound. Mr. Goodwin can make it stop. I hear his pen hacking at the clipboard. Loud. But he knows that his voice would be unbearably loud. Holds the words so I can see.

"I CAME AS SOON AS I HEARD."

I try to speak. Only a coarse, liquid grunt. Not words. I try again, a dying thing. He motions for me to relax.

"THE DIRECTORS HAVE TAKEN OVER THE DYAD PROJECT."

My wheezing breath comes faster, toxic clouds raking my insides. The shreds of my fingers clench. He writes more.

"THEY ARE DOING THIS TO YOU."

Rage shakes me like an electrical current. I fought the metal inside me. Consumed it. All for them. But it was never enough.

Now they hold me prisoner. Murder me, again and again.

I heave against my restraints, feel them carve into my muddy flesh. Foulness oozes from my pores, cauterizes my fists. Feel the metal in my knuckles bubble as I grasp at the straps.

Mr. Goodwin writes.

"I CAN HELP."

The fight bleeds out of me.

Screeeeee. Screee.

"BUT I NEED SOMETHING FIRST."

What? What could I possibly do?

"YOU WENT AFTER PLUMM."

The name sends a twist of agony coursing through me.

It's true. I ignored my orders. Even worse, I failed.

Mr. Goodwin is angry. That's why he came—to punish me for disobeying. And I deserve it. Deserve . . . this. I try to apologize, but I can't untangle the words in the ruined sore of my mouth.

"IS HE DEAD?"

Instantly, I feel it. My body remembers the sensation with razor clarity. Perfection. Plumm's sternum bowing under my blow. My fist collapsing the ladder of his rib cage. Sweet death in his eyes. I had victory. But they escaped.

I thrash. Howl. Feel my tongue split in my mouth, writhe like worms. I reach my bound hand out to Mr. Goodwin and point. Veins of scorched metal peel out from under my flesh and extend toward him. Then soften and melt back into my body, searing me.

He backs away in horror. But he understands what I want.

Screeeeeeeee.

He puts his pen in my hand. Try to grip it, but my bones bend. The object is so hard and unbelievably cold, sticking to my sickly corpse skin. But I don't dare let go.

Mr. Goodwin holds the clipboard for me. I struggle to work the pen. Every movement floods me with nausea. Vision is cutting out and blurred. It takes everything to write.

Letter. By agonizing letter.

Screeeeee. Screee.

The metal pen softens in my hand, fingers sink in like it's made of putty. Ink spills and puddles on the slab. The pen turns to slop. Finish writing with my fingers, smearing ink and flesh.

Mr. Goodwin's face changes. His eyes widen. I feel a shift in his breathing. He sees. Knows.

I collapse, withdraw to my waking nightmare of pain. But he is pleased. His smiling eyes are my salvation.

Screeeeeeeee.

If he'd only do something about that . . .

Then I realize. He cannot hear it.

I focus on the sound. Everything else drops out. A rattling electronic hum. Feel the hot tungsten coil from a light. Smell of unwashed hair and weeks of old coffee stains. Dirt on a cheap shoe. A man, a Greencoat, watching a machine that's watching me. He's rocking back in his chair.

Screeeeee. Screee.

That's what I hear.

But why? Why can I hear what's happening . . .

Screeeeeeeee.

. . . in another room?

"Kaspar, my boy," *Mr. Goodwin whispers every so lightly. The sound shreds me, but I don't care. I crave his voice.* "Well done."

And I see my one word, a mess of bloody black ink.

My word that made Mr. Goodwin happy.

TUNNELED.

5 FOCUS

Micah breathed deep. He mashed the trigger, and bullets thudded into the iron undergrowth.

Not even close to the target.

Growling, he lowered the Dervish rifle and swept back his hair with a shaky hand. Even though the weapon was quiet as a cat sneeze, its recoil was wicked, and the rounds came out way too fast. Maybe it was broken.

Nah, that wasn't it. The truth was Micah was too weak.

The ore beneath his feet rumbled, and a chorus of clangs sounded from the nearby training field. After the funeral, he had seen the Covenant warriors practicing combat maneuvers.

For a second, Micah had considered training with them, but when he saw the mehkans slamming into one another like crazed Autos in a demolition derby, he set up a training area of his own.

It was a stretch of ground behind some big dome tents and up against those tangled black growths the mehkies called tahniks. He had set up some empty lantern bags for target practice and managed to pop off a few lucky shots. But mostly his aim had gone wild, spackling the surrounding vegetation with white bonding rounds. Empty boxes of ammo lay scattered.

He tensed his trembling arms and hefted the rifle, bracing the stock against his shoulder. Micah fired again. A shuddering burst showered the tahniks and tossed him back. Not even close. Still, he kept on mashing the trigger—*click*, *click*. That sound, just like when he emptied this gun into Kaspar. Killed the man.

No, not a man. He was a monster. Micah had shot him dead.

But it still wasn't enough to save the Doc.

Micah hurled the rifle down as hard as he could. *No good.* He kicked an empty box of ammo. *Idiot.* He wailed on a lantern bag, pounding it with his fists, spraying sweat and spit. *Midget.*

He was spent, sick in the stomach. Seeing red. But he couldn't rest. He threw himself down on the ground and started in on another set of push-ups.

Because he and Phoebe had a job to do. It was a mission from the Ona, so important, so secret they couldn't say a word to anyone. And that was only part of his duty.

Ignoring the aches, Micah scrabbled to his feet and grabbed on to the tahnik branch he had been using as a pull-up bar.

He grunted and gritted his teeth. Four. Five. Six.

Protect her.

Hot, bloody breath in his ear. The Doc's last words.

No matter what.

Thirteen. Fourteen. Fifteen.

Promise me.

The Doc had looked so scared at that moment. At first, Micah had thought it was fear of dying, but that wasn't it. The Doc had been scared for Phoebe, stuck in Mehk, her life in the hands of some stupid servant kid.

Micah's grip slipped from the tahnik, and he collapsed on the ground, heaving for breath.

Footsteps pattered toward him.

"Oh—oh no! Are you ok-k-kay?" Dollop squeaked as he shook Micah. "Sh-should I get help?"

"I'm fine," Micah growled, pulling from Dollop's grasp. He eased himself to a sitting position, wincing.

Dollop nudged a sealed metal case toward him. "I—I got you another one. Ju-just like you asked."

Micah opened the box. It was full of bonding rounds.

"An-and there's more where that, um, came from. Lo-lots of stolen Foundry supplies."

Micah looked at Dollop, noticing him for the first time. His proportions were all screwy, like a reflection in a carnival mirror.

"What's up with you?" he asked the mehkan.

Dollop glanced down at his rearranged parts. He had traded a few mismatched bits here and there to get extra bulk up top, broadening his torso at the expense of creating stubbier legs.

"Oh—oh, you know. So they don't . . . I-It's just so that I—"

"So you don't look like a wimp."

Dollop flinched. "Wh-where's Phoebe?"

"Still prayin'," Micah said as he emptied the cartridges out of the case to take stock.

"Is sh-she okay?"

"Would you be?" Micah shot back, more harshly than he had intended. His muscles were on fire. He wanted to be left alone.

"Sh-shouldn't you be praying wi-with her?"

Micah scoffed and focused on sorting his ammo.

Dollop twiddled his fingers giddily, shifting from foot to foot.

"So . . . Isn't it ama-mazing here? Ev-everyone is so primed with fu-function. Th-they say they're all my clan, my br-brethren, that they would all ru-rust for me. I'm one of th-them!"

Micah ignored him.

"There are so—so many mehkans in the Covenant. Ev-every race, all Makina's children p-p-putting aside differences. No more Gr-Great Decay! All to-together, all getting ready for—"

Dollop strode up to Micah excitedly, stumbling over his neat stack of ammo cartridges and knocking them over.

"Dollop!" Micah hollered. "Just stay outta my way."

The little mehkan cringed as if he had been struck.

Micah immediately regretted it. His freckled face softened, and he crawled to his feet, muscles aching.

"I didn't mean it," Micah said. "I'm a jerk, I know, I'm just—"

"You're sc-scared," Dollop said quietly.

Micah felt his face flush. "Naw, it ain't that," he said, dismissing it with a smirk.

"I-It is. And it's ok-kay."

Micah's self-assured grin crumbled. He felt naked. He couldn't tell if he was about to scream more insults at Dollop or start blubbering like a baby.

"I—I am too," Dollop said. "But we do-don't need to be. Ma-Makina guides us now, don't you see?"

"Not really," Micah said with a shrug.

"You have be-been chosen to serve Her," the mehkan chirped, barely able to contain his excitement. "The ge-gears have engaged! The Covenant has been pr-preparing for many phases. The moment of reck-ckoning is near."

"Meaning what exactly?"

"So-soon we will march. Soon we will ta-take back Mehk!"

A chill rippled up Micah's spine. He snatched up his rifle.

"If that's true," he grunted, "then I got a lotta work to do."

Dollop watched as Micah slapped a magazine into his Dervish rifle, cocked the bolt, and spun the barrels with a whiz. The mehkan held a fist over his dynamo, then slipped away.

Micah stretched his arms and shook his hands vigorously before raising the gun. He got a target in his sights.

The Covenant was going to take back Mehk?

The thought burned away his fatigue. This was his chance to fight back against the Foundry, his chance to prove himself. He thought back to his big sister, Margie, how she had adjusted his grip and showed him how to relax his aim. Micah took a deep breath and let it out.

Then, just like Margie had shown him, he waited for that quiet moment before he needed to inhale again. Stillness came.

He fired. Not a single shot hit the target.

Micah gritted his teeth, ready to try again.

He would protect Phoebe. No matter what.

Muddled sunshine oozed in through the tent ceiling, which was made of a translucent membrane that must have been mehkan hide. A tray of water and rations lay untouched.

Phoebe knelt in the back room of the domed temple where her father's body had lain just that morning. The chamber was intended for solitude, and aside from the walls and the black ore underfoot, it was featureless. She was wrapped in the strange rust-colored shawl that blocked out all sound. The tar-thick silence left her floating. How long had she been back here, pretending to pray? Three hours? Four?

A day? A lifetime?

It didn't matter. Nothing did. She was alone.

No mother, no father. An orphan.

Her breath stopped. That word. How could a concept so

foreign, so other, suddenly have become the one thing she knew for sure? It smothered her every pore like smoke.

Orphan.

Phoebe looked down at his spectacles in her hands. She traced the spiderweb crack on one of the lenses with a ragged nail, crusted red from the ceremonial rust. How far she had come to save him, how much she had risked. And lost.

All for what? To be caught by the Foundry and used to force her father's confession. Then when the Covenant had come to rescue him, they were held back because Phoebe demanded they save Micah. If it wasn't for her, Orei would have gotten her dad out of the Citadel alive, along with Entakhai and Korluth and all those brave mehkan warriors. Right now, her father would be feeding vital information to the Covenant, guiding them in their next attack on the Foundry.

If she had never left home, her father would still be alive.

Why? Why did it have to be like this?

No answer. Just the oppressive rhythm of her breath within the silence of her shawl, magnifying the anguish that threatened to swallow her whole.

Phoebe's shawl was ripped back, and the rush of sound was disorienting. Orei loomed over her, glimmering rings and scythes in orbit, snaring the meager light. The thick cords within the Overguard's throat vibrated with her fluttery, disembodied voice.

"You are done," Orei commanded.

"What?" Phoebe blinked her tender, bleary eyes.

"You grieve too long. Four point eight clicks. Must prepare for your mission."

"No . . . I—" Phoebe felt like she was trying to rouse from a deep sleep. "I—I just . . ."

I just buried my father, she wanted to say, but her mouth wouldn't form the words.

"Rusting rites finished. Urgent matters press. The Aegis comes. Must be ready to depart."

"What are you talking about?" Phoebe gasped, her anger rising. "I can't turn it off. Just like that."

Pendulums and sliders ticked in Orei's ever-shifting body, measuring the air around Phoebe. "Unacceptable," Orei stated. "Loaii must be strong."

"I don't care!" cried Phoebe. "Leave me alone!"

"Core temperature rises two percent. Wasteful. You must—"

"Get out of here!" Phoebe screamed. Her heart thrashed in her rib cage like a wild thing trying to escape. She reached for the tray of rations and hurled it at Orei, who easily sidestepped it. "I hate you! Leave! NOW!"

Orei took a step forward and tilted her head. A strange change came over her as the myriad pieces of her shifting anatomy slowed. It looked as if she were moving underwater, as if some invisible force was trying to grind her body to a halt. She took an unbalanced step back, then abruptly spun through the tent flap and shoved past Axial Phy, who was just entering.

The elderly mehkan seemed undisturbed by Orei's

behavior. The delicate chains dangling from her vestments whispered like spring rain as she ambled in. Phoebe looked warily at Axial Phy, expecting another callous rebuke. However, the priestess just shuffled over to the scattered provisions and carefully arranged them back on the discarded tray.

"Sorry," Phoebe whispered, gesturing to the mess.

"Loaii." The axial's words came in a scrape. "Forgive her."

"Why?" she said, curling her lip resentfully.

"Because she must not feel."

"She's evil."

"No, she is kailiak," Axial Phy said. "They have no bonds. They do not feel the way we feel. Cannot." Sadness darkened her voice. "Kailiak are mehkans of precision and measurement. It is their most vital function. Emotion is poison to them, interrupts their systems so that they cannot act, think, or even breathe."

Phoebe considered this.

"Your pain touches us all, Loaii, but none more than Overguard Orei. She is moved by your sacrifice—an unusual tenderness that, for a kailiak, can be deadly."

The diminutive axial set the tray aside and approached. Beneath her crumpled golden robes, Phoebe saw the hint of stubby legs rotating around her body, as if her pelvis were a wheel. Axial Phy reached out her skeletal arms and with broad clamp-like digits, adjusted Phoebe's shawl.

"It's my fault," Phoebe said, lip quivering. "It's my fault he's dead. I—" She burst into full-throated sobs, shaking violently.

Axial Phy wrapped her in a tight embrace. Phoebe had never been this close to a mehkan before. She could feel the axial's hard, knotted form beneath her shimmering robes.

"I am a worker. A mere jaislid, born to serve," came the axial's coarse whisper. "But I obey no ore-bound master. I serve Her. And from my labors, there is one thing I know for certain."

Phoebe looked up at her.

"The gears do turn," Axial Phy said. "Their purpose is unclear, yes, but there is purpose all the same. The components interlock, all integral to the whole."

Phoebe felt warm, flat fingers petting the tangles of her hair. "But what does that even mean?" she asked. "That doesn't change anything. He's dead. Because of me."

"Because of the Everseer. Your father was taken beyond the Shroud, returned to Her Forge. You did not cause it, nor could you have ever stopped it."

"But what . . . What am I supposed to do?" Phoebe pleaded.

"Use the whist," the old mehkan said, indicating the rust-colored shawl. "It is a rare thing, an ancient art nearly lost to the epochs. The whist is bestowed to mourn a fallen hero. Never has it graced one who is not Waybound, much less a human."

"I tried to pray with it like I'm supposed to," sniffled Phoebe. "But there's . . . nothing."

"You burden yourself. Do not pray. Use the whist to find

comfort, to feel fiercely the love of your father. Embrace its silence, and I promise, your pain will melt like flux into the ore."

Axial Phy's face eased into a crinkly smile.

"Then, Loaii, in that nothing, Her voice will guide you."

Phoebe gently pulled out of the embrace.

"What is 'Loaii'? What does it mean?" Phoebe asked.

Beneath the veil of clinking chains, the mehkan's eyes flickered. "There is no word in your tongue. It means . . ." The axial thought for a moment. "For you, the path is . . . illuminated. She guides you. Few have borne the title."

"Loaii," Phoebe said softly.

"Loaii," Axial Phy repeated and bowed deeply. "Use the whist to find peace. Makina will come to you in time." The old mehkan pivoted, her robes rustling as she withdrew from the tent.

Phoebe closed her eyes and draped the whist over her head. The axial's words had made Phoebe feel lighter, like she wasn't such a fraud after all.

But her head was still swimming with questions, especially about her mission. She didn't understand much of the Ona's cryptic words, and there was no one to ask—she and Micah had been sworn to secrecy. The Ona had said she would explain everything once their escort arrived, but Phoebe couldn't wait.

She needed Micah. They needed to figure this out.

Phoebe stared down at her father's spectacles. One thing the Ona said rang perfectly clear.

His function was. To save Mehk. Now it is. Yours.

6 UNDER THE SURFACE

Banks of floodlights flared on as night congealed in the sky. A toxic CHAR cloud lingered over the vast blackened pit where the Citadel once stood. The area was cordoned off and accessible only to workers in protective suits. Any metal brought within its slowly expanding perimeter would decompose into poisonous slop, so all operators were equipped with specialized gear made from high-fired ceramic, reinforced glass, and wood.

Goodwin peered out at the haze from the paltry lean-to shelter. After his unexpected meeting with President Saltern, he had returned to Mehk to face Chairman Obwilé and the four directors. First, Goodwin had learned that they were taking the Dyad Project from him, then he had been tasked with his new assignment: managing the aftermath of the Citadel—glorified janitorial work.

"You were responsible for this mess," Obwilé had purred, taking far too much pleasure from Goodwin's fury. "It is only fitting that you should be in charge of cleaning it up."

So they had shipped him out here, to this mobile command center, little more than a tent village, a handful of open-bed cargo trucks, and a closed circuit Com-Pak relay dish. Goodwin reapplied mentholated cream beneath his nostrils and adjusted his filtered facemask as he surveyed the charts and blueprints.

He had twenty Watchmen at his disposal, but they were useless near the CHAR. This meant he had to rely on a team of fifty or so human employees, a few of whom had already been evacuated to the Depot with respiratory problems. Even though he was well outside the Alpha Zone, his ear throbbed fiercely, a sign that the fumes were affecting his implanted metal earbud.

This cleanup was pointless. Nothing of worth could possibly be salvaged within that foul morass. He was understaffed and poorly equipped with no further support coming.

And yet despite it all, Goodwin's mind churned with anticipation. Kaspar's intel could change everything.

Assuming it wasn't just the wild raving of a madman.

Or whatever Kaspar was now.

"What is the current status?" nagged a voice in Goodwin's ear.

"We have been waiting," said another.

"Com-Pak sets cannot enter the Alpha Zone, so I am unable to correspond with the crew. There will be no updates until this work shift ends," Goodwin explained. "However, there have been no significant changes in the past six hours."

"Your point being?"

"The ferro-crotic spread has advanced exactly as our models predicted. It is unlikely that anything can be salvaged."

Silence in his earpiece.

"Of course, if I find anything unexpected, I will notify you at once," he continued calmly. "Is that all?"

"What are these figures we're seeing?"

Goodwin turned his attention to his Scrollbar and sifted through the most recent upload from his Watchman unit. He had equipped them with perimagnetic densometers and assigned them to specific quadrants outside the Alpha Zone. Quickly, he made notations on an elevation map, which was already blanketed with red hatch marks and X's.

"What are you up to, James?" a voice asked.

"We understand the outward spread of CHAR, but I am gathering information on its subterranean impact as well," Goodwin lied. "I have the Watchmen taking samples of ore at various depths to augment our data."

"A blatant waste of resources."

"Recall the units."

"Focus on the task at hand."

"Of course," Goodwin said. "This is merely an exploratory measure." He spoke into his Com-Pak. "Watchman Unit

4J-729. Adjust subsurface sounding frequency to minus fifty feet."

There was a pause as his order was processed and obeyed. Numbers on his Scrollbar flickered as new data rolled in.

Goodwin felt his skin flush. There it was, the reading he had been waiting for—his road to redemption. He scribbled on the elevation map, pressing so hard the tip of his pencil snapped.

"Wait," commanded one of the directors in his ear.

"What on earth?"

"Just what are we looking at here?"

A warm, caustic wind blew, and the poles of the tent creaked around him. A sprout of jarring pain grew in his ear. He had to hold on to the table to remain steady.

"Unbelievable . . ." Goodwin said, feigning surprise for maximum dramatic effect. "It cannot be."

"Report!" came the response in his vulnerable ear.

"Yes, yes!" Goodwin said urgently. "There is an anomaly beneath the surface. It . . . it looks like a channel seven feet wide with eighty percent reduced density and it . . ."

"What?"

"A tunnel?"

"Exactly! And it is leading out from the Alpha Zone."

"Meaning?"

"Prepare an assault team," Goodwin commanded.

"Remember your place, Deputy Manager."

"Ladies and gentlemen of the Board," Goodwin interrupted. "This is an escape route. I have found the Covenant."

7 GLIMMERS

Micah stood beside Dollop, trying to appear at ease while they waited for Phoebe, but his insides were jumping. Nearby, a huge complex of gray hide tents bustled with the Covenant. He had seen at least fourteen different types of mehkies swarming in and out of the domes, and he had only just started counting. There were chraida and those weirdo sheet-metal langyls, warriors like Orei, and others like the tripod creatures they had seen in Sen Ta'rine. Many were so strange he couldn't make heads or tails of them.

They were people—that's what still rattled his brain. So many *kinds* of people. Sure, wandering through Albright City you'd see all kinds of folks—dark skin, light skin, long hair or no hair, big people and little people. But humans weren't all that different from one another, not really. Not like mehkies.

But the things that really lit Micah up were the siege engines. War machines, though that seemed like the wrong name since many were clearly breathing. He saw a walking catapult with a payload of spiky egg sacs and something like a wrinkly bulldozer with gnarls of serrated blades. Mehkies stoked fires in the bellies of cantankerous creatures. It was hard to tell the beasts from the equipment. There were warriors strapped into machines, and machines strapped onto warriors.

It was too much. What was he doing here? A ten-year-old kid from Sodowa couldn't measure up to this lot, even if he did have a Dervish rifle. But that just made him want to join the madness all the more. He dreamed of hopping on one of those siege engines and leading the charge with the Covenant at his back.

His fantasy evaporated as he noticed the camp had fallen still. Mehkies bowed their heads and stepped aside to allow a figure to pass through their ranks—a sliver of rust, a silky veil draped over bony shoulders. Clad in her new shawl, Phoebe shuffled forward, ignoring the ripples of awe in her wake. She pulled back her hood in a splash of dark tangled hair, and Dollop touched his dynamo in respect. Micah just stared.

He hadn't seen Phoebe since the funeral. Her face was dead white with shiny scars of tears carved in her cheeks. Dark pouches weighted her gaze, brimming saucers ready to spill over any second. Yet her raw eyes were aglow. Maybe it was the patch of sun she was standing in, or maybe it was all the crying she had done, but Phoebe's pupils seemed lit from within. They were chopped wood, bristling with splinters, sparkling with sap.

They were so sad. So . . . pretty.

"What?" Phoebe asked in a sandpaper voice.

"Huh?" Micah mumbled stupidly as he looked away and adjusted the gun strap on his shoulder. "No, nothin'."

"Are you ok-kay, Phoebe?" Dollop asked. "I—I mean Loaii."

"What's with the 'Loaii' stuff anyway?" Micah asked, feeling his senses snap back. "Why's everyone callin' you that?"

"I . . ." Phoebe said. "I don't know." She glanced at the surrounding mehkies, who slowly resumed their business.

"I tried to get in to see you," Micah explained, "but the axials wouldn't let me."

"I know. Thanks," said Phoebe. "We should get started."

"Sure thing," Micah replied. "After you, Dollop."

Their little friend perked up at the sound of his name. "R-r-right! Follow m-me!"

He led them through the crowd to the central domed tent. Inside was a stuffy, jumbled commotion, with Covenant warriors hustling through passageways, hauling massive bundles to and fro. A few of the mehkies paused to stare at the kids, nodding in regard, but most ignored the humans entirely.

Dollop saluted his comrades and watched for some sort of acknowledgement, but he received none.

"Th-this way. I—I think," Dollop chimed as he led the

kids through a low corridor. "Be-behind the indruli dens. Th-they're nocturnal and can get kind of . . . b-b-bitey if you wake them, so . . ."

Micah snorted. "Full of comforting lil' tidbits as usual."

He stole a glance at Phoebe, but she was lost in thought.

"B-but they're lo-lovely if you c-catch them at the right t-time. Everyone here is. You know, I f-feel like I have known some of th-these mehkans f-forever. Th-this is what it truly means to be an equal, to—to interlock! It's exactly how I always . . ."

Micah tuned out Dollop's chatter as they followed him through the winding tunnels of black ore. A lantern bag flickered as they descended, and Micah looked through its sinewy skin to see bluish lights twinkling inside. Not just lights—critters. Little geometric guppy things swam around in the sludge, glowing whenever they collided.

". . . learning the b-basics of def-fensive theory. I—I even taught them a th-thing or two. Soon I'll be highest ra-rank in my unit. Honestly, I d-don't know how they managed without me—"

A hissing stream of Rattletrap interrupted Dollop. Up ahead, Micah saw a Covenant warrior looming over their hapless friend, snarling. He was dull green with a hexagonal pattern like hammered scales, and his four stout, hydraulic legs stamped the ground while his segmented tails lashed about.

"Hey!" Micah called, rushing to Dollop's side. "Cut it out!"

The stranger whipped around to reveal eyes and teeth on shifting dials, spinning like a slot machine. The mehkan flexed one of its praying mantis arms with a menacing buzz, and Micah backed up. Its limb was wrapped with whizzing spikes and blades, some kind of wackadoodle chainsaw.

Dollop pleaded with the mantis mehkan in Rattletrap. Then the Covenant warrior shoved a weighty foil bundle into Dollop's arms and stalked off without a second look at the kids.

"What was that all about?" asked Phoebe.

"Th-that what?" Dollop asked, playing dumb. "Who, um, hi-him? Oh, haha! No, nothing. Ju-just a little job I forgot to do."

"Whaddya mean, 'job'?" pressed Micah.

"I—I have to peel this bu-bunch of kolchi nuts for Brother Nuhlarg. Tiulus like him ca-can't be bothered with menial tasks. Such is the li-life of a Covenant warrior. This a-way!"

Micah cast a wary eye back at the departing chainsaw mantis before following behind Dollop and a solemn Phoebe. They shuffled down another corridor, past a series of reinforced reed hatches. Security gates, Micah supposed. Probably for those flesh-eating droolie thingies that Dollop said were sleeping nearby. The thought made Micah move along a little faster.

They emerged into a dark chamber with a low ceiling draped in clumpy root wires. The air shook with the muffled tromping of warriors above ground. Micah fussed around with his rifle for a moment, then activated the light that was mounted on it. He flashed the bright beam around to reveal crates glinting from niches carved into the ore. A lot of them.

"S-s-so? What do you th-think?" Dollop asked.

Micah opened a few of the cases. They were packed with random stuff, like someone had tossed in whatever they could find. There were wet and dry rations, framed photos and jewelry, protective gear, reams of papers and Computator parts. Then, in the jumble, Micah spied a familiar logo on a cardboard box.

"Jackpot!" he whooped, tearing into it. He tossed a little foil-wrapped thing to Phoebe, who fumbled it.

"Wackers," she read aloud, picking up the crinkly object.

"Ya bet yer butt it is!" Micah hollered with his mouth already full of creamy white chocolate and salty macadamia nuts. "Oh man, never thought I'd taste that again!" He ripped open another Wackers bar, peeled off the paper lining within, and crammed the whole thing into his overstuffed cheeks while he rummaged through the goodies. There were cans of soup, pouches of dried fruit, dehydrated meal packets, and aluminum bottles of water. "There's enough chow here for, like, a hundred years."

"The Ona said our mission would only take a day," Phoebe replied, poking into a crate. "We just need a few essentials."

"We'll eat like kings!" Micah said. He started sorting the supplies. "Why'd the Covenant keep this human junk anyway?"

"It wa-was for . . ." Dollop trailed off, shifting under the weight of his bundle. His bug eyes darted at Phoebe. "You know . . ."

Micah felt the room go cold.

Stupid Dollop. Did he *have* to bring up the Doc? Phoebe turned stiffly and wandered off. Micah had to do something.

"Say, where's the ammo?" he asked. "I'm runnin' low."

"Oh, yo-you won't need your gun," Dollop assured him. "You and—and Loaii will be escorted by th-the Aegis."

Dollop said it as if it explained everything. Micah stared at him wide-eyed, motioning for more information.

"The Aegis are Em-Emberguard, the Ona's silent-sworn, fiercest war-r-riors in, err, all of Mehk. It is said they can—can vanish into the thin air. Th-they are as noiseless as the Shroud, and—and unmatched in battle." His voice lowered. "Only th-they can tame the kav'o . . . which is to wield the living weapons."

"Wicked," Micah whispered back.

Dollop nodded sagely. "Y-you w-will have nothing to fear with them p-protecting you."

"Bleh—creamed beets? Seriously?" Micah scrunched his nose at a can and tossed it back into the crate. "Aegis or not, I ain't goin' unarmed. You might wanna get yourself some heat too, chum. No tellin' what we're gonna be up against."

The mehkan shifted awkwardly and looked at the ground.

"Dollop," Phoebe whispered somewhere in the darkness. "You're not coming with us, are you?"

"Say what?" Micah shot back. "No way, Dollop. You have to!"

Phoebe came back into the rifle light, her sore eyes shimmering wet with fresh tears. "What about us?" she said.

Dollop offered a feeble smile. "You two have been ch-chosen by the Ona. By Makina. I—I'd l-like to join you, but I'm in the Co-Covenant now. We have ma-many preparations to make. All our ca-camps, we all—all must come together."

"There's other camps?" Micah asked.

"The Covenant is scattered throughout Mehk, embedded in ev-every city. The—the time has come for the Children of Ore to unite. I have to b-be ready for that. My br-brethren need me."

"To what, peel nuts?" Micah snorted. "No way. You belong with us. Come on, Phoebe. Let's just tell him about the Ona's secret mission. He ain't gonna blab."

Phoebe shook her head, and Dollop covered his ears.

"N-no! The Ona has reasons for her se-secrets. I—I have to earn my pl-place here." He touched the silver splattered scars on his chest. "We are all vital co-components."

"That chainsaw dude didn't think you were all that vital."

"I . . ." Dollop hugged his foil bundle and hurried away. "I have to get back to my—my duties."

"Wait!" Micah called after him. "That ain't what I— You're vital to *us* and stuff!" Dollop's footsteps echoed away down the tunnel. "Geez Louise, I was tryin' to be nice!"

Bony fingers clutched Micah's arm and drew him back.

"We have to talk," Phoebe whispered.

"Look, I didn't mean to hurt the guy's feelings, I just—"

"No, not Dollop." Her eyes darted to the doorway, making sure they were alone. "The Ona."

He lowered his voice too. "Oh, you mean the whatsit we're supposed to be findin' for her? The . . . the Occulips."

Phoebe giggled. His old, familiar anger at her snootiness bubbled up again, but it dissolved in the sound of her laughter. For an instant, he saw the real Phoebe glimmering behind her mask of grief. It was a little victory.

"Occulyth," she corrected. "There's got to be a reason we can't talk about it," Phoebe whispered. "Here's what I think we—"

The rhythmic stomping of the Covenant training overhead came to a halt. A familiar musical wail groaned down through the ore. It was that weird windup device from the funeral.

"The fusion chant," Phoebe said. "Axial Phy is expecting me."

"But wait!" pleaded Micah. "What were you gonna say?"

Phoebe headed for the exit and turned to face him. "Let's talk tonight. I'll sneak out. Meet me at the stables." She lowered the cowl of her rusty shawl over her head.

"Stables? What stables?" he cried out, but there was no reply. Phoebe was already gone.

DEAD OF NIGHT

The lantern-blue darkness seemed to sharpen Phoebe's senses. The air was awash in a damp earthen scent, and her skin prickled at the slightest breeze. She pulled the whist tight around her like a blanket as she snuck through the camp, weaving between dome tents that buzzed with sleeping warriors.

Did mehkans dream? The question had not occurred to her before. Of course they did, and apparently they snored too.

A deep harmonic sound drew her attention. She followed it, making her way past the tents and across the practice field, rutted with scars from the day's training. Phoebe descended to the lip of an abrupt slope that led to trenches and tunnels below. Within them, she saw dozens of pale salathyls, the subterranean behemoths like drill-headed squids. Their pearly bodies and flowing tentacles made them look like ghosts.

A joyful fluting passed between the giants. She spied a young salathyl, nearly transparent, diving into the ore as if it were water. The adults slapped the ground playfully with their striated tentacles, and the baby sprang out in a somersault, then disappeared underground again. The salathyls emitted a bubbly sound that Phoebe could have sworn was laughter.

"There you are. Whoa, whoa!"

Behind her, boots skidded on loose ore as Micah came sliding down to join her. She grabbed him to steady his descent and noticed something clunky on top of his metal-fiber coveralls. He had outfitted himself in rust-and-gray-camouflaged combat gear made of interwoven triangular panels. The pieces were mismatched, oversized, and almost certainly on backward.

"Thanks," he said, regaining his balance. He noticed Phoebe eyeing his bulky ensemble and self-consciously adjusted the straps. "Had some time to kill while I was gathering supplies in the storehouse, so I decided to suit up. Can't be too careful."

She offered a little smile.

"Anyway, I been lookin' for you but wasn't sure what stables you meant. All kinda weirdo critters holed up around here."

"They're not critters," she said. "Salathyls are people.

Axial Phy said they are very intelligent, and that they believe in Makina. That's why they help the Covenant."

"Where I come from, you live in a stable, you're a critter. But whatever," Micah said with a shrug. "Listen. I think I got it all worked out—this whole Occulyth thing."

Phoebe held a finger to her lips, and Micah glanced around.

"It's a weapon," he whispered. "The Ona said it's mega-important, and that it'll save Mehk, so what else could it be?"

Phoebe shook her head. "Then why can't we talk about it?"

"'Cause it's a *secret* weapon," he said with a wink.

"But that doesn't make any sense."

"Neither did most of what she said. All that babble about a 'Bearing' and a 'white star.' I hardly understood a word."

"But why send us to get a weapon?" she wondered.

Micah chuffed a little laugh. "'Cause she wants to kick some Foundry butt, obviously."

"She has an army. If it's so important, why send *us*?"

"I dunno, maybe . . ." But he didn't have an answer.

"No," Phoebe began, working through it in her mind. "It must have something to do with the Way. Maybe it's something—"

The salathyls' melodic tones shifted, becoming discordant. Phoebe looked down at them. The mehkans seemed to be annoyed by her and Micah's presence.

"We should go," she spoke over the rising salathyl voices.

"Yeah, what's up with them?

The agitated beasts lurched. The adults gathered up their

child, wrapping it in writhing tentacles. Beneath the shrill cries, there was another sound, a growing moan underfoot.

An earthquake?

The kids scrambled back up the incline. The salathyls were thrashing now, trumpeting as their tentacles whipped dangerously through the air and pounded into the ledge.

Phoebe and Micah dashed into the practice field. There were chaotic Rattletrap voices. Members of the Covenant were bolting from tents and perches, shouting orders.

Were the salathyls attacking? No. They were fleeing.

Then the world went purple-white.

WHOOMF.

A gale of ore. A salathyl lifted off the ground, tentacles flailing. Like a violet tidal wave, a magnetic detonation hurled everything back, including Phoebe and Micah.

Geodrills. Blinding searchlights shattered the darkness, and the caustic reek of engines singed the air. Then came a hailstorm of bonding rounds as the Foundry opened fire.

Phoebe and Micah found their feet and ran.

Covenant warriors streamed from tents. Others flocked from above, scurrying down the canyon walls and soaring through the air. Frightened salathyls spilled out from the trenches, crashing through the Covenant's ranks.

The kids rushed into a labyrinth of tents as a nearby mehkan war machine blasted out jets of liquid fire. An explosion knocked the kids off balance. Micah bolted to the right.

"What are you doing?" Phoebe hollered. Acrid smoke

pooled around them, obscuring everything and burning her throat. She chased his silhouette down a narrow path and into a tent.

The instant they stepped inside, a strobing light blinded them—the lethal spit of rifle fire. Micah yanked Phoebe down, and they covered their heads as bullets shredded the tent wall.

"Oh n-no! I'm so s-sorry!" Dollop sobbed. The smoking Dervish rifle shook in his grip. "I th-thought you were—You could ha-have been—Sweet Mother of Ore, are you all r-r-right?"

"Are you nuts?" Micah ripped his rifle from Dollop's grip. "You coulda killed us! You okay, Plumm?"

Phoebe checked herself for bullet holes, then nodded. Dollop was pressed against the wall, eyes wide, body rattling in terror.

A brilliant purple boom erupted outside, another magnetic explosion. The tent convulsed as if in a cyclone, and they held on tight. Then came a dazzling orange blast and horrid screams.

"Last time I leave you behind," Micah grunted.

At first, she thought he was talking to them, before realizing that he was actually addressing his rifle. Micah strapped a field pack on to his back that looked like the shell of a giant pill bug. Phoebe glanced around and saw deadly weapons piled everywhere. Micah had taken enough from the storehouse to turn his tent into an arsenal. He thoughtfully perused his stash.

"Micah!" she hollered, nervously spying a bunch of explosives in a heap. "We have to go!"

He was about to snatch up a sinister machine gun that was as tall as him, but he held back with a sigh of disappointment.

"Right," Micah said, strapping on a tarnished copper combat helmet instead. "There's a path that leads to the jungle floor above. Scouted it earlier. We can get out that way."

Phoebe nodded. Dollop stared, catatonic.

"Stay right on my six, okay?" Micah asked.

"Your six?"

"Behind me. Let's roll." With that, Micah poked his head out of the tent to scan with his rifle, then raced out into the smoke.

He's actually enjoying this, Phoebe realized in disbelief.

She hurried close behind with Dollop clutching on to her flowing whist. Through the gloom and the deafening crunch of metal, they made their way to a jagged stairway of knobby branches that wound between tahniks. There was no railing, just plank-like paths with the promise of a fatal fall for any misstep.

The three of them made their way up, ascending from globe to globe. Phoebe ignored Dollop's whimpering and her sinking stomach to focus on the rickety steps. The air was fractured with battle cries and jarring blasts that made it hard to concentrate. She peered down into the camp to try and make sense of it all, but dense tahniks and thick smoke obscured the scene.

They were so high now that Phoebe began to feel dizzy.

A shearing metal shriek from above. The roof of the camp tore open. A blaze of light.

They spun to retreat, scrambling back down as fast as they could. A breathtaking blast of purple from below. The network of walkways shifted and groaned around them. Above, a tangle of growth broke free and plummeted. It smashed down, shredding the suspended paths beneath them. Trapped.

Hydraulic arms descended from hovering Aero-copters, punched through the ceiling, and lit up in a rapid flurry of fire.

Dollop motioned down to the tendrils twisting from growth to growth. Now that the walkways were gone, their only option was to climb down those branches. They scooted over the edge of the tahnik, slipped down, and grabbed a limb. Then they scurried across it to another orb, slid down a tendril like a firefighter's pole, and worked through the growth with Dollop leading the way.

An explosion. Tahniks jostled like ornaments on a tree.

The limb that held Dollop broke. Phoebe tried to grab him.

He fell.

But his body extended. As the shattered tendril dropped beneath him, Dollop unfurled his form. His legs wrapped around the nearest bough, and his arms stretched across the gap. In a split second, he had replaced the severed branch between dangling tahniks with a ladder made from his own body.

"How did you—" Micah said.

"Just G-G-G-G-GO!" came Dollop's chattering plea. No

time to hesitate. Phoebe crawled gingerly across the chain of limbs, feeling Dollop wobble beneath her. Then came Micah, scrabbling across. But his body armor was too heavy. Dollop lost his grip.

Micah lurched forward. Phoebe yanked him to safety. Dollop retracted his string of disjointed parts, and they all slammed together in a human-mehkan jumble.

They were back on their feet in a flash and ventured into the haze, climbing lower and lower. The heat of battle crackled against their skin. The scorched ore came into view, strewn with rubble and the fallen.

Thirty feet away. Now twenty.

Their vision flashed purple-white—a resonant blast. Tendrils cracked, globes twisted. The suspended system of tahniks and walkways bowed. Iron squealed. Formations tore loose.

Phoebe and Micah dropped. They smacked the ground and slammed into a shallow indentation in the canyon wall.

The network of tahniks collapsed like shelves of glacier ice.

BOOM—Massive orbs—*BOOM*—thundered to the ground. *BOOM*—Like a—*BOOM*—meteor shower.

CRASH!

The kids took shelter as the world tremored in a barrage of tahniks. The colossal boulders settled. Phoebe and Micah coughed, fumbling for the facemasks built into their coveralls.

With the hoods sealed, they peered out through their visors. The Covenant camp was an unrecognizable hellscape. The symphony of war continued unabated.

"Dollop!" Micah shouted, plunging into the haze.

Phoebe realized their friend was no longer with them.

"DOLLOP!" he screamed again.

"Micah, wait!" she pleaded, trailing after him.

A shape emerged from the smoke ahead, lit in dream-like flashes of distant fire. The figure was tall, stalking with precision.

A Watchman soldier. He was facing away.

Micah snarled and fumbled for his gun.

"No!" Phoebe reached out to stop him.

But it was too late. Micah's rifle flashed to life.

The Watchman whirled sharply out of the way.

Micah had missed. He released the trigger, and his spinning barrels whispered to a stop.

"What are you doing?" Phoebe shouted.

Micah had given away their position.

Bonding rounds pocked the ground around them as Watchmen returned fire. Six enemy soldiers charged. Micah bolted, dragging Phoebe with him. They stumbled behind a fallen tahnik that sang with ricochet.

A silvery-blue tornado enveloped the enemy from behind—a demon of whirling blades, born from the smoke. Her scythes flurried between the legs of a Watchman, sundering the group of attackers and sending them reeling. Her rings hooked around another's midsection, using the victim as a shield to soak up rifle fire before lashing out in a swirling dance.

Watchmen fell to sparking pieces before Orei. One of those thrashing mehkan worms that powered the Foundry automatons wriggled free from a mechanical brain casing and slithered away.

"Follow," Orei commanded.

"What about Dollop?" Phoebe insisted.

Orei turned her hollow, unreadable face to the kids. The apparatus of her shifting body measured them.

"Headed to stables. With Overguard Treth."

Phoebe looked at her, unsure.

"Follow."

Overguard Orei inverted her body and raced back into the smoke-swollen dark. They sprinted after her. Phoebe and Micah faltered over the cratered ground, but Orei was effortless in her flight. She swept charging Watchmen from her path with wide, arcing slashes to open an escape route.

Mist swirled around the kids. A brilliant flash of white blinded them completely.

Micah grabbed Phoebe's sleeve. "Stay close!"

"Orei!" Phoebe shouted. As her vision returned, she thought she saw a glimpse of the Overguard, just a flicker of movement. But her shifting and twisting silhouette was impossible to follow, and it was soon swallowed in dust and gunfire.

The kids stumbled away, tripping on roots and wreckage. They hit the canyon wall and felt their way along its surface, finding a tahnik sphere embedded in the cliff face. The kids wedged in beside it, hoping for some cover.

A crack in the wall gave way. Phoebe fell back, toppling into a nest of jungle growth. Micah helped her up.

There was a narrow crevice behind the embedded tahnik. A gust of sweet, soot-free air hit their faces.

Phoebe wriggled in, trying to scramble around the obstruction and up into the cramped crawl space.

"Wait!" Micah rasped. "We gotta stick with Orei!"

They glanced back into the battlefield behind them.

A wall of Watchmen advanced toward them.

The kids crammed into the crevice, ripping through the undergrowth. Another purple blast. Approaching thunder, spheres flung across the camp like marbles. A wrecking ball tahnik smashed through the wall, closing the path behind them.

Phoebe and Micah coughed, clawing their way up and up.

Above the thicket and the dust glimmered a trickle of light.

A way out.

9
NEW LIGHT

A Foundry soldier presented a polished pewter mug to Goodwin, who savored the aroma of freshly brewed coffee. It was a well-earned luxury after a strenuous, yet exhilarating night. Goodwin surveyed his surroundings and sipped himself awake.

What was once a circular courtyard marked by gentle

sloping mounds was now a pit of smoldering debris. Masses of mehkan bodies had melted during the intense heat of battle, fusing into a grim knoll. It reminded Goodwin of the skin of corpses that once cloaked the Citadel—a fitting, even poetic payback to the Covenant for its destruction.

"Your instincts appear to have served you well, James."

"This time," cautioned another voice in his earpiece.

"Although you exceeded your authority."

"Of course. My apologies," Goodwin said with a smile.

He did not need the Board's commendations. They knew the significance of this victory. Goodwin had caught the boogeyman. He had smashed the Covenant, and now he felt a sense of completion.

Goodwin took another drink of coffee, enjoying the fullness of its flavor. Through the gauzy atmosphere, he saw Watchman soldiers march another mehkan prisoner to a magnetic corral where captives snarled in their grating language. There was no telling what intelligence he would gather once the translator arrived and interrogations began.

"Have you identified the remains yet?"

Goodwin approached the dark, crumbled plinth at the back of the courtyard where a tarp-covered form awaited. He pulled away the sheet to reveal a body burnished in gold with a crusted red mark on its chest. Goodwin recognized this bizarre mehkan rite, but he never imagined it might be done for a human.

"Dr. Plumm is dead," Goodwin announced, his voice heavy.

It was a solemn prize. Jules may have been a traitor, yes, but he had also once been a friend.

There was a soft click, followed by a moment's silence. Then his earpiece came alive once more.

"That will be all. Return to the Depot with a full report."

Goodwin ground his teeth in annoyance. The coffee cup quivered in his hand. "I have only just begun. There is still—"

"Chairman Obwilé will be overseeing the Covenant camp."

A spark ignited in Goodwin's blood. His ingenuity had led to the discovery of this camp. He had orchestrated the assault and secured a cache of Covenant materials, including military plans and maps that charted unknown territories. Goodwin alone deserved the credit, and he would not forfeit his spoils so easily.

"Ladies and gentlemen," he said, addressing the Board with complete emotional control. "I have uncovered evidence that the enemy's network extends far beyond what we previously imagined. Give me time to exploit my discovery and—"

"You have your orders, James."

The coffee had gone sour. Goodwin tossed out the remnants and stroked the coarse stubble on his cheek.

"Acknowledge," demanded a voice of the Board.

Goodwin did not unclench his jaw. "Right away."

Within seconds, two Watchman soldiers were flanking him, their dead, black gazes fixed upon him from behind glossy face shields. He was escorted out of the ravaged courtyard.

Goodwin crunched over the scorched ore, fuming at this

newest humiliation. He passed under a Mag-tank, its coil-tipped cannon humming as it was recharged by a generator. The loud rumble almost caused him to miss a nearby croaking voice.

"Ashtal incorrieki il gha Phoebe t'lar Loaii."

He stopped short and turned to find who had spoken.

The words came again, and this time he found their source—the glowing purple corral occupied by Covenant prisoners of war. Mehkans were gathered around a diminutive creature clad in tattered veils. The wounded thing's face was hidden behind a headpiece of golden chains, adorned by that symbol he had seen throughout the camp—a circle bisected with a jagged line.

"Ashtal incorrieki il gha Phoebe t'lar Loaii!"

The words meant nothing to Goodwin, but the girl's name was unmistakable. Fumbling, he withdrew his Scrollbar, slid it open, and recorded the peculiar phrase.

The crumpled creature pointed a clamp claw at Goodwin as it growled the words again.

"Ashtal incorrieki il gha Phoebe . . ."

The mehkan slumped back into its comrades' arms, spent.

Far above, the smoke parted as an Aero-copter arrived to return Goodwin to the Depot, dousing him in a brilliant bath of orange morning light. The clouds parted in his mind too.

The children had been in this camp.

Goodwin was beginning to see a way forward.

And his future was bright.

NUMB

Phoebe awoke in the fetal position, the whist encasing her like a silent womb. Time was a deck of scattered playing cards, moments strewn haphazardly across her mind—climbing after Micah through the crevice, stumbling through the jagged jungle. Then finally, fragments of fitful sleep.

The air was humid with a loamy scent. Phoebe peeled back her whist and heard the distant thrum of Aero-copters mingling with the groans of suspended metal and a drone of insects.

She lay in the muddy ore, surrounded by iron vines that trailed across the ground. Above was a dense tangle of tahniks, ebony planets fringed in a canopy of red, swordlike fronds that permitted only a few drops of light.

Micah was perched a dozen feet above her, playing lookout amongst the tahnik branches. Phoebe did not stir. Her body felt heavy and lifeless. She wished she could drift off to sleep again.

He saw her rousing and started to make his way down, that idiotic body armor and helmet of his clanking like pots and pans. Of course, Micah had that stupid rifle with him too, as if simply lugging it around made him somebody. She wanted to rip it out of his hands and throw it off a cliff.

Instead, she rolled over and turned her back to him.

"You up?" Micah said, landing with a clatter.

She ignored him.

"So . . . what now?" he asked.

A long moment passed while he waited for her to respond. Phoebe heard his footsteps plod around to face her.

"Come on, I know you're awake. We gotta figure this out."

She pinched her eyes shut and didn't move.

"That how it's gonna be? You just gonna lay here in the mud like some kinda—"

Phoebe pulled the hood of the whist over her head to silence his words, but he tugged it back.

"Oh no, you don't," he warned.

"It's over."

"Bull crap it is!"

She didn't budge.

"Don't be all . . ." Micah gnawed his lip, clearly trying to turn his words into a whip. "It ain't over till I say it is. Now get up."

"They're dead. Axial Phy, Dollop, all of them."

"No way. Dollop's fine. He was with that big ol' Treth guy."

"She lied," Phoebe breathed.

"Say what?"

"Orei was lying. She didn't see Dollop at the stables. He fell right near us. She lied so we'd follow her."

"But . . ." Micah said, considering her words. "You don't know that. Anyway, we can't stay here. It's crawlin' with Foundry."

"So what?" she whispered.

"So we gotta go, that's what," he said, raising his voice. "The Doc told me to protect you, so that's what I'm gonna do."

Phoebe's lids slid open, unsheathing honey-brown daggers.

"Like you did back in the camp?"

"What's that s'pposed to mean?" he said, his hand flexing on his rifle's grip.

Her voice was barely a flutter. "Pretty sure using your pop-gun to lead the bad guys to us doesn't count."

Micah's face pinched up. "Why you little—"

"If that's protecting me, I'd rather just die here."

"Shut your mouth!"

"Learn how to shoot," she said blandly, neither fearing his rage nor savoring it. "Better yet, give up now."

Micah shook in place, bristling, then he stomped out of view in a clash of body armor. She lay there, listening to the mehkan insects buzz in harmony with the Aero-copters.

"I . . ." she said, not caring if he was listening. "I'm done."

The words sank in, hearing them as if from outside herself.

"I'm done. I just want to—"

"You, you, you!" Micah hollered, marching up to her again. "You haven't changed one bit, ya know that? I thought your little liodim stunt back in the Vo-Pyks was somethin', but you prob'ly thought that was all about you too. Well, guess what. It ain't. None of it is. So get over yourself!

"Do it for the mehkies. Do it for . . ." Micah's prepubescent voice broke. "Do it for the Doc, who died to save them!"

He released an animal growl and stormed out of sight, splashing through a trickle of vesper.

Phoebe stared into the crimson canopy above. Her heart was tight. Heat scalded her cheeks. She felt her father's spectacles in her pocket, weighing her down like an anchor. With tremendous effort, she pulled her body up to a sitting position and glared at Micah, concocting how best to cut him down.

And then she realized why she was so angry. Not because of what he said. What galled her more than anything was that he was right. In fact, he had never been more right.

Phoebe barely recognized herself.

"*My greatest secret. Tell no one,*" she said quietly, reciting the Ona's words. "*You alone can. Make the descent. To the heart of prayer. Where my Bearing once lay . . .*"

Micah joined in, and they spoke the rest together.

"Retrieve the white star. My Occulyth. And Mehk will. Prevail."

The kids locked eyes for a hard moment.

"It's not enough," Phoebe sighed. "The Ona didn't get a chance to explain it to us. We don't know anything."

"Yeah, we do," Micah argued, taking a few tentative steps toward her. "If she wants us to retrieve it, it's gotta be some sorta object, right? Not a star in the sky or anything tricky like that."

"And we know we have to go down somewhere to get it."

"Down into some kinda holy place," he finished. "We know that much, even if the rest is gobbledygook."

"But where? Where are we supposed to go, Micah?"

"Dunno," he said honestly. "Away from here."

"But we don't know where here is," she protested. "We don't have a map. Or food, or water. We won't last out here for . . ."

Phoebe couldn't believe it. The twerp was actually smiling.

"What?" she demanded.

Micah opened a compartment on his hard-shelled pack to reveal two tubes, one orange and one clear, then he knelt down by the trickle of vesper. He hit a button, dipped the orange tube into the oily liquid, and put the clear one in his mouth.

"You were sayin'?" he said between gulps.

Phoebe was speechless.

"A soldier's always prepared," he declared, tossing off his pack and retracting its segmented steel casing. Inside there was a heap of rifle ammo and a crinkling nest of Wackers bars. It was a ten-year-old boy's treasure trove—bullets and candy.

He offered the tube to her. Without a second thought, she

snatched the line, and water spurted into her mouth, sweet with a vague citrusy flavor—the remnants of purified vesper.

Phoebe looked at him, stunned.

"Called a VooToo. Vesper to H_2O Conversion Unit," he said, grinning proudly. "Saw it when I was goin' through all that junk in the camp. Pretty standard Foundry issue and—"

She kissed him.

It was a spasm of chaos. Spontaneous combustion. A tart, wet punch of lips on his grubby cheek. It lingered.

Two seconds. Three.

Now it was Micah's turn to be struck silent. He stared into space like an invalid, flushed and utterly frozen.

"I'm sorry, I . . ." she said, taking a few steps back. "I just . . ."

Half of her wanted to collapse into a mortified heap, and the other half wanted to bolt away screaming into the jungle.

"I . . . I really thought we were going to die here," she burbled.

"Figured you might need somethin' to protect yourself with," he muttered as he dug around in his pack, trying with all his might to continue as if nothing had happened.

Phoebe's self-consciousness gave way to concern for Micah's health. He was turning as red as a boiling lobster—how was he even breathing? It looked like he might burst.

"Since you ain't all that into guns," he said, thrusting a stout piece of metal in her direction. His hand was trembling.

She fought an unwelcome urge to burst into laughter. Well,

now she knew his greatest weakness. All she had to do to win the next argument was give him a kiss.

Then Phoebe noticed that she was shaking too.

"Thanks," she said, trying to grab the thing nonchalantly.

It was a survival knife in a matte black case, and much lighter than it looked. Phoebe slid open the magnetic snap, and a dark steel blade hissed out. The weapon was layered in pleated geometric patterns like a feather.

It probably was *a feather,* Phoebe thought ominously.

"Multi-Edge," Micah mumbled, taking the knife from her. He adjusted a ring marked with little icons around the base of the hilt. With a series of clicks, the tiny layered plates of its blade danced into a new shape. In half a second, the Multi-Edge had become a hacksaw. Then with another twist of the knob, it became a pair of scissors. *Click*—a fork. *Click*—a trowel.

She fished around in the hidden pockets of her skirt. Phoebe's hand grazed her old sniping supplies, but now they felt childish to her, as if they belonged to some distant stranger.

"Not bad," she smiled. "But it's no match for . . . a needle and thread, a packet of itching powder, a ball of rubber bands. Oh, and a receipt for . . . a self-counting coin purse from T&S Finch."

Micah's volcano of a face was going dormant, and he chuckled. She couldn't help but notice the shiny smudge on his filthy cheek—an excruciating reminder of her regrettable gush.

The guttural chug of an Aero-copter got louder, and the

red-bladed jungle canopy shivered. Phoebe and Micah took cover beneath the nearest tahnik sphere.

They stood still until the sound faded.

"Seriously," Micah whispered, "we gotta move."

Phoebe was about to ask him where, when she looked down at her oversized boots. The trickle of vesper ran between their feet. She followed it with her eyes as it slithered through the jungle like a strand of orange yarn.

"In our world, people gather where there is water," she said.

"Yeah?"

"Maybe it's the same in Mehk. Maybe if we follow this," she wondered, pointing at the stream, "it'll lead us to a river."

"Where there might be a buncha mehkies."

"Which isn't necessarily a good thing."

"Considerin' our options . . ." Micah pondered, screwing up his face, "I say it's our best bet. 'Cause we ain't stayin' here."

He whipped a couple of Wackers bars out of his pack before strapping it on again. Tossing one to Phoebe, he marched off.

"Good work, Plumm," he said over his shoulder.

Phoebe wiped the dirt from Micah's cheek off her lips and tucked into the candy bar. A savory-sweet taste of home.

Home, she thought.

"You too, Tanner."

11 RESISTANCE

"It be running subterraneally along this thoroughfare," Mr. Pynch said, his disc of nostrils ticking. "Me nozzle never lies."

He and the Marquis were three blocks from an imposing Foundry compound that was protected by a glowing barricade. The cluster of buildings stuck out like a buzzing purple cyst in the heart of Sen Ta'rine. Its powerful magnetic field had affected the growth of the nearest mehkan skyscrapers so that the golden sendrite trunks bowed away.

The Marquis was on lookout, twirling his umbrella in an attempt to appear nonchalant to the passersby, swiveling his lenses on their stalks to peer down every street. He fumbled the umbrella and whopped Mr. Pynch on the back of the head.

"Watch that blasted bumbershoot, will ya?" He rubbed his scalp as his partner flickered an apology.

Mr. Pynch flashed his grimy gold teeth at a few nearby mehkans in an ingratiating smile, trying to not draw attention.

"Stop yer paranoiding," Mr. Pynch grumbled under his breath. "Just don't get observated by any bleeder-types, seeing as how we are most assuredly on the Foundry's wanted list. As for the Covenanters, they be in hiding, waiting for us to do their dirty work. They don't know yet how much you've fouled it up."

Blinky-flicker.

"It most certainly was yer fault!" grumbled Mr. Pynch as he sniffed his way into a narrow alley. He fumbled inside his overcoat and pulled out the floppy, hairy thing the Marquis had mistakenly stolen. "Whaddya call this monstrosity?"

Flash-flash-blink-flicker.

"No, I said steal a *headset*!" he blasted, cramming the thing back into his pocket. "Not this revoltilating . . . whatever it be! The bleeder's headsets all have a door-lock release sensor."

Strobe-flash-glare-flicker-glare-blink.

"Fortunately for yerself, I have an alternate infiltratory plan." He kicked at the ground and took a big sniff. "Right under here."

Mr. Pynch extended a clump of quills from his mitts and scraped a hole into the ore, revealing a fat black pipe.

Flashy-flick.

"Got a better idea? This tube leads directly inside. Now strip off yer duds. If we don't deliver on our side of the bargain, the Covenant will never let us go." Mr. Pynch unscrewed a hatch on the pipe and gagged at the stench of human sewage. He pulled out his nozzle cap to affix it, but it slipped from his grasp and clattered into the darkness of the foul pipe. "Puddlemudge!"

The Marquis took off his gloves and his jacket, dusted off a spot of ground, and laid his clothing in a tidy pile. He paused before removing his pants, his opticle light turning pink.

Mr. Pynch rolled his eyes and turned away to offer his partner some privacy. "When you return, knock three times and I will reopen this here conduit. Then our debt will be paid, and we can scarper off to more prosperous territories."

He turned back to the Marquis, who was standing naked, dipping one elongated toe into the pipe like a swimmer testing an icy pool. His body consisted of a single flexible tube that bundled into a dense anatomical muddle in his torso and snaked out to form his hose-like limbs. The Marquis looked sharply at Mr. Pynch and flickered a rude message: *Flashy-blink-blink.*

"Well, I won't fit, so it has to be you. The faster you get in there and do what the Covenant be demanding, the faster we can wash our hands of this whole demeaning affair."

Heaving a deep sigh, the Marquis plunged his foot into the narrow opening. The long coil of his body unraveled like a cheap sweater. In five seconds, he had vanished into the sewer pipe, wriggling through it like a metal noodle.

Mr. Pynch slammed the hatch in place and screwed it tight. He wiped his greasy brow and pressed himself into the shadows, his wonky eyes scouring the alley for signs of trouble.

How long would it take the Marquis to navigate his way inside? Like all lumilows, he'd been raised in the pipes and firkins of Dyrunya, so it shouldn't take more than five ticks, ten at the most. Time dragged on. Mr. Pynch picked at his teeth with a protruding quill, willing himself not to worry.

"What here you do?"

The garbled Rattletrap words snapped Mr. Pynch alert. The bald Foundry bleeder charging toward him had probably learned them phonetically. Two armed guards were with him.

Mr. Pynch composed himself and offered his pleasantest smile. "Salutations, me friends!" he said, noting with pleasure their shock at hearing him speak Bloodword. Clearly, they didn't know that balvoors had a knack for languages.

"State your business!"

"I was merely on a constitutionary stroll, when I stepped into this shadowed recess to escape the overwhelming torridity." His words seemed to confuse the guards, so he added, "Rapturous day, but a modicum too hot for me particular penchant."

The bald guard looked at the hole in the ore and the exposed sewer pipe within it. "You been digging?"

Mr. Pynch's heart valve churned. If the Marquis knocked on that pipe now, they'd be in a whole heap of trouble.

"Mercy, no! I found such disarray when I arrived here.

Mayhaps a jaislid laborer was attempting to access the roots of this sendrite tower and forgot to cover his exertions."

"That pile of fancy clothes yours?"

Mr. Pynch chuckled. "No mehkie this side of the Shroud would be caught dead in apparel of the human varietal."

Baldy's gaze lingered on Mr. Pynch's garish green necktie. Then he spied an object sticking out of Mr. Pynch's pocket—it was the furry thing the Marquis had stolen. Baldy's eyes bulged.

"Little thief!" he snarled, snatching the pilfered toupee and slapping it onto his gleaming bald head. The fuming man squinted at Mr. Pynch and snapped his fingers. "ID this one."

A glowing handheld scanner was shoved in Mr. Pynch's face.

Blip-blip-blip-blip . . .

He watched Baldy's hands move to the magnetic club at his belt—it was a Lodestar, just like the one Mr. Pynch had stolen from Micah, then lost in a lousy bet shortly after.

Now Mr. Pynch was beginning to feel ill, like he had a viral case of rustgut. He could see no easy way out of this. Was the Covenant watching? Would they come to his rescue? Surely, he would be shot dead in his tracks if he tried to flee.

And what about the Marquis?

PING!

"It's one of the saboteurs!" Baldy growled.

The guards drew their rifles. The yawning barrels pressed in so close that Mr. Pynch could smell how recently they had been fired. Fingers hovered over triggers.

A low groan startled them, followed by an ear-shredding glissando. The electronic thrum faded along with the purple glow that had tinted the area. An eerie silence settled.

The magnetic barricade of the Foundry compound was down.

An emergency siren wailed.

Mr. Pynch didn't miss a beat. He inflated with a pop, his body expanding so fast that he launched a few feet into the air. The men were flung back, their rifles skittering away.

Baldy scrambled for his Lodestar, but Mr. Pynch rolled end over end, flattening the bleeder. He deflated, snatched the magnetic club, and fired it. A purple bloom of force hurled the metal-armored men down the alley like stray fluff.

Mr. Pynch was preparing for a second assault—"hit them when they're down" was his default brawling philosophy—when he heard three muted knocks. He unscrewed the hatch on the sewer pipe and shielded his delicate nozzle.

"Took yer sweet time down there, didn't ya?"

The slime-befouled bundle of naked tubing that was the Marquis emerged, none too pleased. He looked at the trio of groggy guards and blasted up a message.

Blinkety-blankety-flashy-flick.

"You most certainly did NOT save me!" blustered Mr. Pynch. "I was handling meself most adequately, thank you very much!"

The Marquis scraped off handfuls of muck and got dressed.

"Though yer obliteration of the Foundry's security

apparatus will surely satisfy the Covenant's needs. You have me regards."

The Marquis tipped his top hat.

"Shall we vamoose?"

As they raced down the alley, a fireball erupted. Mr. Pynch and the Marquis glanced back over their shoulders to see a gang of Covenant warriors streaming from their hiding places, weapons drawn as they breached the Foundry compound's vulnerable perimeter. Among them was the thiaphysi who had captured Mr. Pynch and the Marquis. She saluted them with a fist over her dynamo—their obligation was at an end.

Black smoke curled into the sky above Sen Ta'rine and the Living City rang with a triumphant Rattletrap battle cry:

"Blaze the Way!"

Though it had only been a few days since the Citadel's collapse, the Foundry's relocation to the Depot was nearly complete. They had engaged the NET system, a glowing magnetic lattice suspended over the premises to deter aerial assaults. The watchtowers were overflowing with soldiers, and multibarreled Frag-cannons scanned the premises in agitated arcs.

Security had never been tighter.

Transloaders, hulking Tier-trucks, and Over-cranes clogged the arteries of the complex. All seventeen railways were occupied, yet more behemoth locomotives rolled in through the security gate, awaiting their assignation. The entire Depot teemed with personnel, with most of the commotion focused on trains idling by the tunnel to Albright City.

The shipment to Trelaine was being assembled, Goodwin realized—without his involvement.

He observed from an enormous plate-glass window in the circular conference room on the top floor of the Control Core. This impressive, cylindrical tower was the Depot's high-rise heart of glass and steel. At the room's center was a lengthy copper table inlaid with a golden image of the Crest of Dawn. Trapezoidal chandeliers hung overhead, and supple burgundy carpet spread underfoot. Workers laid cable, carried in plush furniture, and hung paintings on the walls.

Goodwin sat in a chair opposite Chairman Obwilé and the four directors, whose faces were lit from beneath by Computator panels. Their attention was fixed on the voices coming through their earpieces—removable ones, Goodwin noticed irritably, still feeling an ache where his own earpiece had been implanted. Apparently, he was not important enough to be included in this conference between the directors and the Board.

Once they were done, Obwilé and the others fixed Goodwin with indifferent stares. He took that as his cue to begin.

"Good morning, and thank you for your time. Materials gathered from our raid reveal fifteen Covenant encampments scattered throughout Mehk. If we attack from the region marked here"—he pressed a button on his Scrollbar and the map appeared on their screens—"we can drive them to—"

"Thank you, James," cut in Obwilé, "but stick to the facts. My team doesn't need your advice in these matters."

"Of course, but I urge you not to delay. They are scrambling to recover, so we are perfectly positioned to strike."

"You were summoned here to deliver a report. That is all."

There was a click in his earpiece. By their reactions, Goodwin could tell the rest of the directors heard it too.

"There has been an attack on our compound in Sen Ta'rine."

"Nine Watchman units destroyed. Six injuries, two fatalities."

The directors exchanged glances.

"Eighteen enemy mehkans killed, five escaped. Minor damage to our facility. We have a team in pursuit."

"Is the threat ongoing?" inquired Director Santini, a jowly man with a haughty air and a black, manicured goatee.

"No, but it appears to have incited riots elsewhere in the city."

"You see? We must act now," Goodwin said gravely.

"You believe this is the Covenant?" Director Layton asked.

"Unlikely," interjected Obwilé. "There is no reason to think—"

"Let James speak." Her voice was frigid.

"Without a doubt," Goodwin replied. "With our new intelligence, we can cripple them, but time is of the essence."

There was a tense moment while the four directors huddled. Chairman Obwilé adjusted his gold-rimmed glasses and touched his earpiece. Evidently, the Board had something to say to him alone. Perhaps they had a secret purpose for him—it wouldn't be the first time the Board had played one of its pawns off the others. Or perhaps they were reprimanding him.

"James, we are granting you a temporary advisory position on the Covenant Task Force," Director Layton said at last. "You will serve under General Moritz. Don't make us regret it."

Goodwin nodded and made sure not to glance at Obwilé, enjoying the man's frustration from the corner of his eye.

"You have my thanks," he said. "There is one other matter."

"Yes?"

"The children are alive. The Covenant is protecting them."

"What makes you think you know this?" Obwilé asked.

"In the camp, one of the prisoners, a sort of priest, said something. I had the words translated: *'The infidels will wither. Phoebe is the light of Loaii.'* It is unclear what the term 'Loaii' means, but they appear to believe she is a kind of saint."

"What of it?" inquired Director Santini.

"Are these delusions relevant?" Director Layton asked.

"Yes." Goodwin looked at their scowling faces. "If we hope to eliminate the Covenant, we need to understand their objectives. I propose we send a recon team to track the children down and—"

"You waste our time," scoffed Obwilé.

"No, Mr. Chairman," Goodwin said calmly. "If the Covenant thinks they are important, then we should do the same."

"As I recall," Obwilé sneered, "you dismissed us when we told you to find those children."

"They were not a priority then," argued Goodwin. "And I did, in fact, detain them—"

"Only to lose them once again."

"*Enough*," stated a voice in their earpieces.

"*We cannot spare resources to mere hunches.*"

"*The children are of no consequence at this time.*"

"Report to General Moritz, James," Director Malcolm said with a flash of his white-capped teeth. "Focus on the Covenant. If you find evidence that the children are pertinent to our interests, then we can revisit this matter."

"*Dismissed.*"

Goodwin nodded, burying his contempt.

Heel. Roll over. Play dead.

His time would come.

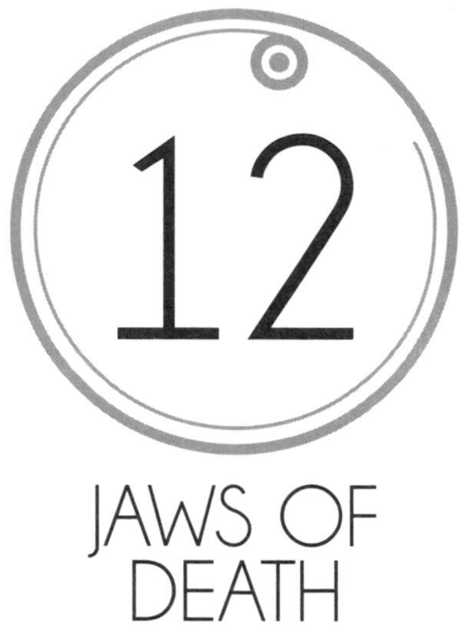

12

JAWS OF DEATH

Just as Phoebe had suspected, the trickle of vesper swelled to a stream, then became a creek that carved through the lush jungle. They had been hiking for hours, and while her coveralls felt like a Toast'em Oven, the trek was not at all unpleasant.

Much like the rain forests she had heard about back home, this jungle was a torrent of life. Magenta, parrot green, and fluorescent yellow blooms dominated the creek beds, their vibrant faces turning like pinwheels. Amid the tahniks, trees with hinged, zigzagging trunks sagged with purple punching-bag fruit. And a rainbow orchestra of flying things was

rehearsing in the canopy. Phoebe couldn't call them birds exactly, because most of them didn't have wings. There were propellers, soaring kites, leaping springs, and some that hovered like flying saucers.

It was sensory overload—too many kinds of plants and animals to take in at once. And that had her kind of worried.

Earlier, she and Micah had stumbled upon a host of carnage-splattered mehkans like miniature jackhammers on stilts. Startled by Micah's armor, the horrific, oversized mosquito things scattered, leaving a blackened carcass behind. Whether they were predators that had brought the poor creature down or just scavengers, she couldn't say.

"Hold on a second," Phoebe said. She loosened the straps on the Multi-Edge's sheath and cinched it around her slender waist.

"Not like that," Micah chuckled. "Put it 'round your leg."

She realized he was right, but her beanpole legs were too scrawny for the straps, so she continued fastening it at her side.

Micah just shrugged and clattered ahead through the florid pinwheel flowers. He paused for a moment by the vesper, activated his VooToo, and dipped the tubes in to get a drink. He marveled at the blooms surrounding him. Spatters of electric blue forked through with streaks of oven red and orange, and as the petals turned, their colors swam in a hypnotic whirlpool. He leaned in to inspect one of the beautiful blossoms.

A little spritz of glitter squirted out of the pinwheel into Micah's face. He backed off and brushed the dust away.

"You okay?" Phoebe asked as she approached.

Micah sneezed. "Yeah, I'm fine, I'm . . ." He sneezed again, knocking his helmet askew. "I'm just . . . ah . . . ahh . . ."

"Don't sneeze."

"Ahhhh . . ."

"Seriously, seriously. Don't sneeze."

Micah's eyes opened, and he scrunched his nose uncomfortably. "Why? Wha . . . what's wrong?"

She looked at him intensely.

"Nothing. But it stopped your sneezing, didn't it?"

Phoebe smirked, and he growled in annoyance, rubbing at the pesky irritation in his sinuses.

She looked around to get their bearings and realized that it must have been midday because the ring of mehkan suns had nearly joined in the sky. Something pale and hazy loomed in the distance. At first, it looked like a massive white flower, hundreds of petals splayed wide. It reminded Phoebe of the dahlias from Mr. Kashiri's garden back on the estate. But it must have been miles away. Beyond it stretched a vast silver ocean, blanketing the horizon like a liquid mirror. There was movement among the flower's ruffles like little bustling ants, and it had creepers too.

Not creepers. Roads.

"It's a city," Phoebe marveled.

"Pretty," Micah said distantly.

She looked at him with a cocked eyebrow.

"Pretty, pretty coconut," he said, sort of to himself.

"What did you say?" Phoebe asked.

He lolled his head around to gaze at her.

"What's that? No, nothin'," he said.

She watched him curiously. "There's Covenant hiding out in the cities, that's what Dollop said. Maybe we can get help there."

"Better skedaddle then," Micah blurted. He marched off, wending his way along the creek. Phoebe watched him stumble and giggle as he regained his footing. She frowned and followed behind, focusing more on Micah than on her surroundings—so much so that she missed a muted sound echoing in the jungle.

A creak. Then a snap.

A scattering of mehkans limped out of the shadows. They helped one another along, some carrying comrades on their backs. Luckily, a hohksyk was with them—he was climbing through the jungle canopy, using his liquid-silver sensor to lead the way. The ragtag Covenant band was headed to a rendezvous.

And Dollop was just trying to keep up.

Back in the camp, falling debris had pinned his leg, separating him from Loaii and Micah. After wriggling free, Dollop had rearranged his pieces to shorten the wounded leg, using the leftover parts to extend one arm like a crutch. With the help of his brethren, he had hobbled to the Housing tent, where Axial Phy opened a secret tunnel. Once they were through, the axials had collapsed the tunnel so the Foundry couldn't follow.

That was clicks ago, and now it was nearly fusion.

There was a voice up ahead, and the survivors quickened their pace. Just beyond the next tahnik, the meager remnants of the camp were gathered around the mouth of a fresh salathyl hole. They were listening to Overguard Orei issue commands, her arcs and sliders moving briskly.

Dollop nearly sang with joy at the sight of her, but he knew such an outburst would be frowned upon.

"Proceed two hundred eight quadrits. Join secondary and tertiary teams. Overguard Zo'rinder commands there."

The warriors were divided into two distinct groups. Dollop wondered what was going on.

"Those are your orders," she said. "From arch-axials. From the Ona herself, may her golden ember blaze. Repeat, this is critical. Her most vital component. Now go."

The mehkans saluted, clenching their fists to their dynamos, and Dollop hastily did the same. One group prepared to depart while the other stayed behind, organizing their thin ranks.

"Ov-Overguard!" he called out.

Orei was engaged with one of her subordinates, and she didn't look at Dollop as he limped up to her.

"You were spared the Shroud," Orei said. "Unexpected."

Dollop didn't know what to say to that.

"You are no warrior," she stated flatly. "Go with Underguard Cya's unit. Departing now."

"Wh-where are they going?"

Orei turned to Dollop at last. "To find Loaii."

Dollop's liquid amber eyes bulged.

"Bu-but I thought they didn't ma-make—"

"Status unknown. My failure." The movement of Orei's apparatus began to lurch and slow down. "I had Loaii. In Hy'rekshi camp. Outnumbered. I—" Her warbling voice quivered, becoming almost unintelligible. "Lost her. No remains detected. Covenant Command requires status of Loaii."

From the confines of her orbiting form, Orei withdrew a long white spike—a salathyl prong, used to summon one of the great mounts. Dollop reached out tentatively and took it from her.

"I-I'll do my best to fi-find them both." Orei's discs began whizzing, and he had to pull back to avoid a painful slash.

"You must," she barked, regaining control. Orei strode past him to join the team of warriors that waited to serve her.

"Wh-what about you? Can't you, um, come with me?"

She stopped and spoke over her shoulder.

"I am strategist of Covenant Command. Not permitted to seek Loaii. Makina guides our hand. The Ona has spoken."

Dollop could hear wind whistling through Orei's scythes.

"And Her word is war."

Something was wrong with Micah.

He had been talking about Moto-bikes for the past ten minutes without a break, and most of it was clearly nonsense.

"See, in '78 they totally screwed up the Mach Three chassis design till it was all *WEEEEEHHHWW!*"

He knocked into her with his oversized body armor and Dervish rifle, then leaned in close and made a lunatic face. Little specks of dust twinkled amid his freckles.

"Which is funny 'cause that was right around the same time they started powering their tire pumps with pinstripes." He staggered ahead of her, careening toward a stand of spinning flowers. "Bin stripes. Gripes. Pipes. Pah, pah, pah."

"Careful. It's steep here," she warned. The vesper creek was rushing past them now, cutting a deeper path into the ore.

Micah tripped over his own feet and took a nosedive into the fluorescent pinwheel flowers. As he crashed into them, they released a hiss of glitter, showering him in sparkles.

"Party time!" Micah crooned. "Party ti . . . taaa . . . Ahhh-CHOO!"

The flowers.

A cloud of shimmering dust rolled toward Phoebe.

With a wild grab, she ripped at the facemask built into her coveralls. She affixed the breathing apparatus just as the tinkling powder rolled past her. A tacky, stale taste of nicotine still lingered in the used tubes, but watching Micah's galloping pony dance was enough to make her fight the urge to spit it out.

He spun around in circles, his helmet rattling atop his

head. Phoebe grabbed his arms to try and get him under control.

"Stop it, Micah," she insisted, struggling to keep her balance.

"Vurbbble, vurbbble, vrrroooooooooooooom!" he sang. "That's the sound a Hyena Turbo makes when it's in ice cream!"

He burst into a fit of sneezing laughter, grabbed her, and twirled around and around.

"I said STOP!"

But that only made him go faster. In a clamor of body armor, they burst through the undergrowth near an embankment where the ground dropped away. Micah scrunched his nose.

"Don't sneeze. Hey, seriously, don't—"

They fell. Phoebe screamed. Micah yodeled.

In a sloppy tangle, they plummeted down a mudslide of ore. They tore through wire roots and jutting branches, clinging to anything to slow their drop. The ground pitched steeper, until there was nothing beneath them but air.

Splat! Phoebe landed on Micah, blasting the air out of his lungs. Even that didn't stop him from wheezing with laughter.

She heard a series of aching metal creaks above their heads. Phoebe grabbed his armor—hauled him back in the nick of time.

SNAP.

Giant metal jaws the size of an Auto-mobile trunk crashed shut right where Micah's head had been. She saw them in terrifying detail—firework orange with canary-yellow stipples, lined in brutal foot-long steel fangs. The massive mouth groaned and retracted in a rustling scrape of metal foliage.

"Ooooooooh," Micah said in dazed wonder.

This was bad.

She and Micah had fallen into a sunken grotto that twinkled with the toxin from countless pinwheel flowers. There were hundreds of fanged shapes settling among the blooms, but she couldn't make them out clearly.

Very, very bad.

"I think the playground's this a-way, Freddy!"

She turned around just in time to see Micah stumble deeper into the glittering darkness. *Snap, snap, snap!* Rainbow-colored mandibles clamped shut, shearing off a panel of his armor like it was made of cardboard. She rushed after him.

"Stop!" Phoebe cried. She spun him around, and he sneezed in her face. A chorus of creaks. She hurled him to the ground.

CRASH. All around them, fanged jaws slammed shut. A wall of teeth pinned them in, every size and every magnificent color.

After a couple of seconds, the mouths retracted, creaking as they hinged back open. It went deathly quiet. Her breath came in constricted gasps. She looked around at the spongy bog as one of the snapping things flattened out, nestling into the stagnant mud so that only the tips of its magenta fangs poked out.

Phoebe was reminded of biology class when Mr. Pomeroy made her feed bugs to a Venus flytrap. She stared in horror at the hundreds of fanged rings lying in wait all around them. Some were as small as coins, others as wide as Aero-copter pads.

More like Venus beartraps, she thought with a shudder.

"Ahhhh . . . ahhhhh . . . AHHHHH—"

"Micah! No, no, no, don't sneeze," she hissed, shaking him.

He looked at her with glazed eyes and rubbed at his nose.

"I said cut that out, Freddy. Or I swear I'll sock you one." He shoved Phoebe, and she took a step back to keep her balance.

Through the sparkling gloom up ahead, she saw an elevated mound that led out of the grotto.

Micah started using a strand of metal vine as a jump rope.

"What are you . . ." Phoebe gaped.

"Coach said I couldn't beat your record," he said, huffing and puffing, "but I bet I . . . ahhh . . . AHHH—"

"Whatever you do, don't sneeze. Don't sneeze!" Phoebe whispered. She snatched his jump-rope vine and tugged him toward her as a couple of jaws nearly snapped shut on his butt.

While he pawed at his nose like a bear swatting a bee, Phoebe spun him around and wrapped him up with the vine.

"Wheeeeeeeeeeee!" he cried, whirling.

The jaws creaked.

"Keep it down, Micah," she hissed. "We're in the library."

"Library?" he scoffed. "I don't care about no stinkin'—"

"It's a Moto-bike library."

His eyes lit up.

"Really?" he whispered.

Phoebe smiled and nodded. "And if you are very quiet and you follow me . . . maybe the little Moto-bikes will come out to play." She tied off the vine, leaving a strand to serve as a leash.

"Ya think we'll see an Afterburner ZX?"

Again, she smiled and nodded. She picked up his rifle and tugged him toward the mound that would lead them out.

"It was discontinued after the recall of 2002. In a tutu. Toodleoo, tutu!" A demented smile spread across Micah's rosy cheeks as he babbled.

Phoebe prodded at the ground with the butt of the rifle. Each time she did so, fanged traps clanged shut, and she stepped around them, guiding Micah while they creaked and reset. It was slow and tedious, and the tension was turning her knees to jelly, but they were inching toward safety.

Until they weren't.

Phoebe faced a tunnel of traps, fangs sticking out of the mud like railway spikes and slung low in a menacing, phosphorescent ceiling. She turned around to go back, but the predatory plants had shifted and closed in behind them.

The way out was only a dozen yards ahead.

But they would be devoured if they took another step.

"I think this may be my favorite gumdrop, I . . . ahhh . . . ahhh . . ."

Phoebe spun to stifle his sneeze. "No, Micah! Don't—"

Then she had an idea.

She kicked at the nearby pinwheel flowers, causing them to spurt out a gust of glitter. Micah coughed and sputtered.

"Ahhhh . . . ahhhhhh . . . AHHHHHH . . ."

Using the rifle, she nudged more of the blooms to raise a cloud of twinkling toxin. Micah was red-faced and huffing.

"AHHHHH . . . AHHHHH . . . AACCHHOOOOOO!"

The splattering blast echoed through the grotto, greeted by a hundred clangs. Venus beartraps slammed shut all around.

"Micah, look!" Phoebe said, pointing to the way out. "An Afterburner ZX! And it's got your name on it!"

His eyes lit up. She released his tether.

Micah tore off through the grotto in a clash of armor, hurdling over hungry plants. Phoebe sprinted after him, ducking around the traps that were resetting and preparing to feed.

Dry ground just ahead.

Micah tromped up the incline.

Phoebe heard the creak. She coiled and dove. There was a whoosh of wind behind her, and she retracted her legs.

SNAP.

The wall of garish fangs slammed closed and she fell to the ground with a thud. She felt a pressure on her boot—one of her laces was clamped in the plant's teeth.

She ripped it free.

"Changed my mind," Micah huffed. "This library's a drag."

13 REFORMATION

I know he is there before I open my eyes. Taste him on the air, through the slime of my skin. It's something I am learning to do.

I can tell the Greencoats apart like this, with my eyes closed. The man with the harelip scar. The woman who blinks too much. Taste them when they come with their probes and their burning wires. But I don't mind the pain anymore.

It nourishes me.

They marvel at my recovery. I do not writhe when they inject me now. Do not sputter and scream when they touch my not-skin. They think I hurt less. Say I must be healing.

They are wrong. Pain flares as bright. Brighter. But instead of blinding me, it illuminates. The pain is showing me the way.

I can smell color now—tangy red and rich, savory blue. I feel light. See in complex dimensions. Spatial relation, heat signature. Beginning to understand. Minute by minute, hour by hour, I feel my brain stitching itself back together.

I am changing. Turning into something new.

My body is a stranger to me. Do not recognize these hands. These horrid lumps that were once feet. I avoid polished steel and glass, anything that might reflect my face.

Do not know how long I have waited for him. Wished him to return and he is here, taste of Durall and moisturizer. Mr. Goodwin. Concerned. Leaning in. No needles in his hand, not like the Greencoats. Just his clipboard. Hear his heart beating, steady. His breath like a warm blanket. I float on the calm he brings.

My eyes are zoomed in like binoculars. Struggle to blink my vision back to normal to read his words.

"BECAUSE OF YOU, WE FOUND THE COVENANT."

I try to answer. He does not understand my gurgle.

"BUT THE CHILDREN LIVE. THEY HELP THE ENEMY."

I moan. Sides of my mouth tear. Skin and lips shearing, peeling, curling away from the black hole of my mouth. He tries not to react, but I feel the flutter of his pulse.

"WE WILL FIND THEM. YOU AND I."

I strain, shake. Furious. My blood bakes me from the inside.

"THE BOARD IS TRYING TO STOP ME," *he writes.*

I rasp an answer. He nods as if he understands.

"THEY KEEP ME FROM SEARCHING FOR THE CHILDREN."

I growl. Their hateful names burn holes into my thoughts.

"YOU MUST BE IN SUCH AGONY. I AM SO SORRY."

His words wrap the wound that is my body like bandages. The sensation is electric. A cough in the next room distracts me, feel it through the wall. The Greencoats.

They hate me. Not half as much as I hate them. Give me the chance and I will shatter them, offer their pieces to Mr. Goodwin.

Mr. Goodwin, who is so kind.

"BUT THE BOARD WILL NOT LET ME HELP YOU."

Cannot control myself. I snap, spray spittle at Mr. Goodwin. He shields himself with his clipboard. My spit froths. Dark ulcers bubble up on the metal tablet. Mr. Goodwin stares at it curiously.

I feel ashamed. Edge away from him. He reaches out and touches my hand with his rubber-gloved one.

Emotion chokes me with joy. And pain.

"I WILL HAVE YOU BY MY SIDE. WE WILL MAKE IT RIGHT."

My face stretches, muscles twisting, skin peeling. But Goodwin is not afraid of my grisly display. He understands.

And he smiles back.

The toxin wore off soon after Phoebe and Micah escaped the grotto, and exhaustion overcame them. She led him to a clearing away from those pinwheel flowers and let him rest.

It was getting late, and she was worried about being in this jungle after dark, but it couldn't be helped. He needed sleep.

She wet a corner of her skirt with a squirt of water and wiped away the glitter clinging to his face—the face she had so stupidly kissed earlier that morning. Micah looked so different now. Without that smug grin, he was just an innocent ten-year-old kid. All that cockiness and bluster, those obnoxious things that made him who he was, all of it was gone as he slept.

Phoebe settled back against a tahnik to relax, but it was impossible. Too many worries pressed in. Would they find a Hearth in that nearby city? If so, they could contact the Ona and get the Aegis to take them to wherever they were supposed to go. If only Orei were here, at least Phoebe would feel safe. And Dollop too—she missed him terribly.

Dollop. What a sad, hard place this world would be without him. But what could she have done?

Phoebe couldn't even save her own father.

The thought of him tightened the screws of her heart.

She pulled the whist over her head and retreated into its comforting silence. Phoebe attempted to purge her mind of doubt, to quiet the chattering voices inside—*to feel fiercely the love of her father.*

All around her, the colors of the jungle were a dazzling, noiseless dream. Her muscles relaxed. She felt herself sink deeper. Her heartbeat was a soothing drone.

Inhale. Exhale. In. Out . . .

Time evaporated.

Had she fallen asleep?

It was a strange, numbing sensation, like being preserved in amber. In the dark, she saw a vague point of dancing light. It slipped away each time she noticed it, so she allowed her mind to drift, to let the shape form and dissolve.

She felt a presence.

Phoebe turned her mind to focus on it, to try and grasp it.

It vanished. In a snap, she was back in her body, aware of the hardness of the ore beneath her. She sat up abruptly and pulled off the whist, welcoming back the sounds of the jungle.

Phoebe's body tingled, thrilling with wonder.

She had come close to . . . something.

"What's up with you?" Micah asked.

He was sprawled out beside her, hands behind his head. He had discarded his bulky body armor and copper helmet, perhaps finally realizing that it was more hindrance than help.

"I . . ." Phoebe whispered, "I don't know."

"I know the feeling," Micah muttered.

"Are you okay?" she said. "You seem a little less crazy."

"Yeah," he huffed. "Sorry 'bout all that." He shifted uncomfortably. "I could use a pillow right about now, though."

"And a hot shower," Phoebe agreed, feeling the dried sweat and ore caking her skin. "Then a bowl of fresh strawberries."

"Even a coupla real trees and clouds would be nice," Micah added. "I'm about ready to head back home."

"We can't."

"Not now," he explained. "After our mission, I mean."

Phoebe looked at him, unsure. "After everything we've seen, knowing what we know," she said, "how could we?"

There was a long silence.

"So what? We just stay here? Like, forever?" Micah grumbled.

She didn't have an answer.

"Well, that's lame. I thought we'd be heroes, y'know? But once we find this Occulyth thingie, no one's gonna know we basically saved the world. If we don't tell 'em, it won't mean a thing to folks back home."

"It will. It'll change everything," Phoebe replied. "Saving Mehk means no more Auto-mobiles, or Cable Bikes, or anything like that. It's all going to stop—because of us. Do you think people in Meridian are going to thank us for that?"

Micah prodded tenderly at a blister on his hand. "Then we'll just have to make them understand."

She stroked the rumpled folds of her whist, pondering the sensation it had given her, of being connected . . . to something.

"You're right," she said at last.

"I am?"

Phoebe nodded.

"People will change," she said. "They'll have to."

She glanced up at the rosy liquid sky glowing beyond the canopy. The ring of suns was expanding toward the horizon.

"It's gettin' late," Micah noticed.

Phoebe got to her feet.

"And we've got work to do," she said.

BLOOD RUSH

Phoebe and Micah heard the city long before they reached it. As the suns sank, a jaunty polyrhythmic clang filled the jungle, something like a cement mixer full of frozen glockenspiels.

A wall of red tahnik foliage was moving up ahead.

No, not foliage.

"Get down," Micah whispered.

The two of them scrambled for cover. Just beyond the undergrowth, a throng of shaggy scarlet lumps milled about, bumping into one another. The musical jangle grew louder.

"What is this place?" Phoebe wondered.

They climbed a tahnik, trying to get a better view.

It looked like a bustling marketplace. Mehkans unloaded shipments from lumbering pack animals that were like giant, scaly caterpillars. There were bushels of ruby wool, crimson foil, and rosy streamers—red material of every kind.

"Are they . . . decorating?" Micah asked.

"No," she said, watching a pair of mehkans purchase a heap of leafy red covering and proceed to wrap themselves in the stuff. Phoebe looked at him with a sly smile. "Costumes."

They shimmied along the tahnik tendrils toward the rear of the huge beasts of burden. Shooting a quick glance around the bustling market, Micah clung to the branch with his legs and dangled his body below it like a possum. He snatched a couple of bundles of red material and handed them up to Phoebe.

They retreated back into the jungle. After a few minutes of wrapping and assembling, they were ready. Phoebe was swathed in fringed red ribbon and a coat of scraggly, wine-colored feathers with eyeholes she had cut out using the Multi-Edge. Micah was draped in a coarse, musky pelt, with a frizzy pink puffball swamping his head.

"Why I gotta get the goofy lookin' stuff?" he grumbled.

"It brings out your eyes," she teased. "Can you see?"

"Sorta."

"Then follow me."

They emerged from hiding and were instantly caught in a surge of mehkans. She and Micah raced along with the horde, plunging through clouds of fragrant cook-fire smoke and passing under giant, multicolored lantern bags. The crowd poured through the marketplace, winding uphill on ground that was smooth and bone pale, streaked with gray and black like marble.

A cluster of crimson-costumed mehkans erupted into a dance in the middle of the crowd.

Phoebe cut around the disruption and trudged up another incline. She looked back through her eyeholes to ensure the pink puffball was still behind her. Then the crowd parted for a moment, and she saw the city looming ahead.

The entire metropolis was carved in a series of ripples, concentric rings that grew increasingly steep as they approached the center. Soaring facades were pocked with oval doors and windows that indicated dwellings within. The heart of the city was an explosion of pearlescent waves hundreds of feet high, ivory swells cresting like fingers that stretched toward the swirling evening sky. It looked like someone had tossed a boulder into a pool of milk, and the resulting ripples had frozen solid.

Phoebe ducked her head as the mob plunged through a tunnel that led beneath one of the sweeping waves. The winding passage buzzed with clattering echoes of music.

"Graz'go roh rohk-li-hee-hee!" laughed a squealing Rattletrap voice as she emerged into bright light. Something grabbed her costume, but she managed to pull free. A swollen face leered at her, pink and crinkled, with hideously warped features and squinty glaring eyes. It took Phoebe a second to realize that it was a mask. The figure spun away.

There was a group of these strange mehkans with oversized heads and baggy pink outfits. They were bumbling into one another, performing tricks, and taunting the crowd. A few got into a pretend fight, and one of them feigned striking the other. In a flamboyant display, the victim spewed a cascade of bright red streamers where he was hit, and the crowd burst into cheers. Next thing she knew, the play combatants were shedding sprays of confetti and foil in a festive shower of pretend blood.

Bleeders. They're pretending to be us.

Mehkan spectators watched the crowd from gaping windows and tossed down spirals of sparkling red wire, obscuring the view. The rowdy mass plunged through another yawning tunnel, and as they emerged onto a main thoroughfare, Phoebe held her breath. The red crowd was spilling over a ledge into a crater the size of a sports arena. It was teeming with costumed mehkans so that the whole thing looked like a porcelain bowl filled with boiling blood.

Micah pulled Phoebe around a secluded corner.

"This is some shindig," Micah remarked, leaning in close.

"And we're the surprise guests," she said over the noise.

"Let's keep it that way. Pretty sure they wouldn't want a couple of humans crashing their 'kill all humans' party."

"So now what?" she asked.

They glanced at the massive crater. The crowd was headed to the far end of the basin, gathering around a brightly lit area that seemed to be the source of the tooth-rattling music. But

Phoebe's eye was drawn to a squat dome in the middle of the crater, barely visible beneath tinkling red banners.

Her skin tingled under the coat of prickly feathers.

"*Heart of prayer*," she mumbled.

"Say what?"

"*Make the descent. To the heart of prayer*," Phoebe called out to him, pointing to the dome down in the crater. It was undeniable—its roof was bisected with a jagged line.

A dynamo.

"That's it. It has to be!" she called out.

"Has to?" Micah asked. "How you figure?"

"It fits what the Ona said, doesn't it?"

"She said only *we* can make the descent. Looks like everyone can go down there but us. And besides," he whispered, "what are the odds that the first place we stumble on just so happens to be the exact thing we're looking for?"

"Do you have a better idea?"

After a moment, Micah shook his head.

"Besides . . ." she said distantly, looking back at the dynamo buried in banners below. "The gears turn in mysterious ways."

15 THE WAY DOWN

“Go freshen this up,” ordered General Bertrand Moritz, holding out his coffee mug to Goodwin. The Deputy Manager glowered at the buzz-cut skin bulging out the back of the general’s hat, took the man’s mug, and handed it to a passing Watchman. Ol’ Bert and his three underlings were clearly savoring the former Chairman’s diminished position.

“Proceed,” Bert said to one of the military executives.

“Yes, sir. I vote we merge all three eastern platoons for a coordinated attack on our target near the Nhel K’taphen mines.”

“I second that, sir,” chimed another.

The chrome-tiled operations room in the Control Core was running at full speed. Bert and his lackeys were as giddy as Nature Scouts on their first rabbit hunt. This was the work they adored, the business of war, and they resented Goodwin tagging along. No wonder they had dismissed his every suggestion.

"Do it," Bert said. "Now let's talk air strikes."

They were tinkering with their digital map of Mehk, drawing colored arrows like coaches planning a game play. They weren't bad at their jobs. In fact, they knew details and figures that were beyond Goodwin. But swept up in their childish enthusiasm, the army boys had made a glaring oversight.

"Where do you want to station the Bloodtalons, sir?"

"I anticipate we'll need maximal firepower along the Inro Coast," Bert said, perusing the map.

A wave of whispers circulated. The officers looked up and stiffened. The directors had arrived.

Now was Goodwin's time to act.

"Do you not see the pattern, gentlemen?" he broadcasted, approaching the map.

"Excuse me?" Bert said, cocking an eyebrow.

The room went quiet.

"A pattern. The attack on our compound in Sen Ta'rine, the unrest in Ahm'ral, this new celebration in Bhorquvaat—what do they have in common?"

Goodwin looked to Bert, who fixed him with a hard stare.

He could feel the room tense as everyone watched him.

And his earpiece was silent, which meant he had the attention of the Board back in Meridian too.

"I shall put it more plainly," Goodwin said like a patient schoolmaster. "What drives our enemy?"

"Get to your point," Bert grumbled.

"Faith," Goodwin announced. "At their root, the Covenant is a religious organization. Ahm'ral is their holiest city. Bhorquvaat contains a sacred landmark. Our compound in Sen Ta'rine is located in the old religious quarter."

"So?" the general demanded.

"So by focusing on the Covenant camps—whose location I, incidentally, discovered—you only see half the problem."

"What do you propose?" asked Director Santini.

Goodwin turned to acknowledge the directors, pleased to note that Obwilé was absent.

"Focus on their faith," Goodwin said. "Occupy holy sites. Detain practitioners. Confiscate all evidence of the Way."

"Hit their cities, and they will retaliate," Bert warned.

"But if we light a fire under their religion, we will smoke out the Covenant," Goodwin said, raising his voice.

"Do it, General Moritz," ordered Director Santini.

"Report once you have mobilized," said Director Malcolm.

"*We knew you would eventually come through, James*," said a kindly voice in Goodwin's earpiece.

"*Your insight and skills are as keen as ever*," another said.

"James will oversee this new initiative," Director Layton announced as she followed her colleagues out the door.

Goodwin looked to Bert, whose eyes flashed beneath his cap.

A Watchman bearing a tray returned. Goodwin retrieved the steaming mug and handed it to the equally steaming general.

Phoebe was certain she was going to be trampled. The music blaring throughout the crater was whipping the revelers into a frenzy. The sea of red mehkans crashed around the costumed kids as they fought their way toward the banner-strewn dome. They pushed through dangling red draperies to feel for a door, but the walls were solid, burnished gold. The kids squeezed through the crowd, working around the structure, until they found a recessed walkway carved along its perimeter.

As they wound around the building and through an arched opening that led underground, the celebratory roar of the crowd died away behind them. The further down they went, the darker it became, until the walkway came to an abrupt stop.

"What is it?" Micah asked.

"The entrance, I hope."

Phoebe poked her head out from under the costume to get a better look. A stained golden dynamo blocked their path. She felt around its edges but saw no way to open it.

Then she recalled the dynamo on the floor back in the Covenant camp, the one that led to the Hearth.

Phoebe pulled out her Multi-Edge. With a shove and a scrape, she wedged the blade into the dynamo's jagged, gear-toothed line. She twisted the dial to the hammer icon, and the shaft of the tool thickened, parting the halves of the dynamo with a groan. Using it as a lever, she pried the door open.

Micah pitched in, cramming his hands into the gap and forcing it wider. Then he mashed his whole body into the opening and used his legs to thrust it wider still. She slipped in beneath him, and he released his hold to spill inside.

The echoing space was musty and cold, pitch black save for a gear-toothed scar of light from the dome above them.

"Hold on a sec," Micah said. She heard a series of clicks, and the bright halogen beam atop his rifle flashed on.

Buzzing wings burst to life overhead. Micah waved his gun-mounted light frantically back and forth. Phoebe clutched her Multi-Edge.

"Whose idea was this again?" he said, scanning the shadows.

"It was probably just . . ." started Phoebe, trying to control her wavering voice, "bats?"

"Right," Micah said, unconvinced.

The cold beam of light revealed this circular structure to be deceptively large. From the surface, the dome appeared small, but the walkway that wound around it must have led them deep underground because the ceiling was at least fifty feet overhead.

Phoebe and Micah shed their costumes and looked around. The dome was made of blackened gold, but the chamber itself had been carved out of bone-white ore. Age and neglect had taken their toll. It looked like a decaying tooth with a rotten golden crown. All around the huge room, gaping cavities spotted the walls beneath etched mehkan glyphs.

"I bet these words would tell us something useful," Phoebe remarked. "What do you think they say?"

"Probably some holy mumbo jumbo," Micah offered. Pale, carved pedestals poked up from the floor like headstones, punctuated here and there by empty metal crates. Other than glittering heaps of what looked like chain-link spiderwebs, the space was bare. "There's nothin' here, Plumm."

"But there used to be," she said, touching one of the alcoves. "Something sat here. Search them all. Look for a white star."

"Like what the Ona said?"

"Exactly," she said. "If one of these shelves has a star carved on the wall, maybe it will show us the way."

"Kind of a stretch . . ." Micah said, scrunching up his face. But Phoebe marched intently around the chamber, and Micah had no choice but to follow her with his light.

Something rustled at Micah's feet, and he leapt back, gun waving. A loose scrap of foil. Thinking of the bizarre langyls, he nudged it with his muzzle, not taking anything for granted.

Nope, it really was just a loose scrap of foil. He picked it up and saw that it was marked with more mehkan writing. The top had a blue insignia—a curved line arching over three dots. The same symbol was stamped on the crates scattered about.

"Over here!" called Phoebe.

She stood before a stout altar that was about chest high, its edges lined with gear teeth. Atop the worn and battered surface was a relief sculpture patterned in tarnished gold details. It showed a figure cloaked by delicate fins and encircled in veils, graceful arms raised in an exalted gesture. Its partially obscured face was depicted in an expression of rapture.

"The Ona," Phoebe said.

"But she looks different."

"Younger."

The molten image of the Ona that had appeared to them in the Hearth had been hard to make out, but Phoebe had seen her eyes, and they were heavily wrinkled. This image of the Ona, on the other hand, showed a childlike face.

"*You alone can. Make the descent*," Phoebe mumbled to herself. "*To the heart of prayer*."

"What's that?"

"Nothing. I'm just trying to figure this out."

Micah scratched his head. "I mean this is interesting and all, but we gotta keep moving."

"There's something here," Phoebe insisted.

"What?"

"I'm working on it."

"Like I was sayin' before," Micah said as he wandered over to his bulky red costume to put it back on. "No way we're gonna find this thing with a buncha dumb luck."

Phoebe glared at him.

"Face it, Plumm. This is a dead end."

"But there might be a clue."

"Doubt it," he said with a groan as he took a seat. He

detached the light mounted to his rifle and held it out to Phoebe. “You just let me know when you’re ready to split.”

She snatched the light from him.

“Thanks for nothing,” she said.

“Welcome,” he yawned.

Phoebe marched back to inspect the shrine.

But she, too, suspected that whatever clue might have led them to the Occulyth was either beyond their grasp or long gone.

DONE FOR

Dollop paused beside a rusting tahnik to catch his breath.

"Und-derguard Cya?" he called out. "A-a-anyone?"

Again, he struck the salathyl prong that Orei had given him and plunged it into the ground. He waited, and he hoped. And again, there was no response.

He could see well enough in the dark, but night transformed the Hy'rekshi jungle into a frightening phantasmagoria. Luminescent pinpods grew everywhere, and when they puckered, they looked like blinking, glowing eyes. There was a djintra nearby too, its eerie, creaking groan like a restless demon.

How had he managed to screw everything up?

For a while Dollop had kept up with the search party, hobbling along using his elongated arm as a crutch. But on the uneven terrain, he hadn't been able to keep up the pace, and before long, he had lost them. The Underguard had said they were planning to regroup, but he couldn't recall where. Even if he knew the location, how would he ever manage to find it?

He was hopelessly turned around.

Dollop had sworn to Orei that he would find Loaii and Micah. Nothing was more important, and he would give anything to bring them back. But he had already failed. What kind of imbecile could manage to lose a search party?

Who was he trying to fool? The Covenant didn't need him. Despite every attempt to be useful, he was only a burden. They were better off without him.

He was about to try his salathyl prong once more, when he heard a rustling sound. Dollop leapt and almost fell to pieces. Was it the Foundry? Were they hiding out in the jungle, hoping to finish what they had started back in the camp? Or perhaps there was something even worse lurking in the shadows.

Uaxtu. He had heard nightmarish tales of the ember-reapers his whole life. It was said the ravenous specters haunted places of death, hunting for lost embers to devour.

Dollop had to get away. He scrambled through the tangled undergrowth. Once he was far from the fearsome Uaxtu phantoms, away from the ruthless Foundry, he would try again to summon a salathyl. But everywhere Dollop turned, he thought he saw ghosts. He felt their chill at his back. The jungle seemed to be writhing with them.

Why had Makina spared him? He thought of all the brave Covenant warriors who had gone to rust back in the camp. Yet somehow, undeserving Dollop had survived.

He knew he must honor his brethren. They were gone, but their embers would live on—the Way was quite clear on this matter. As he tried to recall the well-known verses, his mind cleared. The fear did not vanish entirely, but it did recede.

He was so lost in thought that he didn't notice a celebratory echo ringing from the white city, just around the next hill.

Aimlessly, he fled. Desperately, he prayed.

Makina adored Her creation, yet still was She not content, for Her children lived their limitless cycles without consequence. And lo, they did stray from Her, and there was cruelty and malice among them, and none would heed Her Way.

Again, She spake.

"RUST" was Her command, and so it was that Makina delivered death unto the world.

And thus did the Mother of Ore decree:

"Know this. Thy embers belong to Me eternally. And I shall tend to them in my Forge according to the merits of your spans.

"The wicked who revile their Mother, who sow fear and enmity, for thee there is no eternal home. I shall douse thy embers that they may vanish forever, that thy foul deeds may be obliterated.

"The humble who strive to follow My Way, who long to find your function, those of My children for whom righteousness is an aim not always achieved, to thee I offer the mercy of another span. Thy embers shall be stirred, that ye may return to the Ore whence you came and live again to seek the light of My Way.

"And you, the vital components of My sacred machine, you who love My creation most of all, who spread interlocking harmony amongst My children—beyond the Shroud, My fires shall light for thee. Thy embers blaze eternal."

With her decree, the Great Engineer did smite the Mirroring Sea, and from it rose a mighty wall of impenetrable mist. This She named the Shroud, for it hid the world of the dead from that of the living, home of embers, heart of Her Forge.

Thus, Makina created the Shroud, not to punish Her children with death, but that they might cherish their spans and those of their brethren. Their phases numbered, mehkans wasted not, but instead strove to find their functions.

For when their cycles were at an end, and the rust took them, their embers traveled beyond the Shroud, and the children returned to the eternal bosom of their Mother of Ore.

And lo, the Great Engineer was pleased.

Accord V: Edicts 01–06

Phoebe reluctantly gave up on the shrine and slipped back into the celebration with Micah. They fought through the throng, climbed out of the crater, and navigated the paths snaking among ivory bluffs.

Between the buildings, they saw the sparkle of the ocean. A placid plane of liquid silver stretched as far as the eye could see—and Phoebe didn't want to see any more of it than absolutely necessary. That was easier said than done, as every other winding avenue seemed to end at a dock where hefty barges bobbed, their decks overflowing with revelers.

The city's glaring whiteness reflected the lanterns a dozen times over, so that Phoebe forgot how late it was until she glanced at the sky, where vibrating threads of stars shimmered.

The kids stopped to rest beneath a quiet bridge stretching between two massive ripples. Micah lifted his puffball headdress away from his face and gasped for air.

"So . . . dang . . . hot in this thing."

"Don't take it off yet," Phoebe warned, glancing around.

"Just how long are we gonna keep this up?"

"Until we find what we're searching for."

"I dunno, Plumm, we been—"

She waited for him to finish his thought, but he looked dumbstruck. It took her a second to realize why.

The music had died.

It was as if the city were holding its breath.

Then there came a steady, far-off thud. It got louder. Phoebe and Micah didn't dare move. The rhythmic drumbeat pounded, rising until it filled the streets.

A blast of wind whisked through the passages, forcing the

kids to shield their eyes as they tried to make out the shape.

An army of marching soldiers.

Searchlights slashed down through the alleys.

The Foundry.

Phoebe and Micah broke into a run. Some costumed mehkans stood petrified, others scattered. Doors slammed. Lights puffed out.

Running in their disguises was nearly impossible. Micah's pink puffball wouldn't stop sliding off, and Phoebe kept tripping on her feathered coat. They elbowed through the crowd and clambered up inclines then down again, traversing the enormous ripples of the pale city. Their legs sizzled with exhaustion.

The kids looked back to see magnetic barriers being erected around the crater, sealing it off. Aero-copters and deviously quiet Gyrojets descended. She hadn't heard any shots fired, but rows of black troops advanced down the streets, bellowing orders in Rattletrap through echoing Amplifones.

Nearby, the purple-coiled tip of a Mag-tank rolled into view.

Phoebe and Micah plunged down another street, made a hairpin turn, and climbed a carved stairwell. Confused mehkans clustered in groups and huddled in doorways.

At the end of an alley, Micah caught a glimpse of a massive, scaly caterpillar beast passing by. He stopped short and let out an excited whoop. Before Phoebe knew what was happening, he grabbed her arm and sprinted off to catch up with it.

The creature hauled a tiered freight platform that rolled

on gelatinous tires. Micah ducked behind the bulky cargo and hopped on to the back. Phoebe scrambled up beside him.

"What are we doing?" Phoebe hissed.

With a grin, Micah gestured to the cargo. It was a heap of metal crates emblazoned with that same blue insignia they had seen before—a curved line arching over three dots.

She gasped. He nodded eagerly, unable to hide his pride.

"I thought you said the shrine was a dead end," she said.

"It was," he shot back. "But maybe now we can figure out who took the junk that used to be there."

"Which means you *do* think it will lead us to the Occulyth."

"Never said it wouldn't."

"I'll take that as a yes."

The nervous crowd scattered around the shambling beast of burden, but no one seemed to notice the two costumed figures hitching a ride on its trailer.

Their transportation slowed as it wound through a series of wide, carved passages. Micah nudged Phoebe, and they hopped off, scurrying to hide among another stack of metal crates.

They were in a vast, brightly lit area, enclosed by rippling walls and within sight of a busy port. There were lanes of towering, cone-shaped buildings marked with the blue insignia, and dozens of caterpillar beasts lined up, waiting to be unloaded.

"Now what?" whispered Phoebe.

"Start searchin' some of these warehouses," he replied.

"Where are we supposed to start?"

His eyes settled on the nearest conical structure.

"There," he said simply.

"And what, just wander in?"

"That's the idea. On the count of three."

"Hold on a second," she hissed. "We need to figure this out."

"One . . ."

"Micah, we can't just go barging into—"

"Two . . ."

She growled and gathered her costume, preparing to run.

"Thr—"

A hulking figure stepped in front of them, blocking the way. He was seven feet tall with a fibrous body made from layers of woven strands, like a metal basket. Instead of hands and feet, his elongated limbs ended in frayed bushels. Here and there, metal sinews parted to reveal wet, black orbs—dozens of staring eyes scattered all over his banded body. The blue insignia that the kids had followed was seared onto his chest like a brand.

Strands around his face pulled taut and opened to reveal a flapping mouth. He spoke in a hollow, raspy voice.

Shuddering beneath their costumes, Phoebe and Micah took a step back and shrugged, hoping the gesture was universal.

The imposing mehkan spoke again, his mouth splitting his face open wider. Again, the kids shrugged and shook their heads.

"Three!" Micah cried, and dashed between the crates.

She leapt after him. They only made it a few steps before they heard a twanging sound. Two more banded mehkans cut them off. In a flash, one of them ripped Phoebe's costume away. Metal fibers cinched around her waist.

Micah tossed off his pink puffball and raised his rifle. In a lightning-fast motion, the chest of one of the fibrous mehkans splayed open wide. The metal strands formed thrusting fingers, which wrenched the weapon away and seized Micah.

He fought and flailed, but not Phoebe. What was the point?

They were done for.

HIS SPLENDOR

The three fibrous mehkans covered Phoebe and Micah in their costumes before marching them through the shipping zone. Despite this precaution, they drew a crowd. The kids were rushed past onlookers and ushered to a spot that was terrifyingly quiet. The kids' captors tore their costumes away.

They were standing in a long courtyard flanked by protective walls made of ivory-white waves. At their end, a series of graceful towers swooped up, emitting an angelic radiance. The ground was inlaid with smooth gold flagstones and pebbles groomed into curved lines and concentric circles, reminding

Phoebe of serenity gardens from the Kijyo Republic. A fountain trickled from the wall, liquid silver pooling to form the insignia that she and Micah were beginning to loathe—a curved line arching over three dots.

An oval gate whispered shut behind them, and the kids were urged forward, past dozens of stoic guards. Ahead, a group of silhouetted figures emerged from one of the luminous towers. As they stepped into the light, Micah gasped.

"You little tub o' lard!" he screamed, lunging. "I'm gonna—"

A guard wrapped Micah's face in metal fibers, gagging him. Phoebe saw what had enraged Micah. One of the mehkans before them was squat with spiny muttonchops framing his lumpy face.

"Pynch," she growled. It all came crashing back—the Gauge Pit, the sinister Auctioneer, and their two trusted mehkan guides selling them off like slabs of meat.

"I beg yer pardon?" rumbled the fat figure. His voice was different than she expected, deeper, less pompous. Instead of wearing a chusk overcoat and green necktie, he was decked out in a flowing gown and sash of silken silver.

This was not Mr. Pynch, just another member of his race.

Behind him stood an entourage of hunchbacked, tortoise-like figures. They were similar to one of the Covenant warriors who helped free the kids from the Citadel, but instead of tumorous explosives on their humped backs, these mehkans sprouted brilliant ore gems of every hue.

"You find yerselves at the mercy of His Splendor," announced the squat, Pynch-like mehkan, "foundation of Bhorquvaat, grandgiver to all of mehkankind—the Mercanteer."

He gestured to a dazzling figure amid the jeweled entourage. This mehkan's hunchback was encrusted with long stalactites of the purest sapphire blue. Azure growths extended down his rail-thin arms, patterned his elephantine legs, and emblazoned his sunken head. Symmetrical blue facets lined his face, drowning his deep-set silver eyes. Two of his companions attended his mighty crystals, manicuring the formations with little tools.

"I am but a humble balvoor, his devoted Agent of Tongues, here to translate yer utterances for His Splendor," the rotund figure explained. "Show yer respects."

"You first!" Micah snapped back. The Mercanteer's hunched handlers tittered a clinking sound.

"Micah. Not now," Phoebe warned. "We are honored to be your guests," she said to the Mercanteer. Despite the guard's grip, she managed a bow.

The Mercanteer turned to her, bemused. He made a clattering sound that might have been laughter. Despite the noise, they didn't suspect the Mercanteer was happy.

"His Splendor does not care to find bleeders in his city," the Agent said. "Especially at such an extraordinary time."

"We are truly sorry for the intrusion," Phoebe admitted. "But we had nowhere else to go."

"What extraordinary time?" asked Micah, squinting.

The Agent of Tongues rumbled some sounds to the Mercanteer, who chortled along with his counterparts.

“We celebrate the fall of the Citadel,” the interpreter said. “And we praise those who shed human blood in Sen Ta’rine.”

“Sen Ta’rine?” she gasped. “What happened there?”

The interpreter ignored her question. “His Splendor demands to know why the Foundry would dare enter our city and threaten our fragile arrangement.”

“’Cause they’re jerks, that’s why,” Micah responded.

“Do yer masters think we will tolerate spies in Bhorquvaat?”

“Who, us? No, you don’t understand,” Phoebe said. “We’re not a part of the Foundry. We’re with the Covenant.”

This made the translator smile, his golden gear teeth sparkling. He interpreted her words, and the Mercanteer erupted into a belching fit of laughter, his polished face winking like a hundred flashbulbs. His mouth splayed open to reveal a nauseating cluster of gnarled mandibles that clinked together like a drawer full of silverware. His underlings chimed in too, in the familiar tittering of eager lackeys.

“What’s so funny?” Micah spat, struggling against his captor.

“It’s true,” Phoebe insisted. “We’re on a mission for the Covenant, and we don’t have much time. Please tell him!”

“If you not be with the Foundry . . .” said the leering Agent, “then you be of no use to His Splendor.”

He said something to the sinewy guards, and their grip tightened on Phoebe and Micah. The Mercanteer and his giddy entourage edged in closer to watch.

"Wait! We can help you . . . stop the Foundry!" Micah choked.

"It's true." Phoebe wheezed. "I am Loaii."

The Mercanteer twitched, his silver eyes going wide. He clinked something in a low chuckle.

"What did you say, bleeder?" the translator demanded.

"I . . . am . . . Loaii." She could barely breathe.

The Mercanteer made a gesture, and the guards released the kids. They collapsed to the ground, panting. There was a brief, heated exchange between the Mercanteer and his translator.

"His Splendor demands to know how you know this word."

"My father helped the Covenant destroy the Citadel," Phoebe gasped. "They named me Loaii and gave us our mission. We need to find . . . something important. We think you might have it."

The Mercanteer's jointed mouth twitched angrily. He snapped a harsh, clashing word.

"Lies. You know not what 'Loaii' means," the Agent said.

"It means my path is illuminated," she answered, rising to her feet. Phoebe held out her shawl. "Do you recognize this?"

Their captors were silent.

"It's a whist, created by the axials. To . . . to honor my father."

Tears singed her eyes unexpectedly. *Not now,* she thought. *Please, not now.* Micah rose beside her. He placed a hand on her shoulder, and she felt his warmth. Phoebe swallowed.

"He died trying to save Mehk, and so would I."

"Both of us," Micah added.

The Agent of Tongues translated. The sunken heads of the jeweled mehkans drew deeper into their hunches. They approached Phoebe, circling, clinking back and forth. Their minuscule, many-jointed hands inspected the whist, caressed it.

The Mercanteer did not move. He kept his gaze locked on Phoebe and spoke in a steady tinkling rhythm.

"His Splendor says that there have been . . . rumors. Whispers that bleeders aided in the fall of the Citadel," the Agent of Tongues said. "He had dismissed them as nonsense."

The Mercanteer collapsed his hinged arms over his bejeweled chest, twiddling his tiny, articulated fingers. He strolled to one of the lofty towers, and his underlings scurried after him.

"His Splendor bids you follow," the translator explained.

Speechless, the kids obeyed.

As they entered, Phoebe was forced to squint. The interior of the tower appeared to have been coated in luminous dye, filling the palace with a soft white light. The sweeping arched entrance opened upon an atrium that stretched all the way to the top of the structure. Trickling silver fountains spilled down the walls alongside abundant sprays of sapphire-blue ivy.

"The Way has been dead for hundreds of phases," the Agent of Tongues said, interpreting the Mercanteer's clinking words. "So one calling herself Loaii should be dismissed as mad. Yet if the Covenant can destroy the Citadel . . . then perhaps not all myths be pure fantasy."

As they mounted a braided ivy platform, Phoebe saw that the vines were wrapped around flat seed casings, and the tendrils stretched up like support cables. It was the same elevator plant the Overguards had used to lower her father into the ground.

The Agent tugged on a vine, and the platform ascended. Gesturing to his entourage, the Mercanteer spoke again, and the Agent translated his clattering words.

"We freylani be fertile habitats, bodies we tend and harvest to provide a marvelous variety of goods." The Mercanteer indicated the sapphire mine on his back. "But that not be our only means of making gauge. We be mehkans of commerce. I have no use for the superstitions of the Way, but I collect relics from the age of the Engineer—treasures that fetch quite a profit."

The elevator rose, passing floor after floor. The Mercanteer said something assertive to his translator.

"His Splendor must know what you seek. If it be in his possession," the Agent said, "an arrangement can be made."

The elevator creaked to a stop, and the Mercanteer led them all into a majestic vestibule. Dynamos great and small were on display, some ash-dull and others gleaming as bright as the Crest of Dawn. There were carved tablets and fragments of ancient metal sculptures. A mural had been painstakingly reassembled, though portions of it were missing. This was a veritable museum of the Way.

Phoebe grabbed Micah's hand and squeezed it.

"Do you know what the 'white star' is?" she asked.

"It's somethin' to do with the Ona . . ." Micah suggested.

The Agent told the Mercanteer, who discussed it with his tittering minions before responding.

"His Splendor knows of no such thing," said the Agent.

"Does he know what the 'Bearing' is?" Passion bolstered Phoebe's voice. The Agent conveyed this, and the Mercanteer's silvery eyes lit up. There was a consensus amongst the freylani.

"His Splendor recalls that the accords of the Way refer to the Bearing as sacred vestments worn by the Waybound, usually a headdress. Or a mask."

Phoebe thought about the Ona, about her withered image in the Hearth versus the sculpture of her in the shrine. Had that effigy depicted her mask? Was that why she looked so old now—because her face was no longer covered by her Bearing?

Where my Bearing once lay. The Ona had lost her mask, and wherever it was, that's where they would find the Occulyth!

"That's it!" Phoebe cried. "Does he have the Ona's Bearing?"

The Agent interpreted, and the Mercanteer discussed it with the others. They appeared confused.

"What you seek not be in the possession of His Splendor."

"Well, where is it, then?" Micah shot back irritably.

The Agent asked and received an abrupt answer.

"If the Ona ever existed, she died long ago," the Agent explained. "All traces of her be lost to the epochs."

A searchlight flashed across the wall.

The Mercanteer hurried to the end of the chamber, which opened upon a great balcony. Everyone followed.

The view hit Phoebe with a jolt. The Mercanteer's tower sat at the end of a wharf, bowing out over the silver sea. The shining expanse was punctuated by a scattering of nearby islands, but beyond that it looked infinite. To one side was the city of white waves—it seemed to be festering, teeming with black Foundry maggots on the ground and shiny Aero-copter flies in the sky.

The Mercanteer clattered harshly to his entourage.

"His Splendor requests that I escort you out," the translator explained. "The Assembly of the Grand Mark eagerly awaits his recommendations for how to deal with this Foundry occupation."

"Grand Mark?" Micah asked.

"The old meaning of the name Bhorquvaat," the Agent explained. "The Waybound claim that this was once a city of sin. They believe that Bhorquvaat was formed by the Great Engineer when She came down from the sky to smite the wicked."

Phoebe looked down at the crater with new eyes, its edges now glowing purple from the Foundry's barricades. Long ago, a mighty force had liquefied the ore. The splashing spikes, cresting waves, and the rippling ground—this entire city was evidence.

Bhorquvaat was a crystallized explosion created by Her hand.

There was no doubt in Phoebe's heart.

Makina had been here.

18 OFF THE MARK

Phoebe leveled her eyes at the Mercanteer.

"Your Splendor," she declared. "I am Loaii. I serve Makina, the Mother of Ore. I come to beg for your aid. You must help us."

The Agent interpreted, and the Mercanteer's gnarled mouthparts folded back like the legs of a gem-encrusted crab.

"His Splendor advises that you not outstay your welcome," the translator said. "He has generously offered his assistance, but he does not possess what you seek."

"Then let us hide here while we look for the Covenant,"

she cried, stepping forward. Micah held her back. "If you don't, the Foundry will find us, and we will fail."

The Agent spoke. The Mercanteer turned away.

"His Splendor . . ." The translator paused reluctantly. "He says that not be an option. You not be worth the risk."

Phoebe pulled free of Micah's grip and strode up to the freylani. The group of mehkans clinked, and the Mercanteer's silver eyes popped wide. She grabbed his little jeweled hand and dropped to her knees. Based on the silence that fell, she knew that she had committed a grave offense.

"*Mehk* is worth the risk," she pleaded. "It doesn't matter what you think about the Way. If what the Covenant is doing might help you, if there's a chance it could save the people of Mehk, then it IS worth it!"

The Agent interpreted, and the Mercanteer tore his hand away from Phoebe, caressing it as if it had been burned. The translator bowed humbly and continued to beseech in hurried tones. The Mercanteer did not like what he was hearing. Nor did the other freylani, who flew into a chattering frenzy.

"What did you say to him?" Phoebe asked.

The Mercanteer barked to the Agent, who bowed even lower. The translator grabbed the kids and drew them away from the balcony, followed by the stares of resentful silver eyes. The trio of fibrous guards that had caught them stepped aside.

"I'll take that," Micah said, yanking his rifle from the guard.

The Agent escorted them back through the relic collection.

"We can't leave until we get his help," Phoebe pleaded.

"And you have it," the translator replied. "Hurry, before His Splendor changes his mind."

"For real?" Micah asked.

"There be one who might aid you," said the Agent, "a source that His Splendor hardly ever calls upon, only to find the rarest of treasures. She be a font of knowledge, ancient and feared."

"What do you mean, 'feared'?" Phoebe asked uneasily.

"She be a dread of legend—a great deceiver, a dealer of wretched schemes and lies."

"Sounds perfect," Micah grumbled.

"Then how do we know we can trust what she says?"

"You don't, Loaii. Entreating her be an ordeal, not a thing one would choose. But choice be a thing you sorely lack."

"Who is she? How do we find her?" Phoebe said grimly.

The Agent led them back to the elevator, and they mounted the platform. "Her name be unpronounceable, even in me own language. Could I manage it, speaking her name would take us until the rise. Mehkans know her only as the Erghan word meaning 'to gorge.'" He looked at the kids with one of his independently moving eyes. "This word be Rhom."

"To gorge," Phoebe mused darkly.

"You will find her in a reef system known as the Talons."

"Boy, this is gettin' better by the minute," Micah huffed.

"His Splendor has generously offered you the use of one of his barges, which will provide you safe passage across the flux."

"You mean . . ." Phoebe asked hesitantly, "the silver ocean?"

The Agent nodded.

She clutched one of the knobby vines of the elevator. A barge on the open sea? Her skin felt clammy at the thought. Would it be as bad as riding the vellikran back in Tendril Fen?

They returned to the grand atrium, and the translator hurried the kids across the chamber to a different elevator.

"This was your idea," Phoebe said suddenly to the mehkan. "You asked him to help us, didn't you?"

The Agent smiled, his golden gear teeth flashing, but in a way that was sincere, even humble. Phoebe wondered how she could have ever mistaken him for Mr. Pynch.

He was about to speak when a commotion drifted in from outside. Someone was pounding on the courtyard gates.

"The Foundry be here," the Agent growled. "Hurry!"

The translator tugged a vine, and the elevator began to sink.

"I must remain to speak for His Splendor," he said. "Go to the base. It leads to the dock where his barge awaits you."

"But who will—" Phoebe started to say, but they dropped beneath the floor, and the Agent vanished from sight.

They were in a narrow white shaft, descending through the tower at an angle. They drifted past oval windows that gazed out at the night and the silent silver sea.

"Can you handle it?" Micah asked. "The water, I mean."

"Like he said. We don't have any choice."

"I know, I just . . ." He struggled with the words. "Just wanna make sure you won't . . . that you're gonna be . . ."

She looked at him strangely. A tentative smile crept across her lips. He looked at his feet and took a step closer, scrabbling around in that silly brain of his for the right thing to say.

Voices echoed above. Humans.

The ivy elevator eased to a quivering stop.

"No," Phoebe whimpered. "No, no, no."

The kids strained their ears, but they couldn't make out the muted words up above.

"What do we do?" she asked.

"Wait, I guess."

"What if they call the elevator back up?"

Micah glanced around the wide, circular platform. Dozens of creepers and pulleys grew out of it, running up and out of sight. He threw the rifle strap across his chest, set the gun on his back, and shinnied up a vine to the nearest window ten feet above.

"What do you see?"

"Hrmmm . . ." he said, straining to hold on while he peered out. "Come see for yourself."

Micah climbed off the vine to perch on the window ledge while Phoebe made her ascent. She grunted with the effort, recalling that the rope climb was the very reason she always skipped gym class. She swooned as she stepped onto the ledge beside him. It was a sheer drop down to the vast, reflective sea.

"Don't suppose you're up for a swim," Micah said.

"I don't think so. Flux looks like"—she peered down at the silver infinity—"mercury. That stuff can't be safe."

"But if we climb down, we can get to those rocks and—"

"We can't. The wall is totally smooth. There's no way to . . ."

Phoebe looked at the vines wrapped around the wide seed casings. She tested the lines, chose the fattest coil, and slid out her Multi-Edge. With an adjustment of the dial, the segments of her tool clicked to re-form a hacksaw, and she went to work.

"Leave it to Plumm." Micah laughed, shaking his head.

She severed the vine, and the elevator lurched. The sliced tendril recoiled back toward the seed casing, but Micah grabbed it, unspooled the vine, and tossed it out the window. Its loose end splashed into the flux below. Phoebe looked down nervously.

"Piece o' cake," Micah said as he grabbed on to the vine and climbed out the window. "Just do me one favor. Don't let go."

He vanished over the edge and rappelled down the tower.

She grabbed the vine, fought down her sickening fright, and stepped off the window ledge.

With the vine clenched under her arm and held securely in her hands, she used her feet to ease her way down the tower. The air was crisp, but free of any briny scent or the sound of crashing waves. And yet, somehow it was worse. The tide was a warning—the growl of an enemy you knew was nearby. The flux, however, with its antiseptic smell and its ominous silence, was a clean killer—one that didn't want you to know it was there.

Her arms were straining, but she was in control. Almost there. Just one step at a time, that's all it was. One step at a—

The vine began to retract.

The elevator was ascending.

"Slide down! Slide!" came Micah's hiss from below.

Between her frantic legs, she saw Micah leap off the line and cling to the bluffs at the base of the tower. She clambered hand over hand, but it wasn't fast enough. The vine was carrying her back up. Phoebe eased her grip and slid down. She cinched her hands and tried to control her descent. But the end of the retracting line was coated in flux as slippery as silver grease.

She couldn't stop.

The vine slithered free from her hands.

She dropped, hit Micah. His arms flailed, and she clawed for him. Her body slammed against the bluff. She clung, hands digging into the surface, boots scraping to find purchase.

Micah reached down to her, but it wasn't far enough.

She heard the Sea of Callendon crashing around her, the taste of foam and bile in her mouth. The murderous undertow. Hands thrusting her onto the rock—her mother's last touch.

Micah lowered the butt end of his rifle, and she took it. With all his might, he heaved her up, and she collapsed beside him.

"I ask you . . . to do . . . one thing," he panted with a smile.

But she was shattered.

"Sorry," he said quietly.

Shaking, she waited for the daze to pass.

They caught their breath, then shuffled around the base of the tower, staying away from the edge of the bluffs. Poking their heads around the corner, they spied a curving shore with a dozen bone-white outcroppings that served as docks. At the far end, a lone barge marked with the Mercanteer's logo bobbed in the flux with a group of mehkans waiting beside it.

Waiting for Phoebe and Micah.

Before the kids could start climbing down, a speedboat materialized out of the night. It rumbled up to the nearest outcropping, cutting off their path to the barge. A team of Foundry troops poured out and stormed the docks.

"A stinkin' Sea Bullet!" Micah huffed.

Phoebe felt sick. She squatted up against the tower and hugged her knees. It didn't matter what they did. At every turn, the Foundry was there—always just ahead of them, always right behind them. How were she and Micah ever supposed to—

Micah ran.

He scrambled down the bluffs and hustled along the docks. Out of sight of the barge, he vanished inside the Sea Bullet.

Phoebe stood rooted in place, dread laced with fury. Only a stone's throw away, the Foundry soldiers had their rifles trained on the mehkans. They hadn't noticed Micah, but if they turned . . .

Before the worst-case-scenario part of her brain took over, Micah popped his head out of the boat and waved her over.

This was wrong. This was madness. She climbed down the bluff and rushed along the pier to join him.

The Sea Bullet was a deadly black knife in the flux, about thirty feet long with a low, covered cabin. Hating Micah, hating herself for following him, she stepped onto the boat. The rhythmic sway immediately sent her head spinning.

The cabin was spacious with bucket seats lining the perimeter. It had been a ludicrous gamble on Micah's part, but the soldiers had left it unattended. The boat was dark aside from his rifle light, which he had detached to hold in his teeth. His head was buried in a panel as she approached.

She heard a snap. Micah tossed something to her—a black disc the size of a bottle cap with a tiny green light.

"ID tracker," he said. "Toss it in the flux."

Unable to steady her reeling mind, she robotically did as she was told and dumped the device overboard.

Micah adjusted the controls, then tossed his idiotic grin back at her like a grenade. "Strap in. This puppy's got muscle."

He tweaked a few more dials. They heard raised voices from the nearby barge. How long until the Foundry soldiers returned?

Her brain finally popped into gear as his finger reached for the ignition switch.

"Stop!" she hissed. "The engine, it's too loud!"

His eyes widened. He knew she was right. They had heard the Sea Bullet rumbling from up on the bluffs. If they started it up now, they would be detected for sure.

"Wha [illegible]" He was starting to panic. "What do we do?"

"Get off this boat," she said, using the wall for support.

"No way. This is our ticket out!"

"To where, Micah? We have no idea where we're going."

"Anywhere is better than here," he snapped.

"They'll find us. They'll kill us. They—"

She jolted as her whist snagged on a wall panel. With a couple of tugs, she freed it, and the panel opened silently. But as the folds of her whist slid away from it, she noticed that the panel was, in fact, squeaking on its hinge.

The whist . . .

"Where's the engine?" she snapped.

Micah pointed to a row of vents slashing across the hood like the gills of a shark. Phoebe tore off her whist and reversed the material, so that the inside was facing out. She climbed out onto the hood, stuffed her shawl into the vents, and tied the corners off around rivets.

"Start it!" she ordered.

His jaw dangled open, but he understood.

He rushed back to the controls. She closed her eyes and prayed. Panel lights illuminated his face. The whist puffed a bit as if it were breathing. The Sea Bullet vibrated to life.

And the engine was silent.

Phoebe climbed back into the cabin as the boat leapt into action. Micah whipped the wheel and narrowly avoided crashing into the bluffs. The Sea Bullet sliced through the flux, quiet as a breath.

Phoebe curled up in the back of the cabin and shut her eyes, her innards churning like magma.

Lost in nausea, she didn't see a floor panel ease shut.

Nor did she notice the pair of eyes that had been watching.

19

LOST SOULS

"Bless yer embers," Mr. Pynch purred piously, counting his gauge. "Walk the Way, gentle pilgrims. Many thanks."

The dim, rot-pox-ravaged tchurbs admired their newly purchased dynamos. Mr. Pynch and the Marquis bowed with great devotion as the family of mehkies departed into the night.

The two partners could suppress their giggles no longer.

"How many we got left?" Mr. Pynch snorted.

The Marquis sifted through their foil sacklet of counterfeit sungold dynamos. *Flash-flick-blinky.*

"Nearly sold out!" he chortled. "Keep yer peeper peeled for another patch of ragleaf so we can fabricate some more."

Having just left the village of Orkeyl with full bellies and pockets bursting with gauge, Mr. Pynch and the Marquis were jangling across the Arcs. The land bridges were abandoned and peaceful, aside from the occasional Foundry train rumbling below. The night was bright, lighting their path with a streaking starscape, and a brisk breeze mussed Mr. Pynch's frazzly hair.

He felt good—good and drunk.

Mr. Pynch drew the coiled decanter of viscollia from a flap in his overcoat, took a swig, then passed it to the Marquis.

The Arcs were a magnificent system of stratified ravines that ran from the Vo-Pykarons to the Inro Coast. Over countless epochs, vesper had reshaped this landscape in irregular patterns, leaving the basins staggered like giant stairways. The elements had also formed a network of natural bridges, a crisscrossed jumble of angular pathways interconnecting the ravines. Some were short enough to cross with a stride, and others ran for a thousand quadrits.

Mr. Pynch had always heard that the Arcs were one of the great wonders of Mehk, but to him it was just a pretty view stretching from one town of suckers to the next.

The Marquis flipped back his head and poured a slug of viscollia down his neck. He righted himself, shuddered, and returned the booze to his companion.

Flishety-flack.

"Indeed! Huzzah for the Great Engineer! May Her gears gyrate eternally and so on and so forth." Mr. Pynch took a swig. "I pray Her popularity continues to swell, and that Her gullible followers remain profitous to us until the end of our cycles."

The Marquis, who was no longer capable of walking a straight line, giggled silently with his fluttering opticle.

"Come!" Mr. Pynch guffawed. "I observate the Holkhei land bridge ahead. Perchance we can reach Durl by the rise and fleece another crop of blissful dundernoggins."

They staggered from one land bridge to another, singing bawdy songs and telling the filthiest of jokes. Mr. Pynch chugged from the decanter as they wobbled across ribbons of ore.

"Who was that ill-forged scoundrel outside of Oolee? Y'know, the one with the hideous breed-mate?"

The Marquis scratched his head. *Blink-blunk?*

"That be it! Smooth operator, she was. Remember the time we paid her with her own fraudulent currency?"

Mr. Pynch swallowed some more viscollia and flipped the flask back to his companion. The tall mehkan stumbled drunkenly over his own feet as he caught it.

Blinky-flasharoo-strobe-flickety-flick.

"By me matron's corroded rack and pinion, I nearly forgotted that one! How about the time I got stuck in that bore-hole and almost missed the ambush altogether?"

The Marquis sputtered viscollia with wheezing laughter, liquor spraying out the hole atop his neck like a geyser. He tossed the decanter back. *Strobey-blink-blunk.*

"Oh, that was spectaculous, to be sure! The Vo-Pyks never seen such a conflagration! You hooked that Watchman goon right off his motorized transportator with yer bumbershoot—"

Flashy-stroble-dy!

"Then when I rolled away, you walloped his head clean off. POP! Oh, that was beee-ootimous!"

The Marquis was bouncing up and down he was so excited.

Glow-strobie-flash-blunk!

"Then that Micah boy blew another's face right in with his . . ."

A heavy silence sank the conversation. The rumble of an approaching train grew louder, chattering the little ore pebbles around their feet. Mr. Pynch's face folded in a sour grimace as he caressed his silk necktie, picking at the slipshod stitches.

Blinky-flash-flush-plop.

"So what? I don't care a modicum. It don't change the circumstancials. What did you have to go bring them up for anyway? We didn't owe them two bleeders nothing."

The Marquis fixed his light on the ground. *Flick-flick.*

Mr. Pynch gulped from the decanter and lobbed it to the Marquis with an irritated grunt. The toss was wide, and the distracted lumie almost didn't see it in time. He extended an arm to snag it, but the flask deflected off his hand and spiraled away. The Marquis took two stumbling steps to catch it.

Mr. Pynch tried to hold him back.

Too late. The lumie spilled over the edge of the bridge.

Mr. Pynch blinked boozily.

He staggered to the lip of the land bridge and looked over, steeling himself for the horrific sight of his partner shattered into grisly bits far below. Instead, he saw the Marquis dangling from a jutting lump of ore by the belt loop of his fancy trousers. He was fluttering his opticle in delirious laughter, suspended over the faint glint of train tracks far below.

Blink-blunky-flunk.

"Oh no. This most certainly DOES count as me saving yer life," chuckled the balvoor as he lowered a mitt to haul his friend up. "If it wasn't for me—"

A train roared. Pebbles danced. The jutting ore cracked.

The Marquis fell.

Mr. Pynch's smile fell with him.

The Marquis's opticle blasted a blinding shriek. He crunched atop an open train car of granulated ore. His opticle snuffed out like a candle.

Mr. Pynch stared openmouthed at the blur of train cars below as they sped off into the night.

Dollop knew he shouldn't have eaten that calefactus, but he had been starving. It was only now that his body felt tingly and numb, like his parts were all detached, that he seemed to recall that calefactus was poisonous. Or was that tulum?

Either way, his core was pumping irregularly, and his head buzzed like it was full of zurdyflies.

And he was exhausted. Dollop had been searching for so long that the jungle had given way to a swamp. Skeletal growths drooped low and erupted in scythe-like fronds. Vesper gathered in bubbling, muck-skinned pools, and fetid orange mist clung to the night. Dollop knew he wouldn't last long out here. He didn't know how to make a terra shelter, or how to purify corrupted vesper, or anything.

With shaking hands, he tried the salathyl prong once more.

But no one was coming to save him. Dollop knew that now.

He retrieved the prong with a heavy sigh.

Poor Loaii. Poor Micah. What had become of them?

"M-Mother of Ore," he began to pray, but then stopped himself. She wasn't coming to rescue him now either. The Great Engineer only helped those mehkans who could help themselves.

He continued to trudge through the stinking dreariness of the swamp with his gut roiling. That calefactus was really making him woozy.

Dollop tripped, and a musical tone sang out. He turned, and his arm grazed something, causing an even brighter note to ring.

It was a twisting black strand stretched between two trunks, hidden in the foliage. A nauseating familiarity clawed at him, a sense that he had been here before.

Terror seized him—this was a bad place.

Dollop bolted. He barely made it two steps before he was clotheslined by another concealed black thread and knocked off his feet. A cheerful chord of three notes mocked his cry of shock.

He was surrounded by an intricate web of musical trip wires. The lines ran along the ground and stretched down from branches. He could barely move without hitting the strands.

A shadow whispered past overhead.

Its name spread through his mind like a disease.

Vaptoryx.

Dollop had no memory of encountering one, yet he was overcome with vivid sensations, things he knew but could not have known. He could feel the slick mucus coating its supple black wings, hear the screeching clash of its needle-pointed legs, smell the hot rot of its snapping pincer maw.

It ripped a hole in the mist. Sheet-metal wings unfurled with a warped wobble. The nightmare was coming for Dollop.

He was locked in place, his mind trapped in the nether region between now and some half-remembered other time. The vaptoryx twisted in midair, wove its serrated body through the trip wires, and sailed forth to take its prey.

Its pincer jaws flexed wide.

The fog in Dollop's mind evaporated in an instant.

He scattered his pieces, spilling himself to the ground in a jumble. The predator's mandibles snapped shut as it tore past, narrowly missing his head. His limbs gathered together and bounced off the wires, filling the air with a harmonic cacophony. He exploded into a sprint, ignoring the stabbing pain in his knee.

Dollop looked back—the vaptoryx was so close he could smell the death lingering in its hungry jaws. He looked ahead—a nest of trip wires slashed across his path, blocking the way.

Again, the pincer jaws hinged open wide.

He leapt.

His body came apart in midair, bits and pieces of him tumbling between the wires, slipping through to freedom. The vaptoryx collided with the wall of black strands in a jangling chorus, tangled in its own trap. Dollop's parts reunited to form his body on the other side of the barrier.

The black beast thrashed, using its serrated body to hack at the lines, trying to sever them with its clamping pincers.

Dollop couldn't stop shaking as he raced deeper into the swamp. It wasn't just the vaptoryx. He felt like a curtain had been ripped back, and now light was spilling into the recesses of his broken memory.

20 FULL THROTTLE

Within minutes of gunning the engine, Micah had the hang of the Sea Bullet. Since he couldn't risk turning on any lights, he navigated by starlight reflected off the silver flux. He eased off the accelerator and looked behind them. The lights of Bhorquvaat were too close for comfort. Micah steered the boat toward the scattering of islands that looked to be only a few miles away.

The Sea Bullet died.

The steering wheel went lifeless, and the deck beneath his feet stopped buzzing. He flashed his detached rifle light to read the fuel cell gauge—nearly full.

He swept his light around the cabin. Phoebe was curled up into a ball in one of the seats. Fat lotta good she was gonna be.

No worries. He'd have this jalopy up and running in no time.

Micah found the service hatch in the floor, pulled it open, and climbed down the ladder. He scanned the mechanical confines with his light and saw a narrow walkway with a low ceiling, hemmed in on both sides with equipment.

Who woulda thought a little ol' Sea Bullet could hold such a huge engine room down below?

The power box was as good a place to start as any. A quick search revealed it. To his surprise, the front panel was open.

That was weird.

An arm hooked around his neck.

His light hit the floor. He threw his head back, trying to butt his attacker, but it only allowed the arm to tighten. Micah's vision wavered. He stomped his heels, mashed some toes, but there was no cry of pain.

In seconds he would pass out.

He whipped an elbow back, connected with a rib cage. Still the grip tightened.

The world dimmed.

Then the engine room lit up.

Sparks flew. Something hot screamed past him.

Phoebe stood at the foot of the ladder, firing the rifle in a hissing spray. The arm around his neck loosened.

Micah planted his legs on the wall and shoved. He slammed

his attacker against the low ceiling with a crunch. The choke hold released. He tore free.

As he stumbled and tried to regain his feet, Phoebe stepped forward, the rifle raised and trembling.

"Hold your fire!" ordered the shadow in a husky voice. A woman's voice. "Shoot down here, and you'll kill us all."

Micah took the rifle from Phoebe.

"You almost . . . coulda killed me," he huffed.

"You're welcome," Phoebe grunted back.

The attacker lunged at them again. Micah raised the rifle and pressed the trigger enough to start the four barrels spinning.

"On the ground!" he roared, surprised at the ferocity of his own voice. The woman hesitated, then raised her hands.

"Okay," she said calmly. "Don't do anything stupid, Micah."

"How did you—" Phoebe started.

"I said on the ground. NOW!" he commanded.

The woman got down on her knees, hands behind her head.

"Now back away," he said.

She shuffled backward down the narrow walkway. "Phoebe, look," the woman said. "I know who you are. I—"

"Shut up," Micah ordered. "Get my light, Plumm."

Phoebe grabbed his fallen light and shone it in the attacker's face. The woman was in her early thirties with blunt, curved features that held a quiet confidence. She had light brown skin, and her black hair was pulled into a tight ponytail. The Foundry sunburst logo marked her spotless coveralls.

"Find something to tie her with," Micah said.

"Wait, why don't we—" Phoebe countered.

"Just do it!" he ordered, hardly believing Phoebe would argue with him at this moment.

She started searching the engine room with his light.

"Micah, Phoebe. You kids are in serious trouble, you know that? You have to do the right thing," the woman said, starting to lower her arms. "You have to turn yourselves in."

"If you don't shut the hell up," Micah growled, "I'll shoot you dead right here, right now." The hair on his neck rose.

The woman was unmoved, but she lifted her hands anyway.

Phoebe returned with a bundle of cable, which Micah took along with the light. He handed his rifle back to her.

"She moves," Micah said, trying his very best to sound ruthless, "kill her."

He registered shock on Phoebe's face, but she pointed the rifle at the Foundry worker all the same. Micah approached the woman very carefully.

"Hands behind your back."

"My name is Gabriella," she said, staring down the four barrels of the rifle. "Be smart. I can help you. Don't make this harder on yourselves than it needs to be."

He grabbed the woman's arms and yanked them behind her back. With trembling hands, he bound her wrists to her ankles, wrapping and tying the cable as securely as he could.

"How can you help us?" Phoebe asked.

Micah screwed up the knot he had learned back in Nature Scouts. He undid the cable and tried again.

"Come back with me, and I'll make sure you get treated fairly. You have my word," Gabriella promised.

After hog-tying the woman, he patted her down, powering through the embarrassment he felt at touching her. No weapons.

"Come on, you guys," Gabriella reasoned. "You're not kidnappers. You're not killers. You're scared and for good reason. I'd be scared too, if I was in your shoes."

Micah checked the door at the far end of the engine room—it was thc lavatory. In it, he found a toolbox and a compartment stocked with toilet paper, but other than that, it was empty.

They could hear a sound rising above, the muted chug of Aero-copter blades.

"They're on to you," Gabriella said. "They're tracking the boat. It's just a matter of minutes before—"

Micah wrapped duct tape around Gabriella's mouth. He returned the roll to the toolbox and dragged his captive toward the lavatory. She squirmed and fought.

"A little help?" he said to Phoebe, exasperated.

"We can't do this," she said.

"We gotta," he said, snatching his rifle from her. He used it to prod Gabriella into the lavatory, then slammed the door.

"Micah," Phoebe pleaded.

He ignored Phoebe and dug a flashlight out of the toolbox. "Here," he said, handing it to her along with the rifle. "Find something to bar that door with. Keep her in there, okay?"

Toolbox and rifle light in hand, he stomped over to the power box, threw the core switches, and the electric generators hummed to life. A violent pounding erupted in the lavatory.

"If she gets out, you know what to do," he said, motioning to the rifle in her hands. He clambered up the ladder.

Search beams cleaved the sky, flaring off the ocean of flux. Aero-copters and Gyrojets hovered around the Mercanteer's palace. The Foundry was looking for its missing Sea Bullet.

A radio crackled.

"SB448, this is Control Core. Please respond."

Micah hunkered low and raced to the control panel, setting down the tool kit. Light in his mouth, he frantically set the dials and threw the silent boat into motion with a fishtailing lurch.

"I repeat. SB448, this is Control Core. Respond."

He wrestled with the wheel, pushing the throttle up to fifty knots. Maybe they could lay low in those islands he had spotted.

The radio crackled again. Micah dug around in the toolbox.

"SB448, you have not complied, which is a dereliction of—"

Micah smashed the radio with a claw hammer.

21 SUNK

It was late, and Mr. Pynch was sobering up against his will. The viscollia aftermath left him jittery and weak, with an unrelenting headache pounding behind his eye sacs.

The Marquis was missing.

Had his partner survived that fall, he would have headed for Durl. Yet a thorough search of that back-ore hamlet had produced no missing lumilow. So Mr. Pynch had moved on, hiking across the jumbled land bridges of the Arcs.

He clung to the hope that the Marquis would find a way to contact him. A death-defying fall onto a Foundry train was nothing to a mehkie who had gotten out of tougher scrapes without so much as a stain on his gloves. But that train had been a fast one, which meant his partner might not have roused before Durl. Most likely the Marquis would be waiting at the next town. Wycik, it was, if Mr. Pynch's memory served.

So on he went, though his feet grew heavier with every step.

If Durl was back-ore, then Wycik was submehkan.

Perfect place for a hungover scrap without his partner.

As Mr. Pynch mounted a steeply bowed land bridge, he caught a glimpse of the Inro Coast in the distance and the sparkling silver gulf beyond. That was where the train carrying the Marquis was headed, which meant so was he.

Mr. Pynch sighed and pulled his overcoat tight around his ample figure. He surveyed the elevated pathways, plotting his trajectory through the Arcs toward the distant smudge of Wycik.

And that's when he saw it, a light blinking below.

Mr. Pynch's pump soared, and his nozzle spun. He stumbled down the land bridge and crashed through a patch of iron burrs, picking the painful nuisances out of his skin while he ran.

The light blinked again and again.

Backlit-gurgle-munch, the Marquis flickered nonsensically.

His partner was delirious, talking gibberish. He probably needed medical attention. Mr. Pynch descended, pushing harder and faster, zigzagging from bridge to bridge. He scampered down a pathway and wound around a cliff toward the hapless lumie.

"There you be, ya snaky ne'er-do-well! I was surefied ya—"

Mr. Pynch jiggled to a stop.

His partner was nowhere to be found. He looked back and forth and up and down, but there was no sign of the Marquis.

The only thing here was a monument wedged into the ravine wall. It was a broken-down Waypoint—one of those ancient altars where long-ago travelers sought blessings. The carved figure within it was so savagely weathered that its features were unidentifiable, though Mr. Pynch assumed it once depicted the Ona or a highfalutin axial of some sort.

There were heaps of pink lacepetal scattered at the Waypoint, along with fresh kolchi nuts, aromatic ashcone, and other such devout offerings. There were even a few tinklets of gauge, which Mr. Pynch instinctively reached for.

As he did, a recently planted torchbloom flared to life, incinerating one of the wingnut flies that had been circling. He studied the fiery bloom—this was the flickering light he had mistaken for the Marquis's opticle.

Mr. Pynch's lumpy face sagged into a frown as he pocketed the donated gauge. He slumped to the ground beside the Waypoint and held his aching head in his mitts.

Dollop wandered through the night, clutching his salathyl prong tight, though he had given up trying to use it.

The vine-strangled swamp had thinned out to naked wetlands that were identical everywhere he turned. Rotten trunks huddled like grave markers and knots of coastal kluttlefisk clicked their shells shut as he trudged past. The ground had gone from spongy red to sickly pale mud, as if all life had been leeched from the ore. Flux mixed with vesper in bubbling amber tide pools, the thin, cloudy liquid separating from the heavier silver muck at the bottom.

His mind was tangled with fear. Frantic thoughts assaulted him, and not all of them felt like his own. There was something eerie out here. Not holy like Makina but . . . other. And yet somehow it was connected to him.

Shapes shifted in the mist and coiled on the surface of the tide pools. He looked down with a dull realization that he was sloshing through one of the ponds. Thick bubbles swelled like boils around him before bursting with languid pops.

He was sinking. The mud rose to his waist. His mind was blank. He couldn't remember a prayer, couldn't think to resist.

Now it was up to his chest.

So this is how it all ends? All alone . . .

Amber mud filled his mouth.

Sinking into nothingness.

It sealed over his head.

All went black.

And yet . . .

He was aware. Still breathing.

Dollop checked himself—all his pieces were still in place.

He rubbed his bulbous eyes until the space around him resolved. The salathyl prong lay discarded at his side. He found himself in a huge black cavern beset with millions of tiny, luminous fragments—a twinkling starscape of turquoise and emerald. The lumpy walls looked wet and curdled, with a ceiling of knobby stalactites drooping over an underground lagoon. The mirrored liquid depths glittered with glowing flecks. He rolled to its edge and looked at his shimmering reflection.

A hundred eyes blinked back at him, wide with curiosity.

Dollop spun around.

As he did, something scuttled out of sight.

He heard echoing footsteps, saw a shadow disappear into a light-speckled niche in the wall. A giggle warbled.

Dollop was alert, but somehow not afraid. He wandered further into the cavern, following the movement. Voices spoke in high, excited tones.

"I-it's okay," he hollered. "You—you can come out."

The voices quieted. A splash came from behind him.

"My na-na-name is Dollop."

"Dollop," repeated a dozen playful voices.

He spun around but saw only a ripple in the lagoon.

"Dollop," chimed another voice. He spun again.

Inches away from him was a glistening amber eyeball. It was not attached to a face but blinked and shifted on a long stalk that wound out of sight.

He stared back at it.

Movement shuddered up the stalk. In a blur, bits of rubbery metal whisked forward, forming a mouth to accompany the eye.

"Hello, Dollop," the mouth said.

"Hello, Dollop," repeated a dozen voices.

Behind him, scores of disembodied mouths attached to flexible stalks smiled back, sprouting from the lagoon like a bouquet of grinning flowers. Several of the mouths folded together, shuffled their pieces, and arched out to join the eyeball. The disjointed parts rearranged themselves to form a hand.

It motioned for Dollop to follow.

The hand led him to a glorious cathedral-like cavern lit by a cosmos of glimmering mineral flecks and surrounded by curtains of vesperfalls. Orange streams cascaded from the vaulted ceiling to mix with the churning flux in a magnificent amber lagoon.

Extending out from the pool was an amorphous assembly of shifting body parts, a wriggling riot of color and shape.

Gently, it reached out to Dollop, a mass of cheerful eyes, singing mouths, and waving hands. Individual faces formed and dispersed like ashes. The mass undulated and pulsed, countless arms stretching toward Dollop and then retracting, a thousand millipede legs forming and re-forming to hold the column aloft.

"Hello, Dollop," sang a chorus, a thousand voices strong.

"Who . . ." he said so softly he could barely hear himself. "Wh-wh-what are you?"

But something inside of him already knew.

He was befuddled by a sense of familiarity. His gaze darted from eyes, to mouths, to faces, all unique and yet somehow all one. He tried to get a handle on how many mehkans he was talking to, but they appeared and vanished into the joyful chaos so rapidly that he couldn't pinpoint any individual for long.

"We are Amalgam," sang the chorus.

With a soft clatter, the pieces fanned open and expanded, cascading up and out—a hundred arms and hands spread wide as if to embrace an ecstatic Dollop. Because among the smiling faces, dozens were identical to his.

"Welcome home."

CAST OFF

Dawning suns lit the corrugated walls of the sea cave, refracting off the flux in prismatic patterns. A family of silver-and-white mehkans frolicked in the tide, pistoning their bowling-pin-shaped bodies with endearing squeaks. They bobbed like buoys, bounced off one another, and zipped across the surface.

Last night, after an hour of trolling around the islands, Micah had discovered this little cave. It was a good hiding spot, with an entrance that no one would notice unless they drove right past it. But the flux was shallow, and in his haste,

Micah had struck the bottom. After ensuring that the Sea Bullet didn't have any major damage, the exhausted kids had called it a night.

Micah took the first watch, so now Phoebe was on duty, though she suspected he had slept a good deal longer than she had. She would never be able to relax on a boat (especially one with a Foundry agent imprisoned below deck), but at least her discomfort kept her keenly on guard.

The whist was the only thing that could calm her. Phoebe had retrieved it last night after Micah shut off the engines, and she marveled at how its supple folds silenced everything. This was a mehkan wonder the Foundry had not yet exploited. She yearned to pull the hood down and lose herself within it, but not while she was on watch. Micah would kill her.

Her restless stomach gurgled. She needed to eat something, but the thought of another Wackers bar made her want to gag. Phoebe rose from the bucket seat and shook the tingle from her legs. She wandered to the sheltered helm and searched the panels embedded in the black walls. Most were filled with reams of files and instruments she didn't recognize, but one was carefully stacked with steel boxes. Each contained a metal bottle marked H_2O and a stack of foil pouches labeled SCM.

"Self-Contained Meal," Micah yawned, climbing up from the engine room behind her, rifle at his back. "Military rations."

She tore into a bag and grimaced. "Smells like cat barf."

He took the pouch from her and pulled its activation tab.

"Self-heating cat barf," he corrected, reading the label. "Turkey stew with garlic flatbread. Score! I'll pack some for later."

He tossed the flatbread to Phoebe. It was salty and dry, but she washed it down with water.

Micah scarfed down the steaming contents of the pouch.

"So now what?" she asked halfheartedly.

He ignored her while he gobbled up his barf stew and shuffled through the boat's cabinets.

"Yoo-hoo . . ." she prodded.

"Bingo!" he chuckled with his mouth full.

Micah turned around with a laminated booklet. He strutted to the steering wheel and unfolded a naval map on the console.

"Check it," he said, chewing noisily. "We're probably right around here. Smack dab in the . . . looks like the 'Mirroring Sea.'" He slurped another mouthful and gave the map a flick. "And there, blammo! Just like the fat man said."

Phoebe saw that he was right—to the east lay a stippled area labeled 'The Talons,' just as the Agent of Tongues had described.

She inspected the map further. "Why is that whole area crossed out with red lines?"

"Probably a radio dead zone," he guessed, sucking up the last tidbits of his stew. "Out of signal range or something."

"That wouldn't matter much to us, now would it?" replied Phoebe, gesturing to the destroyed radio.

"Better safe than sorry," he said with a shrug.

"We need to ask Gabriella before we mess anything else up."

Micah's face pinched up. "How 'bout we keep ol' Foundry McStrangles out of it, huh?"

"That's a human being down there."

"A hostage," he corrected.

"You can't keep treating her like that."

"Like what?" Micah shot back with a grin. "Like she's dangerous? Like she might try to kill me or somethin'?"

"We need her help."

"What makes you think we can trust her?"

"What makes you think you can get us to Rhom?"

"Got us this far, didn't I?"

"I mean in one piece," she sighed, crossing her arms. "Or did you forget that you wrecked the boat last night?"

"Not wrecked. *Parked.* Didn't want it to drift."

"I'm no sailor," she said with a snide laugh, "but I'm pretty sure that's what an *anchor* is for, Cap'n."

Micah's smirk flattened.

A silence stretched between them. She regretted her little insult. He stared her down, and she held it as long as she could.

"Sorry, that came out wrong. I'm just saying . . . I meant—"

"Fine. Let's go pick Foundry's brain, if it'll make you happy," he said, tossing his empty food pouch and wiping his mouth.

"Really?"

"But not a word to her about what we're doing. We ask the questions, got it?"

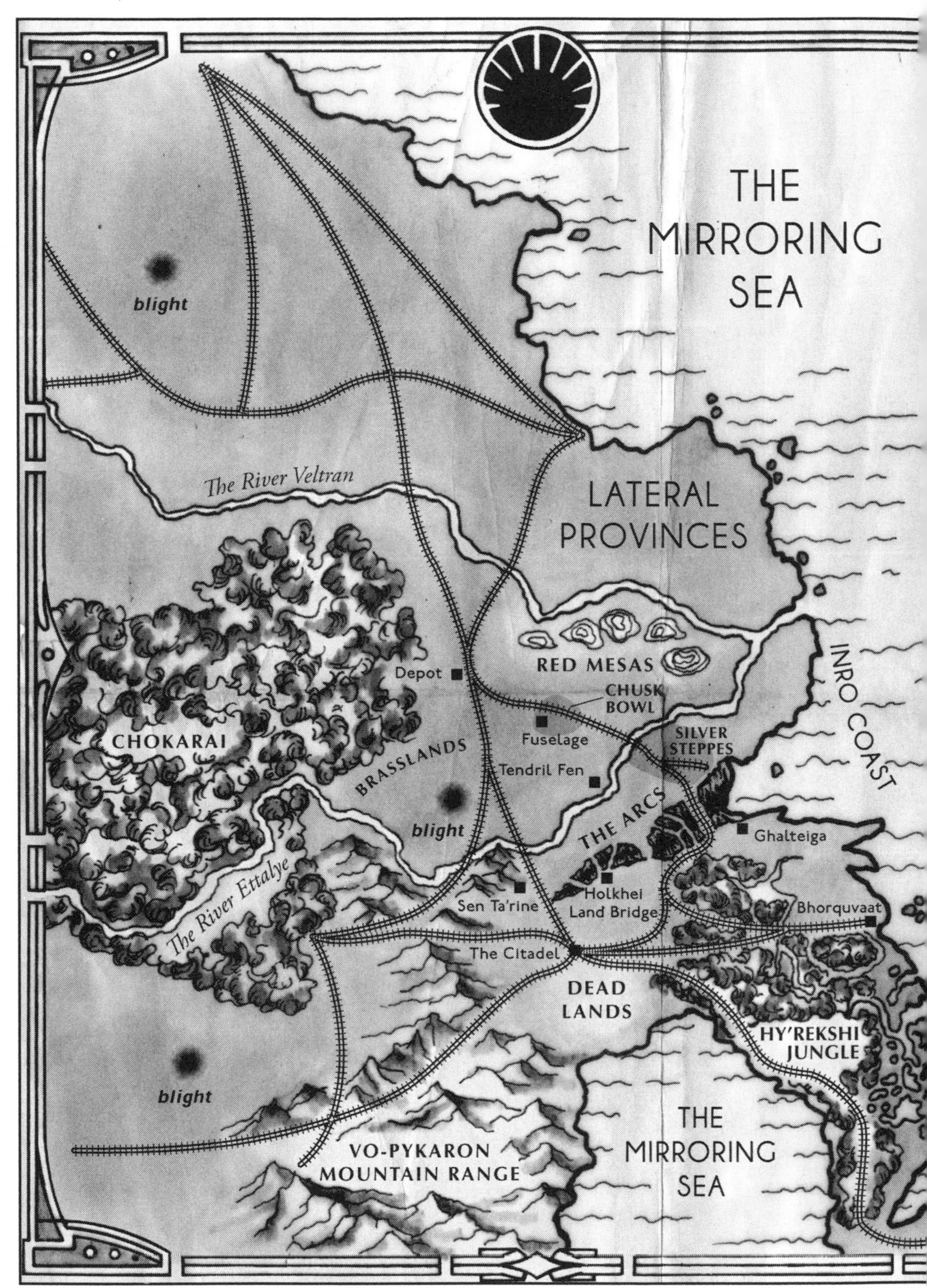
THE MIRRORING SEA
blight
The River Veltran
LATERAL PROVINCES
RED MESAS
Depot
CHUSK BOWL
CHOKARAI
Fuselage
SILVER STEPPES
INRO COAST
BRASSLANDS
Tendril Fen
THE ARCS
blight
Ghalteiga
Sen Ta'rine
Holkhei Land Bridge
Bhorquvaat
The River Ettalye
The Citadel
DEAD LANDS
HY'REKSHI JUNGLE
blight
THE MIRRORING SEA
VO-PYKARON MOUNTAIN RANGE

EPHRIAN
MOUNTAIN
RANGE
Nhel K'taphen Mines
Ahm'ral
Hatchery E-08
THE COILING
FURROWS
Lamp of
the Sea
THE TALONS
EPHRIAN PLAINS
Sen Ephra
0
30
60
120
MEHK-REGIONAL SURVEY

Phoebe nodded.

Down they went with Micah in the lead. He popped on his rifle light and approached the lavatory. He took a breath and whacked aside the pipe they had set up as a barricade. Micah whipped the door open, then leapt back and readied his aim.

Gabriella sat in the dark, calm and alert.

Micah flicked on the interior light. She squinted.

"Don't do anything stupid," Micah said. He leaned in and tore off her duct tape gag.

She didn't flinch. "They're going to find you," she croaked.

"Did I say you could talk, Foundry?" Micah growled.

"We need your help," Phoebe admitted to the woman.

She smiled, but not in a cruel way. "Let me guess. You ran my boat aground last night, and you need me to get it free."

"Hardly," Micah spat, while Phoebe nodded.

"I can do that," she said. "Untie me."

"No chance," Micah snapped, and went to put the duct tape back over her mouth. Phoebe put a hand on his arm.

"Can you tell us how to do it?" she asked.

"Sorry, my boat isn't that simple."

"It's my boat now, Foundry," Micah grunted.

"Relax," Phoebe whispered.

Her advice had the opposite effect. "Start talkin'," he warned.

Gabriella looked at him, almost like she felt sorry for him.

"I know your sister," she said.

Micah tensed.

"Margaret Tanner. She was a cadet of mine in ballistics training. Good soldier, quick learner. Drafted into the Foundry's special engineering corps right out of MIM. Deployed to Trelaine."

"Shut up," he threatened, his voice cracking.

"I bet you take after her," Gabriella said. "You must be smart to have made it this far."

Micah spun and stomped away, rushing up the ladder. Phoebe and Gabriella heard him banging around on deck.

"Hit a nerve?" the woman asked.

"He can be . . . a little touchy," Phoebe admitted.

Gabriella laughed quietly.

"Look," Phoebe said. "We're not what you think we are. We're not the enemy."

"I don't think that," replied the woman softly. "No one does. You're just two kids who are a long, long way from home."

The truth of the statement struck Phoebe like the hot suns reflecting off the flux. She studied the woman's features.

"Don't tell anyone," Gabriella confided, "but you guys have fans. Well, *had* . . . To be honest, everyone thought you two went down with the Citadel. They'll be so glad you—"

The electric generators buzzed to life.

"No. Oh no," Gabriella said. "You have to stop him."

"Why?"

"He's gonna burn out the—"

The woman's words were lost in a deafening scream of

metal. The engine room heaved. Phoebe was tossed aside.

"Stop him!" Gabriella ordered.

Phoebe nodded and closed the door to the lavatory, careful to reaffix the metal pipe under the handle. The boat jerked, tearing against the seabed. She rushed up the ladder and yelled to Micah, but he couldn't hear. He pounded on the console.

Then, in a final bubbling crunch, the Sea Bullet scraped free.

"—right now!" she screamed, finishing her unheard tirade as the boat lurched and she toppled back.

Micah spun around, heaving, his face aflame with rage.

Goodwin perfected the knot in his necktie. It was remarkable what a night's sleep, a shower, and a shave could do. More than once, he had woken in the night, certain he had heard whispers in his earpiece. He suspected that the Board spoke to him while he slept, issuing subliminal messages to his unconscious mind.

But their control over him wouldn't last much longer.

He strode to the bedroom of his living quarters, one of identical hundreds at the Depot. As he slipped into his platinum-pin-striped topcoat, Goodwin checked his Scrollbar.

The screen displayed a topographical map of the red mesas around the Depot. He had found an isolated precipice a few miles to the north, hemmed in by sheer walls and hidden from sight.

It would serve his purposes.

Within minutes, he was strolling into the chrome-tiled lobby of the Control Core. It was practically deserted. Just how many people were attending this gathering?

As he ascended in the plate-glass elevator, Goodwin could hear the muted sound of celebration from up above. The doors slid open and he emerged into a Foundry gala. A bronze Muse-o-Graph belted out a jaunty bandstand tune while Watchmen attended to a room packed with revelers.

A waste of precious time and resources.

The crowd was gathered at the curved wall of tinted glass that overlooked the Cargoliner rails. As Goodwin approached, he noticed a flurry of glances and whispers in his direction.

"*All set, Mr. Chairman*," announced a voice over a conical intercom prominently displayed on a gold pedestal. Reflexively, Goodwin turned toward the voice, before he remembered that it was not addressing him. "*T-112 is ready for departure.*"

The crowd settled and someone turned down the music. Obwilé approached the pedestal, the very image of leadership. "Commence the delivery. And send my regards to Premier Lavaraud," Obwilé said and winked with rehearsed charm.

In the Depot below, the fully loaded Cargoliner blasted its electronic horn and began to inch toward the tunnel. As it vanished into darkness, the crowd applauded. Watchmen distributed crystal flutes of fizzing champagne.

"Ladies and gentlemen, I owe you all a debt of gratitude," Obwilé announced. "I know how trying these last several days have been. We faced impossible odds during our transition, all while mourning those brave souls who were lost in the

Citadel." Somehow, in the midst of his speech, Obwilé's gaze managed to find Goodwin. "But despite these obstacles, we persevered. Together, as the Foundry always does, we have succeeded."

Murmurs of approval circled through the crowd.

"I propose a toast," Obwilé said. "With this first half of our shipment to Trelaine, we hold fast to our dedication to peace and prosperity. May the Quorum be relegated to the history books, and may the Foundry continue to build a better, brighter future."

The crowd raised their glasses.

Goodwin joined in, smiling through gritted teeth.

Laughter rang, crystal clinked, champagne was swallowed.

The music came back on, and the assembled elites resumed their jolly mingling. Goodwin approached Director Malcolm, who was having his drink refreshed by a Watchman attendant.

"A true victory," Goodwin proclaimed to the director, who flashed his bleached-white smile.

"One which we all can share," Director Malcolm agreed.

"How go preparations for the Council of Nations conference?"

"That is confidential information, James," the man replied coolly. "But rest assured, everything is accounted for."

Goodwin accepted the dismissal with a humble bow of his head, though the director's assurance hardly eased his concerns.

"That is a relief. You will be happy to know that my initiative against the Way is proving effective. The cities are on lockdown. Conflicts are escalating at our hatchery near Ahm'ral, but—"

"We are aware," the director said patiently.

"But what still concerns me are the children," Goodwin said, lowering his voice. "They are lost, and the Covenant appears to be doing everything they can to find them. Our enemy is planning something, and I suspect the children are involved."

Director Malcolm touched his earpiece, receiving orders from the Board. He smiled again. "A compelling case," the director said. "Rest assured, we shall discuss it at our meeting today."

Goodwin nodded in satisfaction.

The tinkling of a spoon on crystal silenced the room.

"My apologies for the interruption," Obwilé said, his gold-rimmed glasses flickering. "I just want to quickly embarrass the man of the hour. James, if you would join me for a moment."

The jovial crowd chuckled, and all eyes fell upon Goodwin.

He remained at ease, not wanting to let Obwilé get the drop on him. With a smile and a playful wag of his finger, Goodwin approached the Chairman, but for the life of him, he couldn't guess what the man was playing at.

"We may have had our differences in the past," Obwilé said, patting Goodwin's broad shoulder. "We've locked horns at times, but that's merely a necessity of the job."

Goodwin nodded and smiled even wider as he stared at Obwilé, picturing his hands closing around the man's neck.

"Over the years, I have come to admire a great many

things about this man," continued Obwilé, "but one trait stands above all others. And that, of course . . . is his grace."

The crowd looked on with quiet affection.

"James," Obwilé said warmly. "You have my thanks for a lifetime of dedication to the Foundry."

The Chairman offered his hand to Goodwin, who took it. Obwilé's skin was cold and papery dry.

"You served us with the same grace with which you are so humbly stepping down," Obwilé said, smile uncoiling. "May you live out your remaining days on Olyrian Isle with the satisfaction of a job well done."

Goodwin was riveted. He still clutched Obwilé's hand, feeling the man's pulse quicken as he savored his coup.

This twist of the dagger.

"Mr. James Goodwin, you will be missed," intoned Obwilé.

The crowd erupted into enthusiastic applause.

This gathering was not just to celebrate the shipment to Trelaine, Goodwin realized in a sudden tempest of wrath.

This was his retirement party.

23 MISSING PIECES

Dollop couldn't stop smiling. He had only been with the amalgami for a few clicks, but it might as well have been a lifetime. The twinkling darkness resonated with their harmonic songs, and though Dollop didn't know the tunes, he was overcome with how uncanny it all felt.

A tumbling collection of parts gathered around him. He recognized many of the pieces from his own anatomy—forearms, elbows, and mouths, even segments of heads. They were as varied in color and consistency as the pieces of his own body.

The pulsing mass budded to form six figures that looked

much like Dollop. Still tethered to Amalgam, they lightly touched his body, examining every inch. They did not move in perfect sync, but there was repetition in their gestures, like one action echoed between them. Their fingers tickled the spattering of silver burn scars he had received in the Citadel and caressed the dynamo on his chest.

"We have waited for your return," one of them said.

"We have missed you so," voiced a third.

"I d-didn't know wh-where I ca-came from. I—"

Dollop stopped himself. They weren't speaking Rattletrap. It was a different language, one he didn't recognize, and yet he understood every word and spoke it effortlessly.

They noticed Dollop's sudden confusion and soothed him.

"We are one," came a trickle of voices.

"Eternally we."

"You are us."

"We are you."

"And we are reunited," they said in blissful unison.

Dollop looked from one to another, not sure who was talking or where he should focus his attention. "Do you have names?"

"One name."

"We are Amalgam."

"Am-Amal–" began Dollop.

A delighted wave of laughter rippled through the community. Still tethered to the main body, the six figures dove into the lagoon, sending up a spray of droplets. Dollop watched them swim gracefully through the light-speckled depths.

More amalgami emerged from the mass, pieces collecting on the surface, then blossoming into tethered individuals. With a warbling chorus of joy, they plunged into the lagoon as well. The amalgami swam in intricate patterns, merging bodies and weaving their tethers together.

"Come join us," they chimed.

"Let's swim!"

"Oh n-no." Dollop shrugged shyly. "I ne-never learned how."

Arms extended, hands reached for him. They clutched him tenderly, playfully, and lifted him into the air.

"B-but I—"

They dunked Dollop into the lagoon, which felt cool and tingly. Though he had a momentary fear of drowning, Amalgam held him aloft. He laughed and kicked his legs, sending up splashes that reflected the pinpoints of cave light like blue and amber fireworks.

Dollop was whisked into the air as the cavern rang with jubilation. They reshaped into a long spiral slide and released him. He whooshed around and around, breathless with laughter. Just before he splashed back into the lagoon, he was lifted and swung, end over end, across the cavern like a trapeze artist.

At the peak, they let him go and he spread his arms. He was flying, plummeting through the vesperfalls, sailing among sapphire stars—free.

Amalgam would catch him. He had no doubt.

And they did, as if he were landing on a cloud. Appendages accordioned beneath him, cushioning his fall and returning him to the ground. The titanic mass splintered into a hundred faces and bodies, all linked like paper dolls, cheering and applauding.

"Ag-again!" Dollop hooted. "Again!"

"Of course," replied the amalgami.

"Endlessly," said another.

"Always."

"It-it's . . . I—I mean, you . . ." he struggled to form the thought. "Yo-you are all interlocking. It's, um, it's what the Mo-Mother of Ore intended for Her children."

The amalgami just stared at him with curious, blank smiles.

"Wh-what I mean is . . . You-you are perfect, is all."

"Not *you*. We," they cooed in chorus.

"You are us," suggested another.

"And we are one."

"Wh-what do you mean?" he asked.

"Think with a thousand minds," voices said.

"Feel with a thousand hearts."

"Live without anger."

"Be without fear."

"Or loss."

"Only boundless love." The last word was repeated by every one of Amalgam's smiling mouths.

"We share all."

"Every body."

"Every dream."

"We are one, everlasting."

Amalgam released a hundred contented sighs. Myriad arms lifted Dollop off his feet. He was carried into an anatomical sea, tumbling through waves of smiling, ever-changing faces.

He closed his eyes and savored the warm, all-encompassing sensation. Dollop had a sudden urge to let himself go, to separate his pieces and return to the ecstatic flow of Amalgam.

Yet something in him resisted.

With great tenderness, Amalgam set Dollop down again. A tethered figure grew from the mass and skipped up to him.

The mehkan was a perfect duplicate of Dollop—his misshapen build and lopsided stature was identical, right down to the embarrassingly pink segment on his belly. And yet something about this mirror image was different.

The twin reached out and took Dollop's hands.

"Do not be afraid," the twin sang.

"I'm n-n-not," Dollop said. "It's just . . ."

"You are as strange to us as we are to you."

"Everything is so—so familiar. You, th-this place."

"You are us."

"I kn-know. But it was s-s-so long ago."

"Time is nothing to us."

"N-no," said Dollop, shaking his head. "I mean, I ca-can't remember m-much of anything. I'm t-t-too—"

The twin placed a finger on Dollop's mouth. Slowly, parts began to peel off the amalgami's body, segments extruding from him like pieces emerging from a puzzle.

That's what was different about this duplicate.

Whereas Dollop's anatomy was a mishmash of parts interrupted by gaps and fissures, his twin was complete and whole—a fully assembled version of Dollop.

Pieces fluttered down the twin's arms and shivered across Dollop, sending him into a fit of giggles. The little bits wriggled all over his body, each seeking out its matching gap. Then with soft little nudges, they wedged into place, adhering with the same strange force that held his limbs together.

As each missing piece found its home, an invigorating jolt hit him. He felt alive in a way he had never thought possible. The last of the segments flopped around and slid into position.

Dollop gasped.

He wavered and fell back, but Amalgam caught him, cradled him. A rush of sensations. Unharnessed thoughts.

He lost track of the world around him.

"What . . ." he began.

Dollop clutched at his head, feeling a softly pulsing tether of pieces connecting him to Amalgam.

His mind was being stretched. Compressed. Expanded.

Perfected.

A raging rapid of thoughts crashed into his consciousness. Ideas he could touch, comprehend, and categorize.

". . . is . . ." Dollop breathed.

Awake. Present.

Alive.

". . . happening?"

The words came out of his mouth, but he barely recognized them. His mouth was moving without hesitation.

His stutter. Gone.

His body. Whole.

"This is me," he said, marveling at how easily he spoke.

Amalgam celebrated in a thousand voices, a music so glorious that it caused the entire cavern to vibrate.

The dam in his mind collapsed under a deluge of memories.

PhoebeMicahMakinaJungleCovenantFoundryCitadelSoldiersMakina FurnaceJulesGaugePitMrPynchMarquisLivingCityMakinaTilburyReki ndlingPlasmFoundryLiodimVellikranSyllksFuselage . . .

Dollop receded, plunging weightlessly into his past.

Lost in the brasslands. Phoebe and Micah saving me in the Chokarai. Serving the Ascetic, suffering abuse. Trying to befriend chraida but scorned. Fleeing across plains, running. But running from who? The Foundry. They slaughtered my friends. Who were my friends? A traveling band of kulha. Taught me to forage, how to survive in the wilds. Wandering again, alone. But why?

For so long, his life had been an infuriating patchwork, more holes than recollection, but now his past came crashing in, spilling over the gaps.

Why was I alone? Because I left the Housing of the Waybound to spread Her message. Axial Sha taught me the endless wisdom of the Way. Prayers and ceremonies, kindness of the axials. Their gentle guidance as they adopted me. Teaching me Haizor, and Bloodword, and . . . Rattletrap. I didn't even know Rattletrap.

The tether attached to Dollop's head shuddered. So did Amalgam, its pieces bristling stiffly on end.

And how did I get there? Axial Sha found me lost. In the swamp. Near rusting, starving. Before that, I was in a nest. Black wires, beautiful music. The rumble of unfurling wings.

Snapping pincer jaws.

"Vaptoryx," Dollop gasped. "It attacked us. Grabbed me and tore me away from you and—"

Amalgam detached its tether from Dollop's head, and all the newfound pieces that completed his body wriggled out of him, retracting, returning to their places in his twin.

"Took you from us," the amalgami agreed in unison.

Dollop felt his mind collapse, and the memories, which had seemed so clear only ticks before, faded into faint outlines.

And then they were gone.

"B-b-but—" Dollop began. His mouth was slow and stupid, crippled again by his uncontrollable stutter. He felt weak and inadequate—a half mehkan. "P-please, a f-f-few ticks mo-more."

"You can have an eternity," said the twin, deconstructing before Dollop's eyes. His pieces folded in on themselves, then withdrew to Amalgam.

"You are home, little one."

"Where you may stay."

"If you choose."

Magnificent waves rose within Amalgam, splitting into fractal patterns of arms and legs and faces, all smiling and laughing.

"Yo-you mean . . ." Dollop said, "I can j-j-join you? Ag-again?"

Amalgam spun like a cyclone, a dancing column frolicking across the lagoon. The symphony of voices repeated that same phrase until its words were indistinguishable from the echoes.

"We are one."

"We are one."

"We are one."

24

ADRIFT

The Sea Bullet had traveled far enough from shore that the horizon was identical in all directions. The afternoon suns and swirling atmosphere reflected in the Mirroring Sea so seamlessly that above and below merged into one infinite field.

Phoebe leaned over the side of the boat and threw up what had been sitting in her gut. As she collapsed back into her seat, she noticed a placard bolted to the railing.

WARNING: FLUX IS EXTREMELY TOXIC. IN CASE OF DIRECT CONTACT, SEEK MEDICAL ATTENTION AT ONCE.

Great, she thought. *This stuff is even worse than I thought.*

Were the fumes poisonous too? Probably not, since Gabriella wasn't wearing a mask. Still, the thought of drifting aimlessly on an ocean of toxic liquid metal was not pleasant.

Even more unpleasant was the fact that Micah had no idea what he was doing. He kept gunning the engine, tossing Phoebe around, and lurching to a stop. Then he would check the console compass with a curse and zip off in another direction. She suspected they had been going in circles for hours.

While Micah was definitely being a jerk about it, she understood his confusion. The compass was an obsidian orb the size of a tennis ball half-sunk into the control panel. At first glance, it looked normal, with the cardinal directions indicated as one would expect. But this compass had *two* needles. Time after time, Micah had lined them up to try and navigate, but after a few minutes, the independent needles would go haywire, and he would have to start all over again.

How long could they keep this up? It was growing bitterly cold the farther they traveled, and a brisk wind nipped incessantly at her skin. Which would they run out of first—food, water, or battery power? Or would a Foundry patrol just discover the stolen boat doing donuts out in the middle of the ocean?

She had to make Micah listen to reason, but what Gabriella said about knowing his sister had really sent him over the edge.

Phoebe had barely known Margie. She only came home from the Military Institute of Meridian on holidays, and she was always so polished and polite that Phoebe avoided her.

Really, the only thing that stood out about Margie was how much more attractive she was than the rest of the Tanners.

Maybe she was adopted or something.

"What the . . ." came Micah's voice from the helm. It was the first thing he had said without swearing all day. Phoebe headed into the cabin and glanced through the windshield.

Something peeked over the indistinct horizon, a gray ghost interrupting the hypnotic illusion created by the Mirroring Sea. It was vast, an impossible span across their field of vision. Yet it wasn't land—it was an intangible, gray wall.

Then Phoebe knew.

"Praise the gears," she whispered in awe.

Micah looked at her askance. "Huh?"

"I know what that is," she said, unblinking.

"Looks like a big ol' nasty fog bank."

"The Shroud."

He laughed, then registered her expression. "You're serious?"

"Axial Phy described it. She told me it's a real place. I didn't believe her at first"—Phoebe swallowed—"but that's it."

"You're talkin' crazy."

"Remember what Dollop said at the Rekindling? The Shroud is where we go when we die. Where our embers are judged at Her Forge." A revelatory chill shook her. "That is Makina's home."

"Uh-huh."

"That's the Shroud. I know it is."

"Funny. 'Cause heaven ain't labeled anywhere on the map."

Phoebe stared at him coolly. He didn't understand.

"Aw, come on! You gotta be kiddin' me!" he screamed, pounding his fist on the control panel as the compass needles began to whiz around in circles again.

Phoebe buzzed with nervous energy. Who cared what Micah said? First the Grand Mark of Bhorquvaat. Now the Shroud. If these things were real, what else about the Way was true?

The boat swerved as Micah violently adjusted their course. Phoebe clung to the rails, feeling her stomach squirm. If Micah couldn't get them on course, they would never get to Rhom.

Grabbing a steel case of rations, she headed down to the engine room. She carefully removed the pipe from under the lavatory door handle, opened the door, and turned on the light.

There was Gabriella, bound and the worse for wear.

Phoebe unlatched the box and took out the water bottle. She held it to Gabriella's dry mouth and let her take a long drink.

"Thank you," the woman said.

Phoebe sorted through the foil SCM packets. "Braised short ribs and rice, or herb chicken noodles?"

"Noodles," Gabriella said with a relieved smile.

Phoebe pulled the activation tab and felt the packet heat up.

Gabriella sat in an awkward position, hands and feet tied behind her back. "How am I supposed to eat?" she grunted.

"Sorry," Phoebe said, shaking the pouch. "I can't untie

you." She detached the disposable fork from the container, tore it open, and dug into the steaming meal.

After a gentle blow to cool the food down, Phoebe held out the laden fork. Gabriella looked at her, a weary mix of reproach and humiliation, but she ate.

"Gabriella. I need you to tell me how to use that compass," Phoebe said, gathering up another forkful.

"And why would I do that?"

"Because if you don't, we'll be going in circles forever."

"Not forever, honey. Just until my friends find us."

"The Foundry isn't coming for you," Phoebe said quietly.

Gabriella considered this as she chewed.

"You destroyed the TRS sensor," the woman said, more of a statement than a question.

Phoebe offered another bite.

"Figured as much," Gabriella sighed. "Otherwise, they would have located our signal hours ago." She took the mouthful.

"The Foundry is going to lose," Phoebe said firmly. "You know that, right? We will win."

"Who is we?"

"The Covenant."

Phoebe expected her to laugh, but she didn't. Instead Gabriella just studied her, chewing thoughtfully.

"Do you think they're going to save you?" she asked.

"No," Phoebe said honestly. "I don't need saving."

"What *do* you need?"

"I can't say."

"Then where are you trying to go?"

Phoebe extended another bite but said nothing.

"And yet I'm supposed to help you? What if I refuse?"

"I'll find another way." She surprised herself by adding, "Makina will guide me."

Gabriella looked at her in disbelief. After a pause, she smiled and said, "You're a strange bird, you know that?"

Phoebe couldn't help but smile.

The boat swerved abruptly and Phoebe clung to the door. She had to fight her stomach back into place.

"Seasick," Gabriella diagnosed.

Phoebe shook her head. "No . . . I just . . ."

"Check behind the coolant distributor," the woman said, motioning with her head. "That box with the hoses sticking out."

Phoebe rose unsteadily and obeyed. Attached to the wall behind the equipment was a steel case labeled MED-I-PAK.

"Open it," the woman said. "There's a vial marked PZ."

The box was a fully stocked first-aid kit, complete with sterile bandages, antibacterial ointment, medications, and other necessities. Phoebe located the tube in question.

"Panzamine helps nausea," Gabriella said. "Better take two."

Phoebe eyed the woman suspiciously, wondering if this was a trick—was this a sleeping pill or poison or something? Gabriella cocked an eyebrow as if reading her mind.

Phoebe popped open the water bottle, took a gulp, and swallowed two pills. "Thank you, Gabriella."

"My friends call me Gabby."

"Is that what we are?" Phoebe asked.

Gabby shrugged and offered a kindly smile. "We could be."

They considered each other for a moment.

"Plumm!" Micah screamed from top of the ladder. "Topside—NOW!" His flushed face vanished.

Phoebe rolled her eyes. "Gotta go," she said, closing up the Med-i-Pak and SCM case. She was about to barricade the lavatory door shut again, when Gabby stopped her.

"Wait a sec," she said.

"What?" asked Phoebe.

"Got a tip for you," Gabby said. "Might come in handy . . ."

When Phoebe climbed onto the deck a minute later, Micah slammed the engine room hatch closed with a bang.

"What the hell you think you're doin'?" he demanded.

"Getting this," she said calmly, showing him the first-aid kit. "And information. Now go to the wheel, and I'll explain."

"I said no talkin' to Foundry. Not without my say-so."

"I don't need your permission," she asserted. "And I just—"

"Shut up for a second!" he snapped.

Her mouth fell open. Micah was heaving like a rabid dog.

"You're makin' it real tough to protect you, you know that? Damn near impossible."

"Is that what you call this? Protecting me?" she asked. "You stole a Foundry boat that you don't know anything about, and now you've stranded us out in the middle of nowhere."

"You think you can do better? Be my guest!"

He kicked a box of fuses across the cabin.

"Why are you being such a jackass?" she shot at him.

"'Cause you're bein' an idiot!" he screamed. "What about 'no talkin' to Foundry' don't you understand? You never listen!"

"I don't listen?" she laughed. "That's funny. Because every time I try to tell you anything you just—"

"You think I like cleaning up your crap? You think I wanted this?" He was pacing, pounding his hand into his fist. "I told you, I ain't your servant anymore. I told you I quit, and I meant it!"

"What are you talking about?" she said softly, taken aback. "It's not like that anymore. Micah, I'm trying to—"

He rushed at her, his face warped with fury.

"Then quit tellin' me what to do!" he roared.

Instinctively, she shoved him back, but he barely budged.

"Stop it!" she screamed.

He was right up in her face, mouth flecked with spit.

"OR WHAT?"

Her hand went to the Multi-Edge strapped around her waist.

Micah let out a nasty laugh. "You gonna cut me?" he sneered. "Well, praise the gears! What a brave little Loaii—pfff."

"Don't . . . say that," she muttered, wincing.

"I'm done with all your Makina crap, so just drop the act, okay? The only one you're foolin' is yourself."

"Why are you doing this?"

"You're a phony. Just like your dear ol' daddy."

It felt like he had taken the blade from her hip and plunged it into her chest. Something within Phoebe withered before Micah's eyes, and he knew he had gone too far.

She drifted away from him. He watched her walk to the console at the helm, not knowing quite what to do.

"Phoebe . . . I . . ."

Then he saw her press the compass orb and rotate it. Two red buttons lit up on either side of the compass. She held the buttons down until they chimed and went green.

She looked back—tears flowed freely down her cheeks.

"Just had to calibrate it," she whispered, breezing past.

Micah bit his lip. He needed to figure out something to say, needed to fix this. He turned to face Phoebe, but it was too late.

The hatch to the engine room eased shut with a click.

25
BEGINNINGS WITHOUT END

Dollop wanted to know everything about Amalgam, but they rarely answered his questions. They weren't being evasive—they just couldn't comprehend what he was asking. Their worlds were so different that they often just stared at one another in wonder.

He spent the day with the amalgami, swimming and playing in the lagoons of their glittering cave. When Dollop grew hungry, Amalgam brought him to the shallows of a pool where a school of jelyps flitted. The critters were smooth black tubes about the size of his finger with turquoise speckles that matched their surroundings. They had a spout at each end, through which they expelled vesper, causing them to twirl through the amber fluid.

"Try one," urged several amalgami.

Together with Dollop, they squatted by the lagoon, snatched up some of the darting jelyps, and dumped their harvest in a heap. The cavern was filled with the sound of cracking shells and slurped innards. Dollop tried one and found it to be delicious—a taste he had been craving without even knowing it.

He watched the amalgami gleefully absorbed in their feast, curiosity building within him until he could no longer resist the urge. He tiptoed up to the towering mass.

Tentatively, he reached out and touched it.

Dollop allowed his hand to separate. Like pebbles in a pond, his fingertips sank into Amalgam, then his knuckles, and at last the pieces of his palm slid apart to join the community.

The sensation crept up on him like a dream. Although he could no longer see the pieces of his own hand, he did not lose track of them. Dollop merged with Amalgam, becoming aware of a thousand other limbs as if they were his own. Through them, he could feel the entirety of the cavern, from the top of the dripping ceiling to the bottom of the deep lagoon.

Amalgam was everywhere.

Strange images flickered in his mind, multidimensional feelings of the cavern that were difficult to comprehend. He felt expansive and shapeless as vapor, conscious of every glittering fleck in the ore, all of them familiar as the faces of friends.

The images transformed, scores of eyes shifting focus. It

took him a moment to realize what he was looking at. It was a diminutive figure with half-closed eyes, a stranger. He wondered who it could be—felt he should know. Couldn't quite recall . . .

It's me.

He was staring at himself through Amalgam's eyes.

With a yelp, Dollop pulled back from the mass. He had sunk into Amalgam up to his elbow. His parts retracted and clung together again, re-forming his arm as he tugged free.

The images and feelings vanished in a puff.

"I'm so-so-sorry," he stuttered. "I wa-was . . . curious."

"So are we," they sang together.

"So are we."

Dollop and Amalgam considered one another, and they burst out laughing. While the swirl of bizarre sensations had been startling, Dollop yearned to unite with the community again, to experience that feeling of magnitude—a taste of omniscience.

They played together for a while more, grazing on jelyps until exhaustion overtook them. Still giggling and singing, Amalgam led Dollop to a cozy side chamber with a crescent-shaped pool and knobby walls devoid of those pinpricks of mineral light. This was where they slumbered.

Amalgam spilled itself out to fill every corner of the space, a cushion of innumerable soft limbs. The darkness was warm and alive with a million scattered breaths as the amalgami cuddled and relaxed. Dollop settled himself in the middle of the mass, nuzzling into a nest of embracing arms.

Contentment washed over him. His life before Amalgam didn't feel like it had been his at all. His mind stumbled back through the recent horrors—the attack on the Covenant camp, the loss of his friends, the vaptoryx. He tried to focus on Amalgam's soft snores and its communal bliss, but the pain of the last few cycles was not easily banished.

Dollop pressed his hands to his dynamo and tried to turn his mind to the Way. He had recited the recharge prayer every night since he learned it all those phases ago in the Housing.

But now, try as he might, he couldn't recall how it began.

"Bless me, Ma-Makina," he whispered, certain that these were not the actual words of the prayer, but hoping they would suffice. *"Gu-guard me as I—I re-recharge, and . . . uh . . . sh-shield my f-friends from d-danger. Please protect . . ."*

What was her name again? His mind drew a blank.

What was happening? How could he have forgotten?

They were his friends. He loved them.

What was it? Fee . . .

"Pr-protect Phoebe and Micah," he continued, speaking with more confidence as he overcame his momentary lapse. *"Wherever they a-are."* He squeezed his eyes shut and concentrated.

"What are you doing, little one?"

The question was repeated, sounding from all around him.

"Pr-praying to Makina," he said, opening his eyes to find a circle of sleepy faces studying him.

"Praying?"

"Asking Ma-Makina to watch over my, um, friends. To save them from falling to rust."

"Friends?"

"Who is Makina?"

"Makina . . ." he gasped. "The Gr-Great Engineer. You—you don't know Her? She ma-made us all, Her Ch-Children of Ore."

The faces showed no understanding.

"What is 'falling to rust'?" one asked.

"Ru-rust," Dollop struggled to explain. "When . . . when you pass and your em-ember departs your body."

They continued to look quizzical.

"The end of your sp-span."

"End?" they wondered.

"There is no end."

"Only us."

"Forever us."

His mouth hung open. "You . . . you do-don't . . . ever?"

"Don't ever what, little one?"

"Ne-never mind," he said in a tiny voice and settled back.

Amalgam rearranged itself, purring with sleepy sighs as it drifted off to sleep. But Dollop just lay staring into the dark.

There is no end.

The words rang in Dollop's head.

Could it be true? Did Amalgam live without rust? Without the fear of pain or loss? Dollop touched the spattering of silver scars on his chest. He thought of the terror he had felt when he resigned himself to die in the Citadel.

If he were to stay here, would he be free from rust forever?

But another question tormented him.

He wanted to merge with the amalgami in joyful eternity, but even in the clicks he had been here, he was fading, his memories were receding—his knowledge of the Way, his duty to his friends.

Could he give himself up in order to join Amalgam?

The darkness offered no answer.

26 RAISING VOICES

Phoebe lay huddled in a miserable ball in the engine room, and her tears showed no sign of subsiding. The outline of sunlight around the ceiling hatch had long since gone black. She felt weak, and not because of the seasickness.

How was she going to look Micah in the eyes ever again?

The vibrations of the engine room died away, and blinking indicator lights went dark. She suspected that Micah was powering down the Sea Bullet to grab some sleep. The lavatory was quiet, which meant Gabriella had probably passed out in a hogtied heap. The boat settled, rocking gently in the Mirroring Sea, and silence gathered around her like morning fog.

That's when Phoebe thought of the whist.

She sat against the wall and lowered the cowl over her head. Immediately, all noise snuffed out, leaving only a peaceful void.

And Phoebe gave herself to it.

Blessed relief. She breathed deeply.

Phoebe noted a strange, unfamiliar sensation. It was as if she were drifting upward, her consciousness pulling free from the weary burden of her body.

She did not resist.

Slowly, she departed the Sea Bullet and rose into the night. The air was bitingly cold, but she did not feel it. She was an ephemeral speck of heat and light, an ember soaring weightless, carried aloft through the frigid night sky.

The Shroud called to her. She went to it, a wave of consciousness returning to the endless shore. Unanchored, Phoebe tumbled through the sky.

A murmur of whispers grew as she neared.

In an instant, she understood.

Axial Phy's words rang clear.

In that nothing, Her voice will guide you.

The voice of Makina, it had to be. Phoebe had heard it before—in fact, it had been with her all along.

Follow was Her word, spoken as Phoebe faced the black tunnel deep in the Foundry. It had drawn Phoebe to Mehk.

No, She had said, and Phoebe had saved the liodim.

With every fiber of her being, she longed to hear it again. Now, more than ever, she needed guidance.

Phoebe plunged into the Shroud. She felt lost, confounded by the ineffable gray. But she let nothingness fill her.

To be here she had to not *be* at all.

And then came a laugh so pure that its dulcet tones seemed to kiss the air.

This was not the voice of Makina. It was even more precious.

Not one, but two voices, speaking one word.

"Cricket."

Phoebe tore from the Shroud. Her ember plummeted through the nothing, colliding down to substance in one breathless instant. Her body jerked forward, eyes snapped open.

It couldn't be, she thought.

She had touched the unknown. Part of her insisted that it was just her imagination, a product of her grieving mind.

But was it possible? Could it have really been them?

Her mother was dead. Her father was dead. And yet she had heard them. They had spoken.

They were calling to her from beyond the Shroud.

Normally, the emptiness Phoebe felt was too much to bear. Her mother's death had torn a hole within her, and losing her father had ripped it wider.

Why, then, was she not crying now?

Because hearing them had awakened something.

Her parents were watching over her.

If she could hear their voices, might she discover a way to speak with them? With Makina Herself?

The hole in her heart began to mend.

Phoebe pulled back the hood and reentered the reality of the engine room. The line around the hatch overhead glowed with a dim light. Time had swept past her. Night had come and gone.

There was a hollow banging on the lavatory door.

"Phoebe?" came Gabby's voice. "Are you there?"

She rose to her feet, reeling from the stiffness in her muscles. With a couple of tugs, she removed the pipe and opened the door. Gabby was sitting in the dark on the closed commode.

"You either gotta untie me," she said in a hoarse voice, "or you're going to have to give me some help."

"With what?" Phoebe asked, turning on the interior light.

The woman nodded to the toilet.

Watching for any sign that Gabby might use the opportunity to get free, Phoebe obliged. They avoided eye contact during the awkward process, but Gabby had not been bluffing. It made Phoebe aware of her own pressing needs.

"My turn," she muttered to Gabby.

At first, Phoebe's instinct was to be mortified, but the woman just nodded and turned her back. What a luxury the tiny bathroom seemed now. Between the humiliation of navigating the issue with Micah (meaning avoiding it at all costs and only going when the other was busy) and the impractical nature of doing it in Mehk, this commode was a godsend.

And strangely, it was easy with Gabby. Almost like they were just a couple of girls back at Fort Beatrice—the ones who would only go to the bathroom together, for whatever reason.

When she finished, Phoebe closed the toilet lid and helped Gabby back onto it. They sat down and considered each other.

"It's funny," the woman said, "I'm supposed to be on vacation right now, but they extended my tour when the Citadel went down. Did you have anything to do with that?"

"They let you go on vacation?" Phoebe asked.

"Of course," Gabby said. "No matter what you think about the Foundry, it's just a job to us. A good one too. My fiancé and I were planning to go to Prosper Falls. You ever been there?"

Phoebe shook her head.

"Three hours south of Albright City," the woman explained. "Natural hot springs in Kappermane State Park. You gotta see it to believe it. I miss the woods most of all when I'm on duty here. Our trees, our stars—you know?"

Phoebe had a far-off look.

"What are you thinking about?" Gabby asked.

"I . . ." Phoebe said, looking wistfully at her feet. "You said Albright City, and I thought about downtown. I used to go through it every day on the way to school. It always looked so big, like there couldn't possibly be a bigger world outside of it."

Gabby considered her.

Phoebe caressed her whist.

"But there is. Now I know there is."

Downtown Albright City was seized with traffic as Aerocopters surveyed from the sky. The authorities were keen to maintain the peace below the epic platinum facade of the Council of Nations building. As always when the CN was in session, demonstrators paraded on its plated steps, and heavily geared riot police stood watch.

Inside the golden-glass lobby sat a spectacular column forged from every metal in existence. From manganese to zinc to titanium, the flags of every nation in the world were sculpted upon it, each with its own unique alloy, weaving together in a swirling eddy that stretched up to the steepled ceiling.

Security was especially tight because representatives from all thirteen countries of the infamous Quorum were present.

The assembly hall was packed, its bold metallic décor illuminated by sunlight beaming in like a spotlight. The stage was flanked with Televiewers, gold banners stretched from floor to ceiling, and interpreters crowded a nearby balcony.

If the Council of Nations was a theater, then President Saltern was its star.

Amply dusted in makeup and decked in a stunning gunmetal-blue Durall suit, Saltern's magazine smile was broad. He was mid-speech and just warming up. Saltern noted that the members of the Quorum were the only nations not listening. Greinadoren, the Kijyo Republic, Moalao, Trelaine—the cast of villains was all there, lined up like targets in a shooting gallery. They made a show of being embroiled in their own conversations.

"Of course, trouble runs rampant in the global economy," Saltern continued, the practiced cadences of his speech as masterful as ever. "Yet we see our challenges as opportunities in disguise. By dedicating ourselves to international cooperation, we will ensure liberty and prosperity to our partners. However . . ."

His eyes drifted up to the golden-mirrored lounge above the assembly hall. The faceless Foundry Board was there, he knew, waiting to hear their script come out of his mouth.

Oh, to see the look on their faces.

"There are those who seek to undermine Meridian's progress, those who don't want to play fair in a free market. *Cowards* . . ." Saltern emphasized as he looked to the Quorum, "who scheme in the shadows. Well, I'm here today to draw a line in the sand."

Murmurs clenched the room.

"A secret arrangement was put forth," the President announced, his voice rising with passion. "An attempt to purchase the allegiance of a bully, to buy Meridian an ally. It was a bribe, plain and simple, offered by our very own Foundry."

An uproar. Voices shouted, papers were thrown. The press descended with reporters and Omnicams. Only the members of the Quorum sat deathly still. Saltern savored the outrage he knew must be erupting within the mirrored Foundry lounge.

"Only there was a catch," he said with a devilish grin. "It was a setup. I instructed the Foundry to make a phony deal, a trap bursting with cheese. And guess what?" He let the

Assembly Hall go silent. "We caught a rat. Premier Lavaraud, I'm afraid your so-called payday delivery has been rerouted. Tough luck."

Heated words sputtered among the Quorum as they all directed their shock and fury at Lavaraud.

"Yes, Trelaine," boomed President Saltern. "Once a proud nation, now nothing but a cartel of crooks looking to cash in. And they're not the only ones. Why is the Quorum really here today? To listen? To collaborate? No, friends. They hold world peace hostage, and expect us to pay them a ransom."

Bedlam was taking over the assembly hall, but Saltern's speech gained power and momentum.

"Now I ask you . . . are these the kinds of allies that Meridian needs? Are these the kinds of allies anyone would ever want?"

Together, the members of the Quorum tore off their Council of Nations badges, while the rest of the ambassadors booed. The press was in a frenzy, FotoSnaps flashing and Vocafones shoved into faces. The nations of the Quorum gathered up their attendants and shoved their way indignantly toward the exits.

"I say NO," President Saltern trumpeted, his voice silencing the crowd. "Too long we've put up with your bluster and your vows of retaliation. Meridian does not yield to threats. We do not fear you. This is the line I'm drawing, right here, right now. Stand with us, and you will stand tall."

Lavaraud was the last to depart the Assembly Hall. He

tossed his CN badge to the ground with disgust, and with one last look of malice at Saltern, he took his leave.

"Oppose us"—Saltern grabbed the podium and leaned in—"and you will fall."

The applause was deafening. This was his finest hour.

The President breathed in the adulation. Meridian was the most powerful nation in history, and Saltern was its leader.

He was not about to let the Foundry or the world forget it.

27 HAMMERED

Mr. Pynch was ready to collapse. He had spent two grueling cycles navigating these confounding land bridges with barely a wink of recharge. Fog clotted the sky, leaving the morning so dark he could barely see a spit's distance in front of him. He missed the Marquis's luminous opticle more than ever.

The only good news was that he was near the coast and at the end of the Arcs. The train tracks below halted at a massive Foundry port on the other side of the cliff. If the Marquis had survived his fall, the derelict settlement of Ghalteiga was the last place he could have gotten off before the bleeder outpost.

It was a wreck of weathered squalor built into the precipices above the choppy Mirroring Sea. Battered shacks were scattered across the top, clinging to cliff faces like the stubborn little knurlers that stuck on barges in the wharf below.

If the Marquis was here, he'd be in the Rathskellar. It was a notorious drinking hole where the grizzled volmerids and gohr who worked the docks drowned their cares with viscollia. Mr. Pynch's nozzle could have sniffed it out a dozen quadrits away.

He trotted down a scabby landing plastered to the cliff face. When a drunken roar rose above the howling wind, he knew he had found the place. He shoved the rusted hatch open.

Despite the fact that it was morning, the Rathskellar was packed. Someone was pounding an out-of-tune baritone instrument, but it could barely be heard above the revelry.

Mr. Pynch wedged his way through the crowd and sidled up to the reinforced cage-bar. By the look of the scarred vol bodyguards that flanked this freylani bartender, the Rathskellar had seen more than its fair share of trouble.

"What're youz drinking?" the bartender shouted.

"Greetings!" Mr. Pynch called back with as much gusto as he could muster. "Could you perchance help me with a quandary?"

A jumpy jaislid emerged from a flap behind the cage-bar, his pelvis wheel of legs spinning wildly. He extended his thresher proboscis to harvest the spiny augurweed growing on the bartender's hunchback. The worker stuffed his clippings into a dangling fermentation cask to brew into viscollia.

"What're youz drinking?" the bartender grunted again. Mr. Pynch sighed and dug out a few tinklets of gauge.

"A coil of yer finest, me good mehkie."

Another jaislid slung a spiral shell over to Mr. Pynch. The viscollia within was a chunky, green syrup with a caustic stink.

"Now for me inquiry," Mr. Pynch said. "Have you peeped a discombobulated lumie in your establishment as of late?"

"Don't zerve lumiez here," the freylani snapped.

"Me apologies, but it be of the utmost—"

"Next!" the freylani yelled, and a forceful arm from behind shoved Mr. Pynch out of the way. He took his coil of viscollia and hunkered down at a table slab in the corner.

The Marquis was gone. They had sojourned across Mehk and back during their many phases together. They had done it all and stuck together like ryzooze. He and the Marquis had saved each other's lives too many times to count. Actually, at their last tally, the Marquis had saved him forty-five times, and Mr. Pynch had returned the favor a mere twenty-eight.

"If only," he moaned, oily tears swelling up his eye sacs, "if only them stories about the Shroud was true, we'd meet again someday, and maybe I could reimburse yer generosity."

"Well, rattle my shanks!" shouted a drunken voice. A gargantuan gohr stumbled up to Mr. Pynch with a ragtag circle of mates. "Don't believe I ever did spy a balvoor cry."

"Neither have I," Mr. Pynch replied somberly.

"Must be a mighty big tragedy, friend."

"Words do not express."

The gohr studied Mr. Pynch, then crashed into the seat next to him. The brute clinked his viscollia coil against Mr. Pynch's.

"To forgetting, then," the gohr belted out.

"To forgetting!" repeated his friends.

Mr. Pynch raised the flask and took a swig. His distended eye sacs went catawampus, and he sputtered to the delighted cheers of his companions. It felt like chugging a CHAR bomb, like molten screwgrubs burrowing into his defenseless dome.

It was just the kind of obliteration he needed.

Soon Mr. Pynch's coil was empty, and someone got him another. He drank. The coil was empty again. Then full.

Maybe the Marquis's corpse had been found shattered atop the train when it arrived at that nearby Foundry port. Would he have to break in and reclaim it? It was the least he could do.

Empty. Full. Empty.

That was it. He would go tonight. He would get the Marquis's remains if it was the last thing he—

Full.

The Rathskellar was somehow getting more crowded, and his drinking buddies had multiplied. Or was he seeing doublish?

How much time had passed?

It was like Mr. Pynch was watching someone elshe

operate his body from a hundred quadrits back inside his addleded mind. Whoever was controlling him now was dooing a loushy job.

He watched his own hands spill a coil all over himself.

Empteee.

Fulll.

A face appeared . . . well, Mr. Pynch was pretty shure it was a face. Harda tell with everything so blurrededy. Looked more like an uglee bundla tubes. Stank too, like rot.

"Well, well, well," the bundle said.

Mr. Pynch tried to consetrate. Someone helded him up.

"Long time no see, Pynch," the bundle gurrrgled.

He knew that voice. If he wasn't so viscollia-ized he might manage ta recollect. Mr. Pynch scoooped up his thoughts and lolled his head enough to get his eyesss to stabilize. The Rathskellar shwirled. The face came into focusss. A hiveling.

Instantly, he knew. It was—

Ow.

Somethin' hit him hard on da . . . back of the . . .

Phoebe had zero interest in being around Micah, so she stayed below deck, talking to Gabby. The rocking of the Sea Bullet had been steadily increasing over the hours, and she was forced to take more Panzamine to calm her stomach. She felt at ease, like maybe she was finally getting used to the boat.

"What about Tony's?" asked Phoebe. "Have you eaten there?"

"Which one?" Gabby laughed. "Every place is called Tony's."

"It's in the Financial District, on Central, I think."

Gabby shook her head.

"Seriously? You have to go. Best chocolate twist in the—"

The boat pitched violently. They were hurled to the ground.

Phoebe got to her feet. She clawed her way up the ladder and tried to open the hatch, but the wind forced it shut. With some effort, she shouldered through and scrambled on deck.

What she saw made her want to give in.

The hell-black sky boiled. The sea was at war, waves of silver soldiers swelling and crashing. Flux spewed over the rails. Glistening blobs sloshed on the deck. Phoebe grabbed her hood and affixed her facemask as silver spray burst around her. She raced for the helm, fighting the wind and avoiding the toxic goo.

The control panel flashed with warning lights.

Behind his visor, Micah's face was white as death. "Get below!" he screamed over the squall.

A hail of flux came down. It ricocheted off the roof of the helm. Bullets rained onto the deck. In moments, the floor was blanketed in ball bearings, spilling into the open engine room.

The engine room. Phoebe made a break for it.

She slipped on the flux hail and hit the deck hard. The bullet rain punched down on her. She clambered for the ladder and climbed down, falling the last few rungs.

"Here!" cried Gabby.

Phoebe rushed to the lavatory and drew her Multi-Edge. In a couple of cuts, the woman was free. Gabby winced from the cramping in her muscles, but it didn't slow her down. She drew the hood from her coveralls and sealed it with the facemask.

"We need you!" Phoebe screamed.

They raced for the ladder.

A gush of falling bullets hammered down through the hatch, beating them back. Gabby forced her way on deck, hauling Phoebe along behind her. They sealed the engine room door and clung to the rails to avoid getting blown away by the tempest.

Micah went for his rifle.

"No!" Phoebe screamed at him. "It's her turn now!"

He looked at Gabby, who stood, grasping a handle bolted to the wall. Her face was stony but calm.

Micah stood aside.

Gabby rushed to the driver's seat. "Strap in!" she hollered.

Phoebe and Micah threw themselves into a pair of bucket seats. They fumbled for the straps, almost got the belts on.

Their stomachs dropped to their feet.

The Sea Bullet was sucked into the air, lifted by the fearsome gale. They rose and rose, hanging for a deadly moment.

Gabby dove for the control panel and threw a lever.

Panels emerged from the roof, slid toward the rear, and locked into place. An armored dome enclosed the Sea Bullet.

Then they fell, plunging in prow first.

Phoebe and Micah slammed against the far wall.

The boat was tossed about like a toy. Flux rain pounded on the roof, a dull, persistent resonance in the sealed cabin.

The kids rolled to a stop. Hurt all over.

"In those seats. NOW!" Gabby screamed.

Phoebe could feel the warm trickle of blood under her facemask, but her body was numb. She and Micah limped to the helm, avoiding the globs of flux. They collapsed into the seats and belted themselves in.

Gabby worked furiously at a Computator. A row of lights around the base of the ship glowed purple. The flux bullets and blobs stopped dancing around the cabin, paused, then gathered around magnetic panels in the floor. Drains slid open and expelled the flux.

Then Gabby stared through the windshield in disbelief.

"No," she moaned. "No!"

In the swirling turmoil, gnarled black claws reached out at them. They must have been sixty feet high. So many of them, twisted and broken—a veritable mountain range of jagged spears of ore stabbing up through the flesh of the sea.

"The Talons," Gabby said, defeated.

"Look out!" Phoebe cried, pointing up at the clouds.

A cyclone drilled down from above. Gabby spun the wheel. The funnel detonated on the ocean's surface, and the boat was launched aside. Another sea spout snaked down, then another. Whipping columns of flux and wind writhed around them.

Gabby typed frantically at the Computator, and a purple light flared outside the windows. The Sea Bullet slowed abruptly.

But the waves were shoving them right into the Talons.

Gabby threw open a compartment and mashed a button. They felt a clunking under their feet. A wave smashed into the side of the boat. The Sea Bullet yawed sharply, and they lurched with a jarring whiplash. But the anchor held them fast.

Phoebe blinked away blood. She felt a stabbing pain above her right eye. Bullet rain screamed down.

The Sea Bullet convulsed. The kids looked at Gabby.

She was afraid.

CRACK.

They were spinning. Unmoored.

The anchor chain had broken.

"Down!" Gabby screamed.

The kids put their heads between their legs.

They felt the swell building below them, raising the boat higher, higher. Cyclones raked past. They could see only flux through the windshield, ripping past in glittering sheets.

The view cleared. They were at the crest of a wave.

The Talons were dead ahead—a jagged black wall of death.

The Sea Bullet was powerless in the ocean's grip. They tipped over the top of the wave.

And down they went, gaining speed.

Flying toward the Talons.

So fast they felt weightless.

They braced for impact.

But none came.

Phoebe looked up.

Just beyond the windshield sat the cruel end of a Talon, pointing at them like a finger of doom. The massive barbed spur of ore was only a few feet away. Yet, miraculously, they had not struck it. The Sea Bullet hovered as if frozen in time. Phoebe would have thought they were dead if it weren't for the continual beating of hail on the roof.

Gently, the boat descended. The three of them struggled to look out into the raging storm in an attempt to understand.

Bubbling up from the depths they saw a glint of something dark. Many somethings. Long, serpentine coils like a fleet of tongues, lapping at their boat. Encircling them.

The kids didn't have to ask.

They knew what had caught them.

Rhom.

ONE

Dollop lay on the ground of the sleeping chamber, alone. He could hear echoes of the amalgami frolicking nearby.

He roused and made his way to the cathedral-like cavern where he had been with Amalgam the previous day. Standing silently in the mineral-flecked shadows, he watched them play. They stretched their interconnected bodies across the lagoon, creating hypnotic amber ripples as they undulated in beautiful patterns, like musical harmony made visible.

Amalgam sensed his presence. A tethered individual emerged from the mass and skipped over to greet him at the shore. As the figure approached, Dollop saw that it was his twin again.

"Did we wake you?" the amalgami asked.

Dollop shook his head.

"Then come play!"

Beaming, the twin took his hand to lead him to the lagoon, but Dollop didn't budge.

"I . . ." he began, trying to force out the words.

"What is it, little one?"

"I . . . I ca-can't." He steeled himself.

"Are you hungry? We have fresh jelyps to—"

"That's no-not it."

"You are not well?" The amalgami was concerned.

"I'm leaving," Dollop blurted. It hurt even more than he had expected. His twin just stared at him, confused.

"We will play later?" the amalgami asked with a grin.

Dollop shook his head. "You don't understand. I—I can't stay here. I ha-have to go away. I . . . I wish it co-could be different."

Realization withered his twin's smile.

"Go . . . away?" said another amalgami voice.

"Why?" asked others.

"Be-because I'm needed," Dollop said.

"We need you."

"You are us."

"We are one."

Their voices overlapped, first ringing with confusion, then yearning, growing heavy. Dollop wanted to run to Amalgam, to plunge into their paradise and make this pain vanish. Maybe if he just merged with them once more, he could explain . . .

No. His mind was made up.

"I—I want to be with you," he murmured, unable to look his twin in the eye. "Mo-more than anything. B-but I have someth-thing very important to do."

More amalgami sprouted from the mass and approached.

"My fr-friends are out there," Dollop continued. "Th-they are in tr-trouble, and they need me. I—I have a function."

"Function?" the amalgami asked, pressing in around him. "But what can you do, little one?" asked a voice.

"Dollop is nothing alone," said another.

"You are incomplete."

"Broken."

Dollop winced. Their words struck home. Amalgami hands traced the gaps on his body where he was missing pieces. He longed to feel whole again—to have his memories and his mind intact once more.

"A single drop of flux . . ." they soothed.

". . . is insignificant."

"But together . . ."

The amalgami surrounding Dollop held hands, their parts interweaving to form a loving embrace.

". . . many drops make an ocean," the chorus resounded.

"Without limit," they chanted.

"We are one."

"We were," another corrected. "Until you."

Their angelic faces shined. Gentle hands reached out to him.

"The vaptoryx found us, attacked us."

"Took part of us away."

"Separated."

"That is how you were born."

Dollop took a hesitant step back.

"But you have returned to us."

"Now we can be one again."

"Forever us."

"I'm . . ." Dollop's voice hitched. "I'm so-sorry."

He turned away, unable to bear the sight of sorrow smothering those hopeful faces.

His twin began to weep.

"Please . . ."

Dollop strode from the chamber and entered a narrow passage, determined to not look back. Another voice whimpered behind him, then another. Sorrow multiplied within Amalgam, many voices building into a mourning throng. Dollop swallowed back his tears, but he would not allow himself to waver. He hurried through the labyrinth of passages, trying to recall the path he had taken upon his arrival.

"Please . . ." echoed a desperate plea.

"Don't leave us," moaned another.

Amalgam's sobs seemed to emanate from the cavern walls. The wretched sound filled him with a rending pain.

Dollop just wanted to get away.

But as he continued to search for the exit, the cries seemed to grow closer. He heard shuffling, saw a lingering shadow. Weeping amalgami faces stared at him through connecting passages. Their misery rose to a terrible wail that surrounded Dollop and filled him to bursting.

A hand shot out from a hole in the wall. It grabbed his arm.

An amalgami face appeared, its features warped in agony.

"Please, little one," it begged. "Please don't leave us!"

"I-I'm sorry. I'm so s-s-sorry."

Dollop reshaped his limb to make it thicker.

"You can't go!" Amalgam howled with distorted repetition.

The grip tightened. Dollop squirmed in panic.

He wrenched his strengthened arm free.

"Please!"

Dollop raced down the hall. Hands burst from cavities on all sides, snatching as he hurried past. Amalgam reached out to him through side chambers, faces twisted with sorrow. Their tormented voices were shattering and shrill, so deafening that Dollop had to hold his ears to block them out.

He skidded to a stop. A wall of body parts assembled before him, blocking his escape. A thousand mouths opened.

"We are one," they bellowed.

Hands erupted through the mouths and lunged for him.

Dollop split down the middle to evade their grasp. He slipped past, reassembling as he ran, twisting through the caverns.

Amalgam sobbed, a mother that had lost her child, beating its thousand fists against the ore in despair. And Dollop, too, was crying, overwhelmed with guilt and fear. He wiped heavy tears from his eyes as he fled.

Beneath the howls of sorrow, Dollop heard a trickle of

falling vesper. He hurried toward it and soon saw patterns of glowing blue light and hanging stalactites that he recognized.

"Please!" echoed Amalgam's tortured moan.

At last, the chamber he had been seeking. It was the lagoon and the shore where he had arrived. And there, lying undisturbed, was the salathyl prong he had left behind. He snatched it and looked up at the trickling vesperfalls. Among the dripping stalactites, he saw holes pocking the ceiling. An escape.

He clung to the mineral-flecked wall, re-forming his body, extending his limbs and fanning out his fingers for a better grip. He pulled himself up. Climbing, hand over hand. Foot after foot.

Mournful lamentations gathered like storm clouds, and Amalgam rolled like thunder into the chamber, flooding out of every tunnel. Dollop looked down.

A monstrous face made from countless parts, hundreds of eyes merging to glare. It rose, mouth hinging open, expanding cavernously wide. The face bent, contorted in misery.

It screamed.

"STAY!"

Amalgam came for him.

The howling maw seized Dollop. It plucked him off the cavern wall. Limbs surrounded him in an unbreakable grip.

Instantly, he was crushed by sadness, like the flame of every happy memory was snuffed out. This was sorrow magnified, a million times greater than any he had known. Every ounce of his being trembled with the desperate cry of "STAY."

And as the word bellowed within Dollop, as Amalgam

absorbed him, he felt his mind begin to crumble. He was eroding, every sensation submerged in an ocean of grief and loneliness.

Numbness blanketed him. He could not feel his pieces. They were being taken from him. They no longer belonged to him.

Soon there would be no *him* at all.

There never was, came a sad reply. Not his words, but broadcast into his thoughts. Or what was left of them.

Stay.

Return to us.

We are one forever.

What remained of Dollop? He felt the tingle that had kept him together dwindle, the heat of life fade. There went his belly, then his head. The rest was gone, melted down like liquid ore.

Molten. Like the marks on his chest.

Where had he gotten those scars?

His past was . . .

Fading.

Makina.

Her name stirred his dying ember.

He had almost gone to rust in the furnaces of Kallorax—that's where his scars had come from. But She had spared him.

Dollop was Waybound. A warrior of the Covenant.

Child of Ore, servant to the Great Engineer.

He remembered.

Amalgam grew hot. Dollop's resistance was disturbing it.

Piece by piece, his segments dug their way out of the suffering mass. He willed them to return.

Amalgam tried to hold on, clinging to his every last bit.

"WE ARE ONE!" it wailed.

His pieces retracted. His mouth assembled.

"I. AM. ME!" came Dollop's triumphant cry.

His body re-formed with an explosive force.

Amalgam convulsed, and Dollop was hurled into the air.

He stretched himself out to seize one of the stalactites.

Amalgam crumpled, all flopping limbs and bawling mouths. It recoiled pathetically, hugging itself.

High above, Dollop dangled from the stalactite. He gazed upon Amalgam for the last time.

This was his doing. After searching for so long, he had finally found his clan, and all he had done was cause them pain.

But Amalgam was not his home.

There was no going back.

His friends needed him.

Salathyl prong in his mouth, he scrabbled up the stalactite and pulled himself into a cavity. He found a steep incline and dragged his exhausted body up and up.

The ore shook with Amalgam's muffled howls.

Was the air pressure changing? Was that the drone of the Mirroring Sea? The warmth of suns from up above?

He clawed to the surface like a sprout ready to bloom.

Makina had set him free, and Dollop praised Her.

For Amalgam was right—he was broken and incomplete. But despite his failings, despite his lack, Dollop was himself.

He was one.

29 RHOM

They barely dared to breathe.

Rhom was taking them . . . somewhere.

The Sea Bullet groaned, its walls straining in the leviathan's grip. She had encased the boat in her black tendrils, muting the scream of the storm.

Rhom's tentacles squelched across the windshield. They looked like the shadows of dead trees—thick and darkly translucent with slithering offshoots. They were layered in barbs like meat hooks that gouged channels in the glass. Foreign objects were half-sunk into the gluey black flesh—shells of decomposing mehkans, chunks of indiscernible ore, and rusted shards of machines stamped with the Foundry logo.

Through the meager gaps between the tentacles, they saw that the boat was descending. They were being hauled into a tunnel within the mist-drenched Talons.

Micah snapped into action. He recovered his rifle and field pack, then climbed down into the engine room.

"Please tell me this is an accident," Gabby said. "Tell me that you weren't planning on taking us to Rhom."

Phoebe didn't answer.

"You should have told me." Gabby said sorrowfully. "We might have had a chance, Phoebe. I could have—"

Micah reappeared, stuffing the Med-i-Pak and rations into his case before strapping it on. As he reloaded his rifle, Phoebe adjusted the Multi-Edge sheath around her waist and tucked the naval map into a pocket. Gabby sank into a seat.

Outside, the tempest faded as they were taken deeper into the Talons. The deadly lead-gray spikes curled overhead like clawed hands, shielding them from the ferocity of the storm.

Without warning, the tentacles released them. The Sea Bullet dropped and rebounded heavily. The three passengers sat in silence, bobbing in the flux, too terrified to move.

"Now what?" Micah huffed.

As if in response, there came a blistering screech of tearing metal. The roof of the boat was peeled aside like the lid of a can. The three of them crouched on the floor, shielding their heads.

One of Rhom's tentacles beckoned them to follow, like a giant finger bristling with spines.

Phoebe stood, but her legs felt newly formed. She didn't want to see whatever was attached to that tentacle, especially after Gabby's reaction. But this is why they had come. If Phoebe was to help the Ona and find the Occulyth, she had to face Rhom.

Micah rose and fished a wad of cable out of his pocket.

"Seriously, kid?" Gabby said, watching him tie the severed cord back together. He was about to lash her to the driver's seat when someone grabbed his elbow.

"Plumm," he warned. "Don't even start. I swear, I gotta—"

But it wasn't Phoebe.

Rhom's tentacle drew Micah back by the elbow, then nudged Gabby out of the chair. It drifted to Phoebe, but she got the message—Rhom was herding them off the boat.

Phoebe stepped off the Sea Bullet and took a look around. Late afternoon suns bled through dispersing storm clouds, and light sliced through the Talons, casting prison-bar shadows on a wasteland of shipwrecks. Some were pulverized or capsized, others were husks protruding at severe angles—the crumbling remains of mehkan and Foundry vessels. A few looked new, others so profoundly ancient that they might blow apart in a strong breeze. It was as if all the ships in existence had been summoned here to crash and decay.

The tentacle beckoned.

Phoebe checked the turbulent black-and-blue sky for signs

of rain, then undid her facemask and hood. So did the others.

Her vision swam.

"Whoa, whoa," said Micah, steadying her.

"Your head," Gabby remarked with concern.

Phoebe pulled off a glove and touched her forehead, wincing. Blood. Her fingers were covered in it.

The tentacle approached, as if drawn by the wound.

"That's quite a gash," Gabby said. "Let me patch you up."

"No time," Phoebe said, wiping the blood on her coveralls.

"You sure you're . . . okay?" Micah asked.

Phoebe glared, and he looked down. He wasn't going to get off that easy. She wasn't ready to forgive him for his cruelty.

"Hands behind you," he said to Gabby, holding the cable.

Gabby sighed and rolled her eyes, but she obeyed.

"You know we're marching to our deaths, right?" she said as Micah lashed her wrists together.

Rhom's tentacle beckoned more insistently.

"Yep," he said. "Kinda gettin' used to it."

They trailed after the tentacle. It retracted behind a ruined hull, and another one wriggled at them from up ahead. The debris-littered ground was craggy, like shattered pottery crudely glued back together. They proceeded carefully, feeling it shift beneath their feet. Phoebe led the way with Gabby right behind, her face grim. Micah brought up the rear, rifle at the ready.

Phoebe looked down at the gelatinous blackness beneath her feet, and a terrifying realization gripped her.

They weren't being led to Rhom—they were on top of her.

All this debris was just the surface layer, a weathered shipwreck skin. No wonder the ground was so unsteady.

The tentacles urged them on. Rhom's expanse extended for miles in every direction, filling the Talons. And that was just above the flux. Who knew how far down she went?

They arrived at a hill of inky, viscous flesh. Tentacles crusted with clinking debris surrounded them. A geyser of hot air burst up, and Phoebe yelped. Moist jets blasted out from gloppy, fluctuating sphincters, wheezes that came in rhythmic bursts.

"Uh-oh," Micah mumbled.

Flux bubbled and frothed. Something breached the surface and rose thunderously before them. It was a massive dome with gaping, serrated gills, heaving out plumes of exhaust. As the liquid metal streamed off the thing, Phoebe saw that it was as transparent as a rubber balloon stretched too tight.

The surface was patched with ancient scars, but they could still see into its milky depths. Within was a nightmarish tangle of fluttering valves and nodules. Stringy ducts gathered in bundles, entwined like tangled metal jellyfish. Bloated sacs were linked to fleshy gears, with clouds of dark fluid pumping from one membranous chamber to the next. Giant fish-white hemispheres pulsed and vibrated.

They were Rhom's vital organs, a system so massive, so revoltingly complex, that it seemed like the innards of Mehk itself. And still it rose from the flux.

Sound hissing from the geyser holes coalesced into a word.

"Bow."

The sinister command startled Phoebe. As they stared up at the towering colossus, all resistance wilted. Wordlessly, the three of them fell to their knees.

As Rhom continued to rise, dwarfing them, a shifting circular mass emerged. It was a gargantuan array of concentric metal irises, contracting and expanding—hundreds of them, like the growth rings of an amputated tree.

They trembled before the eye of Rhom. Wet breath gasped out of orifices scattered around them and across the transparent dome. The bubbling voice sounded breathless, inhaling and exhaling simultaneously as she spoke.

"Here you are, lost and alone, hunters and the hunted, so little, so afraid, and oh so very far from home," Rhom gurgled, mirthless, but with a broken intonation that hinted at laughter.

"You know who we are?" Phoebe asked.

"I do," Rhom rasped, "for I am ever eating, ever knowing." Her giant, shifting eye drifted closer, the irises extending like a telescope. "I know they all seek you, wanted by the Covenant and wanted by the Foundry, but I alone, yes, only I have you."

"You don't know nothin' about us!" Micah snapped.

He immediately regretted it.

The eye rotated and widened to take him in. A vesicle within Rhom's head sputtered out thick crimson ink that broke into oily globs as it dissipated.

"I eat then I know," the flapping sphincters spat. "I know the bleeders hunt for your captive, the one they call Flores." A tentacle pointed at Gabby, and she went white.

Phoebe recalled the meaning of Rhom's name—to gorge.

I eat then I know.

"You eat . . . knowledge?" Phoebe asked.

"Ahhhhh . . ." Rhom breathed.

The pinkish fluid in her head rushed away, leaving it clear.

"I am timeless as the sea, my wisdom infinite, my hunger bottomless." There was another steamy snort as Rhom continued. "Living or no, I eat and I know."

The mound beneath them shifted, and the tentacles parted as something else breached the flux—a lost relic, eaten by time and half-buried in a mass of Rhom's black flesh.

"This schooner saw Creighton Albright aboard its maiden voyage, yet I discovered it centuries after his passing, devoured it and, with it, knowledge of the man, his stern voice, his fearful crewmen." The organs within Rhom's head pumped faster, as if she were growing more excited. "But bleeders are a passing trifle, for I have tasted the dawn of life, the birth of consciousness, I ate of the proto-mehkans, they worshipped me, I feasted on megalarchs, consumed nations, fed upon their every thought and memory, so many stories, all mine . . . Just as yours will be."

Phoebe felt the ground beneath her give. Her legs sank into Rhom's black flesh. She threw her hands down to try and push herself up and found them caught in the jelly as well. She was held fast. Heaving and pulling, she turned to Micah and Gabby, but they were stuck too.

They were being eaten. Soon Rhom would know them,

know their secrets and fears. Then their bodies would be nothing more than a bit of debris added to her collection.

Rhom sighed. "The curse of infinity is infinite boredom, so few surprises, so few mysteries remain, and yet still I must eat, for there is still so much to know."

"The Mercanteer sent us!" Phoebe cried.

Glands in Rhom's head gushed out brown and gray ink, muddying the clear fluid and clouding the unsightly organs.

"You do not travel in his vessel, you do not bear his seal."

"No," Micah answered, his prepubescent voice cracking. "We had to split. Bhorquvaat got overrun by Foundry."

"This I know," Rhom stated, uninterested.

"He said you would help," Phoebe pleaded. "That you would help us find what we need. Please! We need it to save Mehk!"

Gabby looked at her in shock. Rhom's eye shifted to Phoebe, and her swirling, murky dome became opaque.

"Mehk does not need you, because Mehk does not need, it merely *is*, nothing more," Rhom said in her constant breathless wheeze. "Yet your delusion is curious, as are your emotions, and curiosity is a delicacy, so I would know what you seek."

"Careful, Plumm," Micah whispered.

Phoebe recalled the warning from the Agent of Tongues—that Rhom was a great deceiver. And it was a risk to reveal too much in front of Gabby, but their lives were on the line.

This was their only chance.

"We have to find the Ona's Bearing," Phoebe said at last.

In a sudden inky detonation, Rhom's dome went red. The irises of her great eye narrowed. Hot flux steam erupted.

"Self-righteous mystic, dogmatic worm she is, slave of tradition!" Rhom sputtered. "I was worshipped as a god, they groveled before me, lavished me with sacrifices, and I feasted, ahhhh, how I feasted. . . ." Spurts of golden ink burbled amid the crimson. "But Makina was displeased with the slaughter, so the Ona turned my flock from me, curse the mouthpiece prophet! My worshippers abandoned me, left me to starve in the deep."

Another jet of exhaust burst from the geyser holes, a noxious smell of rot and putrefaction.

"But this I know, this thing you seek . . ." Her voice was laced with boredom. "The Mercanteer is a reliable servant, always beseeches me with abundant gifts, so I will bargain with his pets, offer you the same exchange I do him."

Rhom's eye backed off, and slowly the blood-red fluid in her head drained away, leaving the horror of her mehkan organ system on full display.

"What exchange?" Phoebe asked suspiciously.

"One for one," Rhom said flatly. "Knowledge for knowledge. I give you an answer, you give me a life."

30 FAREWELL

Although Goodwin's earpiece had been silent since the announcement of his forced retirement, he was certain the Board was still eavesdropping on him. Surely they had more important things to attend to, like the crisis Saltern had unleashed at the Council of Nations. Obwilé had neglected to engage with the disgruntled President, so he deserved the blame for that fiasco.

A train was scheduled to take Goodwin back to Albright City in a few hours. He had been tying up loose ends, saving this moment for last—his final visit to the Dyad Research Facility.

A technician scanned his pass, and the door hissed open.

"Thank you, Wilkes," said Goodwin kindly.

"It's been an honor, sir."

Goodwin entered the sterile white room. For the first time since his CHAR accident, Kaspar was sitting up.

A good sign. He might be able to handle the news.

"Hello, my boy," Goodwin said softly.

He strode past the Omnicam that was monitoring the room. Kaspar's disfigured body had been treated with experimental agents and covered in customized bandages, which were spotted with grease from his seeping lesions. Tubes trailed from glass needles in his veins. A single black eye was all that was exposed.

And it stared.

"I am relieved by your speedy recovery," Goodwin whispered. "It is good to be able to speak to you without causing you pain."

The eye blinked, slow and deliberate.

"May I sit?" he asked, settling onto a wooden stool. Goodwin eyed Kaspar's hands, which were restrained by thick straps secured with high-index ceramic buckles.

"I . . . well, I have something I need to tell you," Goodwin said quietly. "I am retiring."

The black eye went wide.

"It was my choice," Goodwin lied in a soothing voice. "The Foundry no longer requires my services, so I am off for Olyrian Isle. My sole regret is that we can no longer work together."

Kaspar's bandages bulged.

"But together, you and I achieved greatness. We touched

upon something that science is only beginning to dream of."

A new spot of black bled through his dressings.

"You are in good hands," Goodwin said, his voice tight. "Wilkes and the others, they are going to fix you up."

The eye narrowed.

"Please, do not worry about me," Goodwin whispered with a smile as he glanced up at the Omnicam. He withdrew his Scrollbar. "They sent me some photos of my retirement villa. Would you like to see?"

He held his device out to show Kaspar.

"I know, I know," he chuckled. "I do not much care for the color either, but just look at that view. Magnificent."

Kaspar's eye twitched in surprise as he studied the image on the screen, taking it in. Goodwin held the device closer to him, making sure he got a good look. Kaspar gurgled and blinked in understanding. Goodwin put his Scrollbar away and gently laid his hands on the straps that bound the soldier's wrists.

"Dialsets are forbidden on Olyrian Isle, but I hope they will at least allow me to send you letters. Perhaps the Board will even keep me abreast of your progress." Goodwin rose and wiped his eyes. "I will think of you often, my boy—of our Dyad Project. How we held Mehk in our hands. How we glimpsed the future."

He stood, staring deeply into the exposed black eye.

"Be well. There is still so much for you to achieve, but you must continue without me. Until we meet again, dear Kaspar."

Goodwin leaned forward and gently kissed the misshapen,

bandaged forehead. As he walked swiftly from the room, Kaspar released a rattling gasp. It was either tears or laughter.

He did not look back to find out which.

Rhom released her grip on Phoebe, Micah, and Gabby, and they scrabbled to their feet.

"What do you mean, 'give you a life'?" Phoebe demanded.

"This is not the right question," Rhom said in a patronizing sigh. Golden ink streamed into her dome, glittering like metallic snow. "You should be asking . . . *whom* will it be?"

The three of them shared a devastated look.

"The choice is yours," Rhom rasped.

"Forget it!" Micah called out.

"You can't do this!" Gabby cried.

"I do as I please," Rhom gurgled.

"But why?" Phoebe asked.

"Because it is . . . delicious." Her golden fluid gushed. "I could consume you all. Instead, I allow you to choose your own fate."

"You disgust me," Phoebe said.

The black hill of flesh rumbled. Micah and Gabby looked at her fearfully. Rhom's tree-ring irises narrowed at Phoebe.

"The one called Plumm, masquerading as savior of Mehk," Rhom hissed. "And yet you would be so selfish as to allow this simple dilemma to impede you? Choose, for I am hungry."

"All right already. Give us a sec, will ya?" Micah called.

Rhom released a hot blast of moist air.

"Sit," Micah instructed Gabby, gesturing to a withered beam protruding from Rhom's hide.

"Phoebe," Gabby begged. "I know what you're both thinking, but, please—let's discuss this rationally."

"Sit down!" he shouted, raising his rifle. Gabby obeyed.

"Don't do it. Please, Phoebe. Don't let me die."

A blissful sigh emanated from Rhom's cavities. Her transparent head was now a twinkling dome of gold.

"It's okay," Phoebe reassured Gabby as Micah pulled her away. "Just give us a minute."

Once they were out of earshot, the kids faced each other.

"So?" Micah asked, his eyes and weapon trained on Gabby.

"We have to kill her," Phoebe said.

He was taken aback.

"Whoa," he said. "Just like that?"

She stared hard at him. "Not Gabby. Rhom."

Micah laughed. "Haha, that's funny!" He glanced nervously at the swaying tentacles surrounding them, then whispered from the side of his mouth. "Pretty sure she can hear us."

They looked up at Rhom's eye, but the leviathan just stared, offering no sign that she had detected the threat.

"Use your gun," Phoebe said. "Shoot her eye."

"Please tell me you're kiddin'."

She knew how stupid it was.

"Well, then we have to run for it," she offered.

"Where? Across her back? Sure, Plumm, bet we'll get real far." He sighed. "Funny, that Agent guy forgot to mention Rhom's little life-eating exchange with the Mercanteer."

"He said Rhom couldn't be trusted."

"Which means she might not keep her side of the bargain."

"Exactly," Phoebe grumbled.

Micah glanced at Gabby's pale, stricken face. "What choice do we have? It's Rhom's rules or nothin'."

"I'm not letting Gabby die."

"Well, I ain't all that eager to volunteer. How 'bout you?"

Phoebe's head throbbed. She touched her wound—the blood was tacky, which was an improvement, she supposed.

"That's what I thought," Micah continued. "Now look. I ain't any happier about this than you are, but—"

"I doubt that."

"What's that s'pposed to mean?"

"You know what it means," she said. "You wanted to get rid of Gabby from the very beginning. And this is your chance."

"Yeah, but I ain't no murderer!"

"You are if you give her to Rhom," she insisted. "So am I."

Micah jutted his jaw. "Well, what, then?"

Rhom's hungry eye was upon them. It wasn't fair. They had to make a choice, but how? There was no right way, no easy way out. They were going to lose someone no matter what.

It was up to Phoebe.

Her eyes leveled at Micah, hardening like tempered steel.

"I know that look," he said nervously. "What are you doin'?"

She turned from him and strode toward Rhom. There was a cold, calculated confidence in her step, a fearless resignation.

"Wait. No, stop!" he shouted. "Hey, I said stop!" He reached for her, but she evaded him. The fleshy ground seized his foot.

"You want a life?" Phoebe called out.

"Don't you dare!" Micah screamed, struggling to free himself.

"You have chosen," Rhom sighed contentedly.

"Not you!" he cried. It was too horrifying to fathom.

"I give you the most important among us. The one who brought us here, who united us, who has already changed the world of humans and of mehkans."

"Phoebe!" Gabby gasped.

"You flatter yourself," breathed the geyser holes. "So be it." Debris-armored tentacles drifted toward Phoebe.

"No!" Micah screamed again and ripped his foot from Rhom's grip. He ran to Phoebe's side, raising his gun.

She peeled off her whist and held it aloft.

"I give you my father, Dr. Jules Plumm."

Bursts of red bled out into Rhom's dome. Her eye extended, focusing its compound irises on Phoebe.

Micah's jaw dropped. He lowered the weapon.

"That is not the exchange," Rhom hissed.

"I am Loaii. This is my whist," Phoebe declared. "I am the first human to bear both. My father was responsible for destroying the Citadel. He died trying to liberate Mehk, and what remains of him . . ." A knot in her throat tensed her voice. "His memory, his life, are bound to this whist."

Rhom's eye was inches from Phoebe's face. She looked

into its hollow depths, like staring into a well, and felt the leviathan's ancient, ravenous hate. But the red globs within the transparent dome had dispersed, replaced with brown and gray murk.

She had Rhom's attention.

"The whist is a secret of the Waybound," Phoebe said. "That must be of interest to you. Knowledge for knowledge."

Black jelly tentacles twitched around her, their clinking hooks agleam. Buried in their flesh, Phoebe saw the tarnished skeletons of mehkan sea creatures, layered like strata.

A tentacle grabbed the whist.

Phoebe clung to it. The dream that she might once again hear her parents calling to her, the answer to the mystery of Makina's voice—it was all contained in those rust-colored folds.

Rhom plucked the whist free and pulled it under the flux.

With a bubble and a blip, it was gone.

Micah stood beside Phoebe, waiting.

Rhom's eye dilated. The muddy fluid within her dome drained away, replaced by a strange new hue—a placid, pale blue. The machinery of her innards slowed to a languid rhythm.

"Cricket," came the ancient mehkan's whispered response.

Phoebe went numb.

Hearing her father's pet name for her in Rhom's voice felt like corruption, like she had sold an irreplaceable part of herself.

"Silence," Rhom said, her voice strangely distant. "Deep silence . . . profound suffering . . . these I now know. . . ."

"Tell us," pleaded Phoebe. "Where is the Ona's Bearing?"

Black ink clouded her innards. "I curse her, she who took from me all that I once had," Rhom growled. "I am not the Ona's pawn, not like you, yet something is at work here that I do not comprehend. . . . I will allow it that I may one day know."

The tentacles retracted, and the placid blue ink returned.

"The Ona was a prophet of pomp and artifice, never without her façade." Rhom exhaled. "That which you seek fell with her, in the place where two worlds left her for dead."

Everyone assumed the Ona had died, but after speaking to her through the Hearth, Phoebe knew that was not true. She tried to remember the story—what was it? The Ona had been attacked by the Foundry four hundred years ago by . . .

"CHAR," Phoebe gasped. "But that means—"

"The Bearing is no more," breathed Rhom. "Lost in the blights at the foot of the Shroud." A trickle of gold appeared amidst the clear blue. The leviathan was clearly enjoying this.

"*Where my Bearing once lay*," Phoebe repeated the Ona's words. "That's where we're going. Please. How do we get there?"

Gabby's eyes widened, and she struggled against her bonds.

Rhom's great eye considered the kids. Then clouds of silver and gold flooded her translucent dome. She rose higher, her nauseating organ system chugging. Rhom was excited about something, and that made them uneasy.

"Join the Broken . . ." she wheezed, "for only your father can show you the way."

Phoebe gasped.

"What's that supposed to mean?" Micah cried out. "That's no kinda answer. You're cheating!"

"You did not fulfill the exchange," Rhom said. "Nor shall I."

"I don't understand," Phoebe said. "How can my father . . ."

"Again," the leviathan spoke in a hitching tone that could only be laughter, "you ask the wrong question, my dear Cricket Loaii, you should ask . . . why have our three become two?"

It took the kids a moment. They spun around.

A frayed cable lay by the sharp beam where Gabby had been.

Micah bolted. Phoebe ran after him. Musty geysers huffed from the holes around them—Rhom's sinister chuckle.

The kids tore back the way they had come, racing for the boat. They balanced across masts and bounded over breached hulls. An engine sputtered up ahead. With a screech, the Sea Bullet tore away from Rhom's shipwreck skin and sped off.

Micah raised his rifle and fired.

A flurry of rounds peppered the flux. Bullets pinged off the boat, but it was already thirty yards away. Then forty. Fifty.

Gabby was gone.

31 DARKNESS MADE FLESH

I have a secret.

They don't know it, not yet. Think I am sedated. That's why the Greencoats mill about, inserting needles, changing dressings. As if I am sleeping, as if I am lifeless as these pillows.

But I am aware. Ready.

I wait until the worst of the Greencoats are in the room, the ones I hate most of all—the blinking woman and the man with the harelip scar. They discuss my latest readouts from the machine.

I tear my arm from the loosened restraint. Sense their heat fade as they go pale. Smell their fear. I should barely be conscious. Should be held fast by straps and buckles.

How can I be free?

They will never know.

I snap the rest of my bindings. Yank the needles from my arteries. There is pain, but as their poison stops dripping into me, my muscles come alive.

The man with the scar runs for the door, screams that stab my ears. Have to stop the sound. I am on him before he can reach the handle. Fling him into the glass equipment. An explosion of sparks.

He twitches on the ground.

I do not toy with the other. She dies in a red mist.

I shed my bandages, rip off wrappings that smother me.

Sirens shriek. They're too loud, driving into my exposed brain.

I escape the wail. Doors yield before me. Crash through, toss them aside. Guards are coming, but they are slow. In the hallways, Greencoats cower and flee. They are lucky I ignore them.

I smash through the barrier that leads outside. What was muffled is now a roar. Every sensation magnified. Bare muscle fibers, raw bone, naked to the cutting air and sizzling suns.

I race through the Depot.

Head to the Control Core, glass dazzling in the daylight.

Alarms blare because they have lost me. Will never find me because I feel when they're near. I hear them breathe from far away. Every vibration of their vehicles, their footsteps. I smell the clicking Omnicams, know the ping of their motion detectors.

My confusion is gone. I see layers of light, feel atmospheric patterns. My nerves weave into a new grid of ever-present pain. But the grime has been flushed from my mind.

My new senses are awake.

The world is mine to savor.

I reach the Control Core and climb. Metal beams yield to my touch, soften as I squeeze. Climb higher. Exposed in the light like a rat on a wire. The cursed suns sear my not-skin. Someone will surely see me pulling myself up.

Let them see.

I leave sizzling handprints on the building's skeleton. No reach is too great—the next handhold is always in my grasp. I stretch and twist like a hallucination.

Every second their poison drains from me I grow stronger.

I arrive.

Leer through the window, cling to the frame. Muscles do not ache, they burn with desire. Watching my targets behind the glass.

The directors. They do not see me.

My bloated heart throttles. I trace the course of boiling CHAR flooding my veins. Shatter the glass with one blow, send a blizzard of shards at my prey. Their wafting fear fills my nostrils.

I leap.

They scatter.

Guards emerge, Watchmen and humans.

No matter. I charge the machines, which raise their weapons. Vomit my toxin at them. Their empty faces melt like wax. Plunge my hand into one of their heads, rip out its living AI-unit. The sparking, spastic worm turns to slop in my hand.

The human guards aren't prepared. They expected a wild mehkan, perhaps a madman. Not the thing that is me.

Bullets thud into the wall, into me. Icy spike of bonding rounds. The chemical is released, wages war with the living metal within. White bubbles froth like acid in my wounds.

But the pain does not slow me. My joints unhinge.

I strike. Then they are in pieces.

My body twists like a screw. The directors cluster in a frenzy. The bald one with the gold glasses holds up his hands, as if he could ward me off. He is the one that took me from Mr. Goodwin. He gave the order to torture me. I will save him for last.

But the others are not innocent. They all must pay.

This is why I have come. A killing wind.

Darkness made flesh.

PICKING UP THE PIECES

The lobby of the Control Core was packed with troubled employees. Everyone had heard the commotion. Goodwin shoved his way through the crowd until a soldier recognized him and allowed him to enter the elevator.

"Once I am up, shut off power," Goodwin ordered. "No more access. Double the guards at all exits and notify me if anyone attempts entry. No one is permitted upstairs. Is that clear?"

"Uh . . ." The soldier looked around, unsure. "Yes, sir."

"Clear these people out. Lock down the building."

Goodwin straightened his cuffs as the elevator ascended. At the top floor, the doors slid open, and the setting suns that blasted through the shattered glass walls nearly blinded him.

The room was chaos. Executives scurried about in aimless panic. Grisly evidence of the recent violence was painted across the windows and soaking into the lush, burgundy carpet. Some guards were documenting the bloody tableau with Fotosnaps, others moving the bodies or covering them with sheets.

Goodwin climbed onto a table.

"Stop!" he shouted above the disorder.

The room fell silent.

"Perry," Goodwin addressed a nearby soldier. "Gather your people. Secure the stairwells."

The man snapped to attention and assembled his team.

"Dietrich. Confiscate all Fotosnaps and Scrollbars. Absolutely no information or images are to leave this room."

The officer did as he was told.

"This is a crime scene," Goodwin declared. "Nothing is to be disturbed. Investigators are on their way. Until then, everyone will remain on the premises. Understood?"

A few nods amid the silence.

Goodwin stepped down from the table and crossed the room, feeling everyone's stares as he crunched through shards of glass. He looked down at the corpse of his old colleague, Director Malcolm. Strange, after all these decades of working together, he had never learned the man's first name.

Leaning out of a broken window, Goodwin eyed the scorched, sunken handprints Kaspar had left on the beams. The strength required for such a climb was astounding.

"We must speak," said a voice in Goodwin's earpiece. *"Notify us when you're ready."*

"You are in charge here until I return, Dietrich," Goodwin told the officer. He cast one more glance around the room. Satisfied that things were now a bit more in order, he stepped through a gold-inlaid mahogany door and closed it behind him.

Obwilé's office was sparsely furnished, though that might have been due to the recent move rather than taste. The desk was onyx black, polished to a mirror shine. Tidy stacks of documents lined with Obwilé's meticulous handwriting sat beside a glowing Computator screen. Across the room hung an uninspired painting of a sunset. It did not surprise Goodwin that Obwilé displayed no taste for art.

Goodwin settled his broad frame into the high-backed armchair. There was a single photo in a chrome frame on the desk. It showed Obwilé standing beside his wife and two small children, smiling before a waterfall. Goodwin saw his face reflected in the glass, superimposed over the happy family.

"I am alone," he announced.

"*James*," spoke a voice of the Board. *"We appreciate your decisive action in this matter."*

"The chain of command has been disrupted," stated another, *"and we knew we could depend on you to handle the situation."*

The Foundry's five directors in Mehk had just been brutally murdered. Yet the Board appeared unmoved.

"Of course. We are all in shock," Goodwin replied sincerely.

"This attack has come at a most inopportune time."

"International tensions are elevated in Meridian, and it appears that the rebellion in Mehk is not yet under control."

"I tried to warn Obwilé that it was a mistake to treat Kaspar with such cruelty," Goodwin intoned. "I wish he had listened. Kaspar was my creation. I feel . . . I feel somehow responsible, even though Obwilé had assumed full control of the project."

"It is unfortunate."

"Can you guess where the Dyad might be?"

"Information from your recent visit to him, perhaps?"

Goodwin considered this. "Unfortunately, no. He was barely responsive. But Kaspar still looks up to me. Once we locate him, I will use that to elicit his surrender."

"And if that fails?" a voice replied.

"Then he will be dealt with accordingly."

"Our investigation will determine exactly what went wrong and how the Dyad managed to escape."

"We will discover who is responsible for this catastrophe."

"And their punishment will be unprecedented."

The Board let this foreboding statement linger.

"That is a relief," Goodwin said. "Please keep me informed."

"On to other matters."

"We face significant gaps in our operational capacity."

"It will take time to reconstitute a fully functional leadership."

"Indeed," Goodwin acknowledged.

"We are working to find replacements."

"But we must maintain stability until new directors are vetted."

"Someone to coordinate departments."

"One with experience and oversight."

"Have you spoken to Winslow?" Goodwin suggested.

"He is not familiar with our current diplomatic situation."

"We need someone who already has a deep understanding of the manifold complexities we are up against."

"While we smooth over the chaos caused by Saltern's speech."

"Yes," Goodwin said. "His arrogance has proven disastrous." Goodwin checked his watch. "My train leaves in an hour, but if it pleases the Board, I could speak with the President. As you know, we have a strong relationship, and I manage him easily."

"Yes."

"But forget your train."

"Your retirement has been postponed."

Goodwin's eyes opened wide. "Pardon me?"

"You are reinstated as Chairman."

"Until a suitable replacement is selected."

"And new directors are in place."

"I . . . I see," Goodwin said. "I am honored."

"But there is no margin for error."

"Briefing documents have been filed in your accounts."

"A medic will be dispatched to uninstall your earpiece."

"But you must continue to wear it."

"We will be in touch."

"Chairman Goodwin."

Then with a soft click, the Board was gone.

A warm feeling of satisfaction filled Goodwin. He pulled out his Scrollbar—his passwords and access had all been restored.

Goodwin smiled. He looked at his new desk and dropped Obwilé's family photograph into the trash can.

His first order was to find a replacement for General Moritz—he had endured enough abuse from ol' Bert. Next, he would organize a summit with the military executives to ramp up the Covenant Task Force. He had no faith that the Foundry's fight against the rebellion had been handled adequately. Once that was taken care of, he could deal with Saltern's blunder.

Then, the children. That last thread needed to be snipped.

33 UNITED

The sea was harsh, the night wind harsher. It hacked at Phoebe and Micah, cutting across the flux with arctic fury. Their arms burned, their bodies screamed with exhaustion, and there was nothing left to do but row.

Back in the dying light of dusk, Rhom had ignored the kids' demands to catch Gabby, instead leading them to the eastern edge of the Talons with her tentacles. There, she dredged up a half-digested mehkan boat carved from a giant seed husk for them to use. The tentacles pointed them toward their destination—a cluster of dark buildings atop a cliff in the hazy distance. Then Rhom sank into the flux.

Now, after hours of rowing, the kids were spent and frozen from the wind. They tumbled among the silvery waves, gobs of the toxic liquid metal splashing into their boat. Phoebe's head felt like a rock that had been split open with a pickax, and blood kept oozing into her eye. Her grip on the oars was slipping, but she kept on rowing because the heat of exhaustion kept the cold from drilling down into her bones.

The sky was black and cracked with interwoven stars. Looming darkly on the horizon was a titanic mountain range. Beyond that, a breathtaking and infinite wall of gray, like a curtain drawn across the world.

The Shroud—the boundary between this life and the next.

The thought of what lay beyond it chilled Phoebe even more. A vast unknown swirling with . . . what? Spirits? Embers?

Flux waves shattered across breakers just ahead. The sea had pushed them down the coast, so they were a ways off course when a dark green beach came into view.

Their boat ground ashore. Phoebe was thrown forward, and Micah was nearly tossed over the prow. They steadied their ringing heads and towed their sad vessel onto the ore. Micah pointed inland to an outcropping where they might take shelter from the wind. They stumbled up the rocky beach and collapsed into the cranny, away from the brutal, biting cold.

They ripped their masks aside and heaved for air.

"That . . . totally . . . sucked," Micah huffed.

Phoebe confirmed his observation with her panting breath.

He looked over at her and blanched. "Holy crap, Plumm!"

"What?" she gasped, trying to sit up.

"Your face. You're bleeding, like . . . everywhere."

She wiped her forehead, and pain screamed back at her.

"Just lay back, okay?" he said, wadding his gloves under her head like a pillow. He pulled off his hard-shelled field bag and withdrew the Med-i-Pak. "Hope you don't need stitches. I ain't so good with a needle."

The thought of Micah sewing her up made Phoebe nauseous.

He dug out a Wackers bar. "Take it."

"Ugh. I can't eat another one," she said weakly.

"You gotta," he said and pulled out a packet of antiseptic wipes. "You lost a lotta blood. You're gonna need energy."

"You don't have a clue what you're talking about."

"Nope. But it sounded good."

Phoebe nibbled the candy bar as Micah dabbed at her wound. It hurt, but he was being gentle so there wasn't much to complain about—other than the fact that it was Micah doing it.

His mouth moved, then closed, then opened again as if he had something he wanted to say.

She looked at him. "What?"

"Nothin'," he said defensively. "It's just . . . I just . . ."

"Spit it out."

Micah avoided her eyes. "Margie basically raised me," he mumbled. "She took care of me when I was sick and stuff, fed me off her plate. She always protected me from Pa. Margie was the only one who . . . who ever fought back."

His eyes were distant.

"She pulled his own gun on him a coupla times. That usually shut him up. That's why she taught me how to shoot. He didn't stick around long enough for me to ever draw on him, though." Micah chuckled morbidly to himself. "Too bad."

He squeezed ointment on a bandage.

"So when Gabby said she knew Margie, trained her and stuff . . . I couldn't take the idea that my sis might be working for the Foundry too. Just like . . . just like your dad. The only two people who were ever good to me."

Micah looked at Phoebe, his eyes foggy. He eased the bandage onto her forehead, careful not to touch the wound. She studied him, a lump forming in her throat.

"It's not an excuse," he said. "Just a reason. That stuff I said to you, it wasn't right. I'm sorry, Phoebe. I can't take it back, but I can promise that it ain't gonna happen again."

She nodded.

He closed up the Med-i-Pak. "Is that any better?"

"Yes," she rasped. "Thank you."

He looked at the half-eaten Wackers bar in her hand.

"You gonna finish that?"

Phoebe and Micah rested for a spell, drank some water from the SCM case, then bundled up and headed out. Micah used his rifle light to guide the way as they mounted the ridge toward the cluster of buildings that Rhom had indicated.

The smoky green beach was like raw quartz crystal, patches of rough ground interspersed with sheer planes as slick as ice.

The kids struggled to climb these, scraping a few feet up only to squeak and slide back down again. Coarse white trunks sprouted in clumps, their skeletal branches bearing bronze knitting-needle leaves and seed cones like threaded screws.

Bit by bit, Phoebe and Micah ascended the shore. With the mountains and Shroud at their backs, they found themselves on a peninsula surrounded by the vast Mirroring Sea. A hundred yards ahead loomed their destination.

But as they drew near, their hearts sank. They could see through toppled walls and gaps in fractured buildings. Smoke sputtered out of it like the heart of a volcano. The structures were pitch black, not from shadows but from scorch marks.

The Foundry had already been here.

Phoebe followed Micah's lead. They stepped over the rubble of blasted black gates to find dozens of collapsed buildings. A single tower stood at the center of the wreckage, like a monument to the fallen. The courtyard was crisscrossed with tank tread tracks and scattered with pale statues.

Micah shined his light on the white shapes.

The kids felt sick.

These were not sculptures. They were mehkan corpses.

Dollop stumbled into the jungle clearing. He struck his salathyl prong on a fallen tahnik tendril. The white spike resonated, and he plunged it into the ore muck.

He had emerged from the flux tide pools before sunfall

and fled back into the jungle. All he could think to do was keep trying the salathyl prong, and he had been at it for clicks.

But he was not afraid. After his encounter with Amalgam, he felt whole. He was his own mehkan, and Makina was with him.

He poked around at a lump in the mud.

"Ko-kolchi nuts!"

Dollop dug out a coarse little nugget and bit through the shell. The tender morsel within was wonderfully sweet. He got on his hands and knees and foraged for more. They were everywhere, a trove probably stashed here by a wandering flyntl.

As he dug, he felt the mud slosh and tremble.

Dollop got to his feet, confused.

Then he understood. He leapt out of the way just as the ore exploded in a splatter of muck.

A massive white drill breached the surface. Coiling, striated tentacles spewed out of the hole as a salathyl hauled itself above ground. Trailing behind the ghostly mehkan was a giant black capsule. With a screech, the back hatch twisted open, and a lumbering gohr stepped out, his huge clamp claws clinched.

It took Dollop a second to recognize the mehkan, but when he did, he squealed with delight. "Overguard Tr-Treth!"

"Dent my hide!" Treth rumbled, holding a fist over his blood-red dynamo. "Our little acolyte. Never thought I'd see you this side of the Shroud. How can it be?"

"Her ge-gears turn in mysterious ways," Dollop said simply.

Treth's black eyes twinkled deep beneath wiry brows. "That they do," he chuckled. "Well, are you primed?"

"Um, pr-pr-primed for what, Overguard?"

"You haven't heard?" Treth boomed. He blew out a jet of steam from the vents in his neck and hunkered down, eye to eye with Dollop. "We fight," he said with a hungry growl.

Dollop looked behind Treth to see two dozen armed Covenant warriors gathered inside the capsule.

"The Ona has decreed," Overguard Treth said. "No more shall the Children of Ore sit idle. We will make the Foundry bleed."

"Wh-what about Loaii? And—and Micah?" Dollop asked. "Please. Tell me they have been fo-found."

"The children are lost," Treth grumbled, "but hope is not."

The Overguard placed a massive claw on Dollop's shoulder.

"It is time to take back what is ours—to return Mehk to our Mother. Will you forfeit your span to save Her sacred machine?"

"I will." Dollop bowed his head.

Treth growled in approval. "Then come."

As the Overguard returned to the capsule, Dollop called out.

"Wh-where?" he asked. "Where are we go-going?"

"To where this all began," Treth barked over his shoulder. "To send the bleeders back from where they came."

THE BROKEN

Phoebe and Micah felt the eyes of a hundred dead mehkans upon them. The bodies in the courtyard were plastered with bonding rounds and crystallized in agony, arms outstretched.

The kids shivered as they scanned the grounds. The buildings that hadn't been leveled were blackened, bombed-out husks. What remained looked ancient, built from large blocks of rough-hewn ore and splintered metal beams, their corners worn smooth by the persistent coastal wind.

Rising above the ruins was a weathered tower, bruised but still intact. It was as good a place to start looking as any.

There was no clear way to reach it, so they looked for a

route through the collapsed structures, entering the nearest one through a ragged wound in its side. Though they could not see any flames, it was hot inside and reeked of smoldering iron. Smoke curled around Micah's rifle light.

"So what are we supposed to be doin' here anyway?" Micah sighed. "Does 'join the Broken' mean anything to you?"

Phoebe shook her head as she looked around.

"I mean this place definitely qualifies as broken," he huffed. "Maybe Rhom's just askin' us to fix up the joint."

Phoebe smiled.

"And 'only your father can show you the way'? Seriously? It's a load of hooey is what it is, and I'll tell you what—"

Rubble shifted nearby. Micah spun sharply, his light illuminating a heap of wreckage.

He and Phoebe exchanged a nervous look.

"We gotta work fast," he whispered. "Don't forget Gabby."

"I haven't," she muttered.

"It ain't gonna be long—"

"Before they come looking for us," Phoebe finished, stumbling over loose wreckage. "I know."

The passage ahead had collapsed, and the debris was too unstable to climb. They turned around and headed back.

"I tell you what, though," Micah mused. "Between the Ona and Rhom, I've just about had it up to here with riddles."

Another scuffle.

Twisted figures lurked at the edge of darkness. Eyes glittered from behind toppled columns and rubble. When Micah tried to frame them in the beam of light, they shrank away.

"Come on outta there!" Micah barked, readying his rifle.

For a moment, everything was still. Then a lone figure shuffled forward, a mehkan who barely came up to their chests. He looked like a skeleton shrink-wrapped in gray foil, a squashed face and sunken eyes on either side of his head. His digits were arranged in circles around his feet and hands, and they looked too stubby to be of much use. As he crept into the light, Phoebe's instinct was to look away—his body was checkered with seeping, rust-colored sores.

"It you. Loaii. You Loaii?" he creaked. His jaw dangled on a rusty hinge, revealing more sores pocking his mouth and tongue.

He limped closer, his bowed legs groaning like tired bedsprings. "We hear you talk of Broken, talk of Ona. We hear rumor. Little bleeder Loaii, sent by Engineer. Please. It you?"

Phoebe nodded cautiously. "Yes, I am Loaii."

"Oh, praise," rasped the mehkan. "She answer us."

"Please," she said, "what does 'the Broken' mean?"

"We," he replied. "This. This Housing of Broken."

Phoebe felt a chill—Rhom had not led them astray.

A group of mehkans emerged from the shadows. There were at least fifteen of them draped in dingy gowns, some the same species as the one who spoke. One was a blind freylani, his telltale hunchback covered in black tumors like rotten potatoes. Two others were swathed in sprocketed helical bands, but their bodies were knotted together and conjoined. There was also a hulking mehkan covered in mangy steel wool, the kind that the kids knew usually had one monstrously oversized arm. But this poor fellow's appendage was flimsy and atrophied, and he clutched a swaddled bundle.

As the mehkans approached, the kids saw how feeble they looked. Several leaned on makeshift crutches, one was being wheeled in a tilbury. They reached out to Phoebe, trembling. She did not flinch. Their metallic skin was shriveled and cold, but they touched her face gently, their mouths moving in silent supplication. Some kissed her coveralls, weeping viscous tears.

Micah stepped aside to give them room, his eyes sharp and his hands tight on his rifle just in case.

"Makina made us this," said the diseased mehkan who had spoken to them. "Embers stirred, reborn this. Punish for evil we do in past span."

"That's terrible," Phoebe replied.

"No, no!" the mehkan insisted. "Makina loves. Axials love. We tchurbs, all carry rot-pox." He gestured to the other diseased mehkans like him. "No one help. Think we bad luck. No one . . . *kashli mya'hr*, touch. Tchurbs wander, no can earn gauge. But—" He broke into a hacking cough, and his bony frame strained beneath delicate skin. "Only axials care us. Feed, yes? Help sore. That why tchurbs Makina's most devote servants."

The mehkans backed away, and Micah lowered his weapon.

"All us the Broken. Volmerid, thiaphysi, ettik, freylani, tchurb. Some no can walk or see. Born wrong, you understand?"

"The axials took care of you all," Phoebe said. "Is that why you can speak Bloodword? What's your name?"

"Tik," he said. "Yes, I clean for axials. They teach for me."

"What happened?" asked Micah.

Tik looked around. "Foundry. Come with machines. Tear things, holy things. Try take axials away, but Broken fight. Then fire in the sky. Destroy Housing, we hide. All who fight now rust, you understand?"

The kids nodded.

"We do," Phoebe said urgently. "But we're here on a very important mission for Makina. Do you have a Hearth?"

"Hearth?" Tik said the word as if he had never encountered it before. He turned to the group of Broken, repeating it, but they only looked back at him blankly.

"You know, a wall of drippy metal stuff used for talking to . . . other people," Micah tried to explain discreetly. "From far away?"

"Nothing like this," Tik said with a frown.

"Did another bleeder ever visit here, before the Foundry came?" Phoebe asked. "A man who was a friend of the Way?"

Tik consulted the others again, and then shook his head.

"Does the word 'father' ring a bell?" Micah tried. "Anything here called 'father'?"

The mehkans just stared at the kids.

"Please. We need your help," Phoebe pleaded. "We were sent here. We were told that my father would show us the way to the place where the Ona died. That has to mean something."

The tchurb's eyes opened wide. "Emberhome?"

"What's that?" Micah asked.

The tchurb coughed again, a hollow rattle ending in an unpleasant clang. "Yes, I show." Tik spoke to his friends, then turned back to the kids. "The Broken go, must bury rusted. Cannot wait for rise. You come. I show Emberhome."

The group of mehkans bowed as the kids were led away.

Tik clambered feebly over debris, his stubby fingers and toes struggling to find a grip. With the aid of Micah's light, they headed through a sunken arcade and squeezed through a collapsed doorway into a round, crumbling building.

An entire portion of the chamber had been reduced to ashes, and what remained was peppered with bullet holes, but nonetheless the space was stunning. The cathedral—for Phoebe didn't know what else to call it—was reminiscent of the shrine in Bhorquvaat, though much larger. Amid the wreckage, she saw raised podiums of dark, polished ore radiating from the center. The curved ceiling was a lustrous, dusky gold, though it was partially peeled back like a candy wrapper, revealing the interwoven stars.

Stretching up from the center of the dome was the tower they had seen from the outside.

"Yes, yes," Tik said, noticing that the tower had caught their eyes. "Lamp of sea. Ward of Broken. Used to glow all cycle. But sungold beacon stolen phases ago. Dark now, only dark."

"Like a lighthouse?" Micah asked.

"House of light. Yes," Tik said. "Come." He led them through the rows of podiums to the center and gestured to the far side of the rotunda. "Emberhome," he whispered.

"Wicked," Micah said.

The rifle light revealed a mosaic enameled onto the curved

wall. It must have once been astounding, but now it was damaged nearly beyond recognition.

The image depicted the Ona cloaked in flowing veils, face obscured by her Bearing as she gazed at the sky. Extending around her was an elaborate temple of intersecting circular arches and dynamo pillars. Black scars gouged the image, obscuring details, and frigid night air blew through a large hole that obliterated half of her body. Despite that, they could see wavy golden halos emanating from her hands, though it was impossible to tell what the shapes might have once been.

"This picture the Ona's *gha-tullei*, uh . . . sanctuary. Place of holy. Emberhome. There she rust, may her golden ember blaze."

"Please, Tik," Phoebe said, unable to hide her desperation any longer. "We have to find it!"

"Was hidden in Coiling Furrows. But the CHAR destroy secret Emberhome."

"Destroyed?" Phoebe pressed eagerly. "Then where was it?"

"Many CHAR. Many Furrows. Cannot say where, you understand? Impossible to find. Emberhome lost now."

"Seriously?" Micah sighed, exasperated. "There ain't nobody who knows where this place is?"

"Not nobody," said the tchurb. "Arch-axials know."

"Where are they?" Phoebe asked.

"Taken by Foundry."

"All of them?"

"Not all," Tik said, motioning to the cathedral.

The kids glanced around the desolate ruins.

"Am I missing something?" Micah grumbled.

But Phoebe understood. The platforms arranged around the dilapidated space weren't merely decorative. They were tombs. The remaining arch-axials were all dead.

"Loaii," wheezed the tchurb. "You pray, yes? Ask Makina. Then arch-axials speak secrets. You understand?"

She nodded halfheartedly.

"You understand," he confirmed. "I go. Rusting rites must be observed. Many to bury. I return, Loaii. Praise be."

Tik bowed low and hobbled out, leaving them alone in the cluttered darkness. Micah flashed his light at the mosaic again.

"*You alone can make the descent*," Phoebe whispered to herself, "*to the heart of prayer, where my Bearing once lay. Retrieve the white star, my Occulyth, and Mehk will prevail*."

"'Heart of prayer,'" Micah blurted all of a sudden. "Tik said Emberhome was her sanctuary."

"And it was destroyed by CHAR," Phoebe thought aloud. "Which means no metal. A big crater where mehkans can't go. Micah, that's why only *we* can make the descent."

"It all fits! It's gotta be Emberhome," Micah agreed. "Now we just gotta find it. Too bad the only people we can ask are in a buncha frickin' coffins."

The word flipped a switch in Phoebe's brain.

"Coffins," she gasped, looking around. "That's it! Don't you see? The axials, the way they're buried. These are the same sort of platforms they used to bury—"

"Your father," Micah finished in sudden realization.

"Rhom knew," she said.

A little shiver passed between them.

The answer was here. Somewhere. It had to be.

And they were going to find it.

CHARGE

Chairman James Goodwin stood like a pillar in the heart of the operations room. The Control Core hummed with activity. It was clear that the Foundry had been missing its leader.

The surgeons had detached his insidious little earpiece, but he still wore it as instructed. He surveyed the digital map with his newly appointed military executives, pleased that the strikes he had ordered in Sen Ta'rine and Ahm'ral were going well. The Covenant's meager resistance wouldn't hold out much longer.

Soon enough, he would tear the whole mess out by its roots.

"Mr. Goodwin," came a voice over the intercom. "I have that call you asked me to connect."

"I will take it in my office," he said. "Pardon me, gentlemen."

The military executives nodded to Goodwin as he took his leave. Guards posted by the elevator stepped aside to allow him to enter, and he rode to the top floor.

The loft was still under lockdown, but changes were underway. The investigators had documented the scene, the remains had been removed, and a team of workers was busy repairing furniture, replacing glass, and tearing up the carpets.

Goodwin closed the door to his office and sat in his armchair before tapping the conical brass intercom mounted on his desk.

"Connect me," he said.

A dark scene appeared on his Computator screen. It showed a lavish room with high ceilings and a golden four-poster bed. The sheets were torn aside, and an askew lamp illuminated two struggling figures—a man and woman in their bedclothes, gagged and bound. Black-suited Watchmen loomed over them.

"Hello, Mr. President," Goodwin said.

The couple stopped squirming.

"Right now, you are asking yourself, what on earth have I done? I need you to ponder that. What . . . have . . . I . . . done?"

Goodwin gestured, and a Watchman tore away Saltern's gag.

"How dare you, James! You know I—"

Goodwin snapped his fingers, and the Watchman threw a punch into the President's gut, folding the man over on the ground. Muffled sobs came from the woman tied up beside him.

"Do I have your attention?" Goodwin asked, interweaving his fingers. "You are the President of Meridian, leader of the most powerful nation in the world. You are this at the Foundry's pleasure. And as you might have guessed, we are not pleased."

Saltern nodded weakly.

"Your role has been clearly defined for you, and for the most part, you have performed adequately. Until now. It appears you have forgotten your place. So allow me to make something clear."

Goodwin leaned closer to the screen.

"You are a trifle. A clown to keep the audience entertained. But the fool who thinks he is king is a sad fool indeed."

Saltern stared murder at the screen.

"Say it with me. The fool . . ." Goodwin started.

"The fool who thinks he's king is a sad fool indeed," Saltern spat. "You've made your point."

"Your livelihood," Goodwin spoke slowly. "Sarah's, that of sweet Annie and little Denton . . ." The woman next to Saltern sat bolt upright. "They all hinge on what you do from this moment forward. It is simple. Obey, and we will provide. Step out of line again, and you will be of no more use to the Foundry."

Judging by their expressions, Goodwin knew that his message was coming through loud and clear.

"Tomorrow evening, the world will be watching your much anticipated campaign rally. A speech will be given to you by Foundry officials, which you will recite atop the Crest of Dawn, begging forgiveness for your idiocy at the Council of Nations. Do you understand?"

Saltern nodded.

"Good night, Mr. President."

Goodwin hit a button, and the image on his Computator cut out. He leaned back in his armchair contentedly.

He had wanted to do that for a very long time.

The intercom bleeped softly.

"Mr. Goodwin? I have someone on the line . . ." The voice hesitated. "Sir, I think you're going to want to take this."

Goodwin frowned. "Proceed," he said.

The line crackled.

"This is Chairman James Goodwin."

"Sir!" came a woman's voice, distorted by a poor connection. "I have . . . urgent . . . and I . . . intel should go to you."

"Who is this?" he demanded. "What is this about?"

"Engineer . . . Gabriella Flores . . ." the woman said amid the static. "I know where the . . . children are."

36 CONQUERING RUST

As the hours crept by and the kids found themselves no closer to unraveling the mystery, Phoebe began to despair. There was nothing here that could possibly refer to Phoebe's father.

"Can't we just ask Tik if he's heard of the Occulyth?" mused Micah, staring at the halos emitting from the Ona's hands.

"No," Phoebe replied firmly. *"My greatest secret, tell no one."*

"Yeah, but she also didn't expect we'd have to figure all this junk out on our own. I think she can prob'ly cut us some slack."

"She trusted us, so we have to keep her secret," Phoebe said. "We need to figure out Rhom's riddle. It's the only way."

He sighed and swept his light around the room. The bulb was dimming. If it went out, they would have to wait until day.

"We looked everywhere," he grumbled.

"Almost," Phoebe said, inspecting a burial platform. She ran her fingers along its edge. "Tik said the arch-axials knew."

"Yeah, but . . ." Micah's eyes popped. "You ain't sayin' you wanna . . . Seriously?"

"Of course I don't," she said, shoving on the slab that covered the tomb. "But it's the only place we haven't looked."

He watched her give the lid another futile push.

"Then let's try one of these," he suggested, motioning with the light. "Some of 'em were blown open by the attack."

They found a tomb whose lid had been broken in half. Working together, they shimmied the pieces aside. A decrepit, musty smell wafted up from the black hole beneath.

"Shine it here," Phoebe whispered.

The light flickered like a sputtering torch. Micah smacked the side, momentarily stabilizing it. Although the hole was deep, their fading beam was strong enough to illuminate the body at the bottom. The corpse was shriveled and rusted beyond recognition, yet it glinted like golden cinders in a fireplace.

Phoebe shuddered. An unexpected wildfire of emotion swept through her. The image of her father's body, rubbed in gold with that splotch of blood on his chest, gleaming as he descended into darkness, was too much for her to bear. She turned away.

Micah was pale. "You okay?"

Phoebe sank to the ground with her back against the tomb. She held her pounding head in her hands.

Micah squatted beside her and gently peeked under the bandage on her forehead. She winced. "That ain't lookin' so hot, Plumm. We should change it soon."

"I think I know what I'm supposed to do," she said.

He gave her a sideways look. "What do you mean?"

"The whist."

He plunked to the ground. "What about it?"

"I . . ." She hesitated to share with him. But Micah's apology on the shore had seemed sincere, and she needed to trust him.

"Last time I used the whist, I . . . I heard him. I don't know how, Micah, but my dad spoke to me. And my mother too."

Micah looked at her, his brows rising.

"I know you don't believe me," she said.

"It-it's not that," he stammered. "Are you sure you didn't . . . imagine it or something? It was really them . . . actually talking?"

"It was them. I know their voices."

"I know," he said, trying to choose his words carefully. "It's just, I dunno. Creepy."

"It's the only way I can make sense of what Rhom said."

"But you don't have the whist anymore."

"I have to figure out how to talk to him without it."

Soft footsteps drew their attention. In the dim light of the vibrating stars, they saw Tik peering through a hole in the wall.

"Loaii," he spoke quietly. "We needing you."

They followed without question, relieved by the distraction. As they left the cathedral, Phoebe looked back at the Ona's masked face, the mosaic crumbled and flaking.

The prophet kept her secrets well.

Phoebe wrapped her arms around herself to protect against the bitingly cold air. The wind shook the needle trees, producing a grating squeak that set her teeth on edge. Tik led the kids through the rubble and across the scarred ground to a gentle slope studded with weathered grave markers. A cemetery.

The Broken were gathered at the lip of a deep crater, a woeful cavity that had been blasted by a Foundry bomb. Countless bodies were piled in the pit, lined up shoulder to shoulder and laid atop one another. The Broken stood silently, watching the kids with baleful expressions. Tik spoke to his companions in Rattletrap, and they murmured in response.

"We not having what need for rusting rites," he explained, miming the turning of a crank. "No *ohneshalo*, you understand?"

She remembered the machine that had wailed a haunting chord at her father's funeral. "What can I do?"

Tik bowed. "You Loaii. Speak, Makina hear."

"But I . . ."

Phoebe didn't know the words. She hardly knew anything about the Way. How could she possibly heal this wound?

The mournful mehkans stared at her, hoping for solace. All except for the hairy mehkan with the withered arm—his weeping eyes were fixed on the bundle he cradled. Slowly, reluctantly, he laid the wrapped body in the pit.

Phoebe breathed in.

She saw herself standing at her mother's grave.

Saw herself reflected in the mirror of her Carousel at home—that selfish, sniping girl who knew nothing about the world.

She breathed out.

Saw herself marching into the tunnel that led to Mehk. Saw herself looking deep into the eyes of the chraida, back when she first realized that mehkans were not machines. Saw herself reflected in the oasis, when she watched her Trinka sink into the vesper—when she finally understood the truth.

In.

At last, she saw her golden father sinking into the ore. He had sought to save Mehk, and now his path was her own. The way had been shaped for Phoebe from the beginning, though she had not seen it. Every step had been essential, preordained, carved for her to tread.

His death was not in vain.

Out.

In the nothing, Her voice will guide you.

Axial Phy had told her that Makina would come to her.

And She had. Because, Phoebe realized as exhaustion and outrage and confusion rose to a boil within her, *she believed.*

At last, the path was illuminated.

"Mother of Ore," she whispered, too soft for anyone else to hear. She closed her eyes, focused on her breath.

Phoebe felt calm. Not even the bitter cold could bother her.

"Mother of Ore," she repeated, this time projecting above the wind. "We are trying to do Your will. Trying to follow Your plan."

Tik began to translate for the somber Broken.

"We have so many enemies, and we are tired and suffering. But we believe in You. We trust in Your sacred machine. And we know that Your children who have rusted here . . ."

She turned her eyes to the stars. They were beautiful, delicate spiderwebs of light connected in the sky, like the entire universe was bound together, composed for this very moment.

". . . that their embers will blaze in Your Forge forever."

Phoebe looked at the assembled crowd.

"Praise the gears," she said.

Tik translated, and the Broken repeated the phrase.

"Praise the gears," Micah said sincerely. She looked over at him. Tears glistened in his eyes.

As the mehkan with the crippled arm stared at Phoebe, the lines of grief on his face softened. He bowed low to her.

The Broken got to work, tossing handfuls of ore into the pit. It clanked dully against the bodies below. Some of them grabbed pieces of debris to use as crude spades.

"Thank you, Loaii," wheezed Tik. "We bury now. You rest."

"You guys need help," Micah said, seeing how much difficulty the feeble mehkans were having with the task.

"No. Our family, you understand? It is for us the burying. Now safe for us work. Loaii pray, keep Uaxtu away."

The word rang a bell—Dollop had mentioned them before.

"Uaxtu?" Phoebe wondered.

"Ember-reapers," Tik said in a nervous whisper. "Evil ones who defied Makina. She punish. They haunt dead places."

"Well," Micah said with a grin, "glad we could chase away all your ghosts and stuff. They won't be botherin' ya'll tonight."

"You not know Uaxtu?" Tik's small, sore-dappled mouth quivered. "Loaii must know. Loaii must beware."

"Tell us," Phoebe said as Micah suppressed a yawn.

The night was patterned with the clank of the Broken shoveling ore. Tik stared into the mass grave for a moment.

Then in quiet, halting words, he told the story.

And in the place atop the Ephrian Mountains, where living blue does not reach and rust red is the crowning peak, dwelt the Uaxtu. There the mountain did not grow, for all was death and corrosion.

And near was the Shroud, den of our Mother of Ore, and near was Her Forge, where came the embers to be blazed and stirred and doused. Beyond its borders did Makina decree no mehkan should venture until the gears of fate decided it was their time.

But wicked were the Uaxtu, for they did not follow Her Way.

And spake the Uaxtu, one to another: "Of all mehkans, we are wisest, and will bow to none. Therefore, why should the secrets of rust be Makina's alone? Let us seek this sacred knowledge, that we may become as She. Let us learn what lies hidden beyond the Shroud, for none have returned from there to tell."

Of foul tongue did the Uaxtu weave evil incantations as they slaughtered their own children. Then did they venture beyond the Shroud, seeking the embers of their slain. And they did steal the embers back and returned them unto the rusted bodies of their young. And lo, the bodies did live again.

And spake the Uaxtu, "Look upon us and tremble, for we have conquered rust, and we are greater than the Engineer."

But Makina was not pleased. These, Her precious creations, had betrayed Her. And with heavy grief, She did condemn them. Upon them She did breathe Her holy fire, and they were turned to ash. And they became as shades, banished to eternal undying.

So spake our Mother, "Seek My Way, find thy function. But woe to those who defy me. Woe to those who profane the Shroud!"

Thus were the Uaxtu damned, eternally hollow, hungry to reap holy embers to replace their own. And only the blessing of the Waybound would repel their lustful greed.

And their forsaken home atop the Ephrian Mountains, where living blue does not reach and rust red is the crowning peak, did the Great Engineer name Rust Risen.

Accord IV: Edicts 06–11

DRIVEN

I do not stop running for hours. Yet somehow I don't tire, like a train rolling downhill.

I am at home in this darkness. But the world feels enormous, wider and deeper than I have ever known it to be. Frightens me, and that is not a feeling I am used to.

Pain grows with every stride, a volcano within where the bonding rounds entered my shoulder and chest. Muscle shreds. Minute by minute, I reach new heights of agony.

But I won't stop. I will the pain to fuel me. And I know that help will meet me at my destination.

I run faster.

Taste blood through my not-skin. Their blood. Try to remember their faces, but they're already fading. How many were there? The images in my head stick together, edges smearing.

I sense my way. Smell the path. Have never been here, but somehow I know where to go. The past is a confusing mess, part dream and part memory, but now is clear. The place I seek is near.

The suns peek over the red mesas, like slanted wedges holding up the sky. I slide into the shadows, shelter from the day.

When I stop running, the pain eats at me. Every sense drowned out by fire. Wounds are gaping, mouths torn open in my flesh. The white bonding agent is gritty and crumbling like sand. Can't stick to me. But the rounds are still inside. Digging deeper.

My mind is a vortex. Can't tell what I have done from what I've imagined. A torrent of images. Bodies melting under my fingers. Death cries pouring out of them, purple as wine. Eyes turning dull. The hours are wax, dripping, distorting around me.

Was it me that did those things? I believe it was.

Thirst. How did I not notice? A startling new pain, wrestling with the bullet wounds. If Mr. Goodwin were here, he would bring me water to drink. Would hold it to my lips, rid me of this torment.

I tense my muscles, contract every fiber of my body. I have gone mad, I know that. Cannot take all these tortures at once.

Warmth trickles from the holes in my chest. See thick ooze coming out, dull gray. Can it be?

The lead bullet casings. Melted.

Pressure in my chest lessens. Yes, the rounds are leaking out of me. I have expelled the objects, driven them from my body.

I clutch at my wounds and discover something new. My flesh is like putty. Smears at the touch, clay between my fingers. I push the edges of the lesions together and they fuse. Flesh becomes one. No trace of the holes in my not-skin. Whole again. Healed.

I am the Dyad. Darkness made flesh.

Shuffle toward my destination, grateful for the pain.

The wind howls in this empty hell. Clumps of razor wire skitter by. Hunger yawns inside. There are white growths like cactus made of salt. I try to eat them, cannot. Find squeaking creatures scuttling about, little ball things made of wheels and gears.

No man has ever eaten the metal vermin of this world.

But I am not a man.

Fast as they are, I am faster. Burst in my mouth like tomatoes, drink their sour juices. They quench my thirst. Feed my hunger.

My strength drips back.

I climb to my destination, a raised basin surrounded by leaning cliff walls. Cool and dark.

Nestle into a shallow fissure, feel the ore soften against my corrosive touch. Burrow into it like a molten womb.

Here I will wait.

I did everything you asked, Mr. Goodwin. All the instructions on your Scrollbar, followed them to the letter. You loosened my restraint in the lab, released me to do your bidding. Then I sat with the secret, waited for the perfect time.

Laid waste to your enemies for you. You must be proud.

Now I have found the meeting place on your map.

I need you—your guidance and wisdom.

Please, Mr. Goodwin.

Come for me.

38

SURROUNDED BY WINGS

It was so cold when Phoebe awoke that she thought her cheeks might be frostbitten. The previous night, she and Micah had huddled together under a foil thermal blanket he had found in the Med-i-Pak. The metal sheet was icy on the outside, but their body heat made it so toasty underneath that the kids had removed their coveralls and slept in their dingy old clothes.

Between nightmares of the fiendish Uaxtu and worries about how to reach beyond the Shroud without the whist, Phoebe had barely slept all night. Now she needed to find somewhere quiet, a private place where she could concentrate.

Somehow, she would find a way to talk to her father again.

Wan light seeped from the gap in the Emberhome mosaic. Phoebe got dressed, then climbed though it and into the shattered cemetery. The cold wind had died away, leaving the world calm and still. Piles of rubble, toppled monuments, and spindly needle trees glimmered in the light of dawn. She wiped a gloved finger across a shining, silvery mound—everything was covered in a shell of icy flux.

Breath fogging from her mouth, Phoebe climbed the slope and looked out upon the placid Mirroring Sea. The Broken had filled the mass grave with ore, and around its perimeter they had etched mehkan runes to consecrate the grounds.

Beyond the site, she spied a semicircular gate embedded in the partially toppled surrounding wall. It hung askew, battered by the recent attack. Phoebe was curious what lay beyond, so she poked her head through.

A shady arbor of rivet-gnarled roots formed a winding tunnel, soot blackened and warped by the recent fires. But as she walked deeper through it, the damage faded away, until she found herself in a secret garden that seemed to have gone unnoticed by the Foundry. It was an unexpected wonderland encased in a shimmering crystal skin. Florid clumps of purple blooms grew alongside lush, bronze needle trees, and yellow, fork-shaped petals drooped from spiraling boughs. Everything was dusted in silvery frost. The only signs of the attack were fissures in the flagstone paths and a few overturned planters.

Phoebe strolled through the garden, feeling its icy silence embrace her like the whist. She looked around the peaceful grove for a comfortable seat while she readied herself for prayer.

A ratcheting trill cut through the quiet. It came from farther down the winding path, behind a wall of purple blossoms. As she followed the trail, the sound multiplied. She rounded the corner to find the way blocked by a curtain of lacy vines. The air was jumbled with chirps and hoots.

She passed through the jingling veil and into an enclosure surrounded by woven copper vine. Blurred violet fluttered past, followed by a twirl of blue and a flap of opal. Fifty or sixty flying creatures flitted about, perching on branches and roosting in foil bushes. Some flew using propellers, others with stacked wings like jittering biplanes. Phoebe saw hydraulic necks and corkscrew beaks, wiry prehensile tendrils and flat paddle feet. They honked like rusty horns, warbled, and sang tinny songs in a delightful musical interplay.

It was a mehkan aviary.

Phoebe realized she was not alone. Tik and a few other tchurbs were here, surrounded by fluttering creatures that swarmed the buckets in their hands. It was feeding time.

"Loaii!" Tik called out in surprise as a small bird with three striped wings alighted on his shoulder. "You well? You safe?"

The other tchurbs put down their buckets and bowed.

"I'm fine. Please, don't mind me," she reassured. "They're beautiful. What are they?"

"Garvhan, tielr, bonji—all kind," Tik said as he fed the

birds handfuls of gray kernels. "Only two escape during attack. Others hide, like the Broken. We very lucky."

"Are they your pets?" she asked.

"Not us," Tik said. "Axials keep. Us duty now."

Phoebe approached the fluttery fray.

"Old tradition, you understand?" explained Tik. "Said 'be surrounded by wings, fans the ember.' You want?"

Tik offered some kernels to her, and she accepted. She held her hand out to the flock, but they cast wary eyes at her, not trusting the look or smell of a human. Phoebe didn't blame them, seeing as how she recognized the parts of a Dish Wand, a Hair-streamer, and other Foundry products within their anatomies.

But one of the birds felt bold. It was the size of a robin, with a vise-like beak and bright yellow eyes. Spiky stiletto feathers splayed at wild angles from its compact form. It flashed a curious lemon-drop eye at her and hopped closer. Then closer.

In a flash, it pecked at her hand and leapt back. Phoebe watched with surprise as its body inflated, revealing a hole in its center like the inner tube of a tire. In a hiss of wind, the feathered ring twirled away with a sound like playing cards rippling through the spokes of a Bike wheel.

She grabbed another handful of kernels from Tik and followed after the ring bird. It wobbled and spun to a tree on the other side of the enclosure. Gathered in a bronze needle nest atop one of the boughs was a family of similar birds. Some were pea green with orange eyes, some ivory white with purple plumes. A few fluttered away as Phoebe got close. Others formed rings around the branches and swung from them playfully.

A golden head poked out of a hole bored into the pale tree trunk. It blinked, then hopped onto a limb in full display.

All became clear in a breathless instant.

These birds looked like the halos above the Ona's hands in the Emberhome mosaic. Phoebe almost laughed at the realization—she and Micah had gotten it backward.

She piled kernels on her shaking arm and held it out to the golden bird. Less antsy than the others, it hopped onto her open hand and sidestepped up to her elbow to nibble at the seed.

This was her chance. She glanced at the tchurbs, certain that they would be upset if they saw what she was doing. As carefully as she could, Phoebe took measured steps out of the aviary, parted the ivy curtain, and stepped into the open garden.

Could this be it, or was she totally out of her mind?

Before she could decide what to do next, the bird dove off her arm, transformed into a feathered ring, and spun away. The creature twirled past the tops of the trees and out of sight.

She winced. What had she been thinking? The cold cut into her again. Phoebe hesitated, trying to figure out how she was going to explain her foolish behavior to Tik.

And then the ratcheting trill sounded out.

The ring bird was back.

It hopped down a couple of branches, trying to get her

attention. Phoebe stared at the brilliant bird in wonder. The creature was anxious—it had a job to do.

They both did.

In the mosaic, the rings weren't coming *out* of the Ona's hands, they were flying *into* her hands. This bird would lead them to Emberhome. She had known it the instant she saw its coloring—shiny gold with a crimson splotch on its chest.

Rhom's riddle was devious.

Only your father can show you the way.

SURPRISE

The courtyard of the Housing was far less grim with the bodies gone and laid to rest. To Phoebe, it seemed as if there was now even a spark of hope in the eyes of the Broken, but that might have just been the warmth of morning.

With Tik's blessing and a sack of gray kernels, Phoebe and Micah released the gold-and-red ring bird, then set out after it. Their guide led them up the peninsula and toward the mainland. In the distance, the sky was strangled with low, pitch-black clouds that poxed the landscape like ravenous fungus.

Toxic remnants of CHAR were everywhere.

The blights were crowded so closely together that Phoebe wondered whether their mehkan guide could safely enter the corrosive region. Beyond the bleak miasma, they saw the shadows of the looming mountain range. Cutting across it was the Shroud, stretching as far as the eye could see. Everywhere the kids looked, they saw a hellish vista.

And yet onward they went—bound for Emberhome.

The scraggly ghosts of needle trees thinned out, the last bastion of life clinging to this ravaged land. With nothing left to perch on, the ring bird was forced to either hover in midair or land on the ground while it waited for them to catch up. The faceted ore beneath their feet was white from the cold and broken into angled slabs. As the kids ascended the foothills, finding traction on the uneven planes became more difficult.

Ahead, something was sticking out of the ground. It was hard to tell what it was at first—a curled lip here, a folded ripple there. But soon they could see that dark gray sheets of metal had burst up through the ore. As the kids continued, the protrusions grew in size, haphazardly piled like messy heaps of fabric. The crumpled metal waves rose, extending far and wide into a natural formation that blocked their path.

"Wild guess," Micah said, scanning his naval map. "But I'm gonna say these are the Coiling Furrows."

"We're getting close," muttered Phoebe. "I can feel it."

The ring bird landed atop a narrow slit at the base of the maze—an entrance. The kids looked at each other for a moment, neither wanting to go first. At last, Micah steeled his jaw and went in. Phoebe followed close behind.

The Furrows were cold and shady, with sunlight coming down in odd streaks. The walls bent and bulged in unnerving ways with occasional gaps opening to expose the sky. The path dipped and twisted, and within minutes they were completely disoriented. If it weren't for the ring bird, they would be hopelessly lost.

For uneasy hours, they navigated the metal slot canyons. Occasionally, the kids could spy the rim of a black CHAR cloud through a cleft in the sheet metal walls. The blights were all around them now.

As the suns began to fuse, their progress slowed substantially. Phoebe found herself dragging her feet.

"Can we take a break?" she said at last, shuffling to a stop.

Micah blew out a breath. "Thought you'd never ask."

They collapsed against the coarse, curved wall of the Furrow. Micah opened his hard-shell pack and dug out the SCM case. While he chugged from the water bottle, Phoebe scattered some kernels for their guide. The ring bird twirled down, deflated, and pecked at the morsels.

The kids dug in to their rations.

"Only five meals left," Micah noted, examining the case.

Phoebe didn't want to think about the prospect of running out of food. She only wanted to think about finding the Occulyth.

"I guess the best thing to do is . . ." Micah sneezed, then wiped his nose with a sleeve. "You got a tissue or somethin'?"

She reached into her pocket to look, and her fingers grazed a folded piece of paper. At first, Phoebe thought it was trash, but when she pulled it out, she wasn't so sure. It was the inner paper lining of a Wackers bar, creased and folded deliberately, as if someone had tried to sculpt it into . . . something. Though what it was meant to be, she hadn't the faintest clue.

"Gotcha!" Micah said with a grin.

Now Phoebe was confused, but she smiled at him anyway, inspecting the wrapper and turning it around in her hands.

"What is it?" she asked at last.

He snatched the wrapper, smoothed the wrinkles, fixed some angles, then gave it back. Phoebe still didn't get it.

"It's a loon," Micah said at last, a little annoyed.

She looked at it again. Now she could sort of make out a neck and wings, patterned with the flashy Wackers logo.

"Like the bird?" she wondered.

"Yeah, like a loon! Cause you're, you know . . . nuts."

"Oh . . ." Phoebe sort of smiled. "Thanks?"

With an irritable whistle and a whisper of feathers, the ring bird zipped out of sight.

"Tough crowd," Micah grumbled, looking between Phoebe and their departing guide. "Back home, I was gonna steal a coupla live ones from the zoo and let 'em loose in your room. But since that ain't happenin', this was the best I could do gift-wise."

"What do you mean, *gift-wise*?"

Now it was Micah's turn to be confused.

"Duh. It's your birthday, dummy."

The word could not have been more befuddling if it had been in Rattletrap. But counting backward, thinking over the time they had been in Mehk, she realized he was right. They had been away from Albright City for almost ten days. Which meant today was the twenty-second—her birthday.

"Seriously?" he asked, continuing to eat. "You totally forgot?"

She nodded absently.

"Well, I guess you've kinda had some other stuff on your mind," he said with a shrug. "That's whatcha got me for, right? Not like it's a big deal or anything. I mean, you're only thirteen."

Another whammy. Her mouth fell open, which caused Micah to snort with laughter. She hadn't forgotten her age, but hearing the number spoken aloud made it sound ludicrous. How many times had she longed for the day when she would finally be a teenager? Now, for the life of her, she couldn't recall what "thirteen" was supposed to mean. Becoming a woman or something? More freedom? It meant . . .

It meant nothing.

That's not what she was supposed to be thinking. Girls back home were wearing makeup and staying out late. But here Phoebe was, putting her life on the line. Her classmates were thinking about how to act around boys, not how to act around zealous warriors who treated them like a saint.

"HELL-O-O-O?" Micah was waving in her face.

"Sorry," she mumbled. "I was just thinking."

"I'll say," he considered. "You all right?"

She nodded and caressed the paper loon in her hands. "Thank you," Phoebe said. "This means a lot to me."

"Yeah, right," he snorted and ate some more.

"It does," she said. "You remembered."

Their eyes got tangled, his hazel snared by her golden brown.

"I . . . You're welcome," he managed.

For a moment, he was barely able to swallow his food.

The ring bird released a harsh trill.

Phoebe and Micah kept staring at each other in silence.

Again, their guide screeched, this time more urgently.

"Give it a rest, would ya?" Micah snapped.

But it didn't stop. The mehkan bird's cries were insistent. Phoebe stood up and pocketed the Wackers loon.

A golden blur whizzed past overhead, then a black one. The two shapes clashed, a ring and an X.

Phoebe and Micah recognized it at once.

She ran. He shouldered his pack and rifle, and bolted after her, leaving their rations behind.

A Foundry drone had spotted them.

Dollop was trying his best to keep up with Overguard Treth.

After a long haul, their salathyl had arrived at an underground Covenant bunker, a hidden staging area dug beneath the ore. The air rang with barked orders and clanging metal as mehkans readied their weapons and assembled to be blessed by axials. Armored salathyls sat in trenches, their tentacles primed to drill. Heaving siege-engine beasts were idling on a series of ramps that led up to the ceiling.

Hundreds of warriors were assembled into battalions—burly gohrs for the front lines, lightning fast aios for stealth, and hunchbacked freylani with their explosive cyndrl. It looked as if all the Covenant camps throughout Mehk had joined forces.

But there should have been more. Word had trickled in from Ahm'ral and Sen Ta'rine telling of terrible slaughter. No one knew how many brave Covenant warriors had gone to rust there.

Overguard Treth worked his way through the troops and climbed a ladder to a high platform. It was peppered with sunlight that streaked in through lookout holes punched in the ceiling. Dollop scrambled after him.

"Two-point-seven clicks late," came a familiar flutter.

"Good to see you too," chuckled Treth.

"Or-Orei!" Dollop cried. He ran up and tried to hug the Overguard from behind, but she detected his approach with her shifting apparatus and held him at bay. Dollop remembered his place and held a fist over his dynamo. "So-sorry, Overguard! I—I never thought I'd see you ag-again, is all."

"You have failed," she said flatly. "Loaii lost."

Dollop gave a somber nod. He realized that there were others on the platform with Orei, a stern group bearing the gold mantle of Covenant Command on their shoulders. He bowed, but they paid him no mind, focusing their attention on the lookout holes.

"Again the Everseer has spared you," Orei said to Dollop. "I do not know why. But it is time to redeem yourself."

"I—I will, Overguard . . . Bu-but how?"

"You fight."

Dollop's bulbous eyes went wide.

"It comes!" declared Overguard Treth.

The announcement rippled through the ranks until their murmurs and clanging came to a halt. Orei joined Treth and the Covenant Command at the lookout holes. Dollop reassembled himself to be taller so he could see out as well.

Squinting through the daylight, he observed a craggy red plain with slanted mesas on the horizon and the imposing walls of the Foundry Depot rising in the distance. Something glinted as it approached the fortress. A train was just arriving.

The purple coils went dark as the outer gates opened.

"Power is down!" Treth announced to the Covenant.

Orei held a hand up—a timer in her palm started to tick.

"Ready!" Treth boomed.

The Covenant crouched in their positions, bodies tense, waiting for the command to attack. Dollop heard a soft rattle and realized that his loose parts were shaking. Was it from fear or fervor? It did not matter. He was whole. Makina was with him, and he was a warrior of the Covenant.

If this was to be the end of his span, then so be it.

"Mother," Orei spoke. *"Some of Your most beloved Children are about to return. They give themselves willingly, sacrifice their embers to gain us the advantage—so we may crush those who stand against You."* She held a fist over her dynamo, and the rest of the Covenant did the same. *"Welcome home your martyrs."*

The dial on her hand stopped ticking.

A blast of blue-white light. A deafening boom. The train, halfway into the Depot, exploded in a nova of flame.

"Blaze the Way!" Treth roared.

The Covenant repeated the words, a rousing war cry.

Dollop was overcome.

"Blaze the Way!" he screamed.

Salathyls bored into ore. Mehkans marched. Ferocious siege engines charged up the ramps. Overguards Treth and Orei leapt onto one of the mehkan beast contraptions as it tore past. Dollop pounced after them and barely hung on.

They erupted through the ore. Dust and sunlight blanketed them. All around, war machines and salathyls exploded into view. Sirens wailed in the Depot. The Foundry's cannons opened fire, but their magnetic defenses were down.

The Covenant charged to meet their glory.

Dollop closed his eyes in exultation.

40

END OF THE ROAD

Goodwin sat on the edge of his seat in the luxury Gyrojet, face illuminated by console lights. His removable silver earpiece—and the Board's words—sat ignored on the armrest. He could barely suppress his smile, but it was too soon to celebrate.

Not until the Plumm girl was in custody.

Engineer Flores had reported that the children were headed for "the blights at the foot of the Shroud." That could only mean the restricted CHAR zone in the eastern sector. So in the middle of the night, Goodwin had assembled a search team and set out with them to ensure success. After landing in the Ephrian Mountains, he had deployed his team and waited.

And waited.

For hours, Goodwin had tried to focus on other urgent matters. There was the fallout from Saltern's speech to deal with. And there was the battle in the mehkan city of Ahm'ral, which had required more resources than anticipated. Still, the Foundry had successfully routed the Covenant's forces.

The suns had risen, and still no sign of the children. But Goodwin was a patient man, and though the day was long, his moment had arrived at last. A Shadowskimmer drone had just detected the targets.

Now the Gyrojet was in pursuit. Below him, the Coiling Furrows extended in all directions like the convolutions of a titanic gray brain. The children were down there somewhere, running through labyrinthine paths full of dead ends and baffling contortions. The Foundry had lost many assets attempting to map it over the years without success. It was nearly as uncharted as the poisonous Shroud, which caused their instruments to malfunction whenever they attempted to study it.

The children wouldn't last long out here on their own.

The Gyrojet ascended higher. The reason for the pilot's caution was plain—CHAR clouds were everywhere, and flying too close was suicide. Four centuries ago, the Foundry's entire payload of the insidious chemical had been detonated here, when Creighton Albright had devastated the leadership of Mehk.

According to Flores, the children were helping the Covenant retrieve something from the Furrows, attempting to find the resting place of their old ruler, the fabled Ona. But it made no sense. The Foundry had scoured these blights long ago and found nothing. It was a wasteland—a tragic result of Albright's ignorance of the permanence and profundity of CHAR's effects.

What could the Plumm girl possibly expect to find?

The ring bird whipped left. Right. Right again.

Rippled gray walls folded over Phoebe and Micah. There were no landmarks, no indication of a route. The contorted walls bent close, forcing the kids to squeeze through a narrow gap. The ring bird hovered for a second to let them catch up, then blurred away around another curve.

They ran blindly after their guide.

Drones twirled past overhead, searching for a clear view. Aero-copters thrummed. The pounding steps of pursuing Watchmen closed in. And then came the blaring sirens of V-Stalkers, the Foundry's mechanical bloodhounds.

Micah whipped his rifle around. Phoebe ducked. He fired a flurry of rounds that ricocheted through the Furrows with a sound like rapid drumbeats.

Her muscles burned. Eyes watered, blurred. She lost sight of the ring bird, panicked. Pushed herself harder.

A pop. A sizzle. Then a horrible, gasping wheeze.

Micah collapsed to the ground.

She skidded to a stop.

He was grunting and twitching, a Watchman's shock prong buried between his shoulder blades. She saw the wires spiraling back to the extended hand of one of the mechanical soldiers.

She couldn't help him.

She wouldn't leave him.

The ring bird circled, squealing.

Watchmen reached for Phoebe.

Then the air came alive. Something whisked past her.

A figure. As soon as she made out the contour of a body, it vanished in a swirl of shade, dissolving into the Furrows.

There was a hiss. A streak of copper red.

A lash materialized out of midair. It lunged at a Watchman like a viper, impaling his chest. Then it retracted and coiled, a living thing poised, seeking a new angle to strike from.

The head of the lash whirred, a deadly drill burning white hot. Watchmen shot at it with their rifles, and Phoebe threw herself over Micah's body to protect him.

The drill viper darted. Soldiers weaved. One of them struggled, caught on something. A bundle of frayed cables—no, an arm—was wrapped around the automaton's neck.

Behind the Watchman stood a mehkan draped in a cloak that liquidly changed to mimic the surroundings. The camouflage was more than color—even its texture seemed to swim in and out of existence. The folds parted, and Phoebe saw the figure within. He was like the Mercanteer's bodyguards, woven from metal bands and peppered with black eyes.

The mehkan held the Watchman fast. His drill lash struck, slashing clean through the automaton's neck. The weapon then slithered out of sight beneath the mehkan's camouflaged cloak.

The remaining Watchmen were on alert, wildly training their weapons, seeking their invisible attacker.

One of the mechanical soldiers went for Phoebe.

A swirl of copper red shot out, an S-shaped blade whistling through the air. It sheared through the Watchman's head as if it were fog. The curved blade parted, fluttered, and returned like a pair of boomerang falcons. A mehkan of rings and scythes materialized to catch the weapon—a kailiak like Orei.

A flurry of violence erupted.

The boomerangs flew out again, only to be snared in midair and redirected by the lash. The blades carved through their enemies. The fibrous mehkan materialized and flung his weapon through the face shield of a Watchman attacking from behind. Another warrior appeared, a crane-claw mehkan flinging a cloud of copper buckshot that swarmed their foes like red hornets.

Micah sat up, woozy from the electric stun. He and Phoebe watched the interplay of mehkans and their copper-red weapons, blinking in and out of sight to level the Foundry forces with savage grace.

Dollop's words came back to her: *Noiseless . . . they can vanish into thin air . . . they wield the living weapons . . .*

"The Aegis!" Phoebe gasped.

Mehkan faces appeared between the folds of camo cloaks,

staring at the kids in cold silence. There were other ripples in space, silhouettes barely distinguishable from the Furrows.

How many were the Aegis?

The echoing purr of engines nearby. Phoebe and Micah knew that sound all too well—Cyclewynders.

The fibrous mehkan pulled the kids to their feet and draped his cloak over them. He grabbed their wrists, black eyes surfacing between sinews to stare at them. The drill-headed viper weapon wove through the mehkan as if his body were its nest.

The Aegis warrior ran, pulling them along.

The buzz of Foundry vehicles grew louder. An Aerocopter chugged. The blaring alarms of more V-Stalkers.

Phoebe focused on keeping up with the mehkan. His strides were silent, and he bounded over the ore with the unerring balance of a jungle cat. They careened through the Furrows, trying to ignore the sounds of fighting behind them.

"What the . . ." Micah blurted.

He was peeking beneath the cloak to see what lay ahead. Phoebe did the same. Their protector was racing pell-mell for a wall. The kids tried to pull free, but the mehkan held them fast.

They hit the wall at full speed.

And passed through. The Furrow rippled.

The surface offered no resistance. Something coarse brushed past, like a sheet of hanging burlap. The same mehkan material as the camo cloak disguised a secret passage.

They were in darkness, dragged forward by the Aegis warrior. Another partition swept aside, flooding the passage with light. They turned again and again, in and out of hidden passages.

And then they stopped.

The Furrows ended abruptly. The walls had shriveled like paper in a fire. The ore was gray, but a few yards ahead it darkened and wrinkled to inky black.

And beyond that . . .

It looked like a monstrous bite had been taken out of the world. The ground dropped sharply into a colossal pit like a volcanic crater. Noxious gray vapor strangled the abyss and obscured its depths with stagnant swirls. The haze rose overhead and bloomed into an impermeable black mushroom cloud that tried to smother the setting suns.

"Emberhome," Phoebe whispered.

They turned around, but the Aegis warrior was gone.

The V-Stalker alarm grew louder, and though the black CHAR cloud hung too low for Aero-copters to pass through, their encroaching growl put the kids on edge.

There was no time for fear. Phoebe peeled off her gloves, unstrapped the Multi-Edge, and removed her skirt. She unfastened her Durall coveralls and wriggled out of them. Micah turned away, pretending not to see, and focused on shedding his metal gear. Phoebe flushed as she stood in her dingy blouse and underwear, but this was no time for shame either.

She slid back into her skirt and turned to see Micah stripped down to his T-shirt and overalls. His Foundry jumpsuit, field pack, and rifle lay in a heap.

"Boots too," she said, bending down to unknot her laces.

"Nah, mine are just leather and rubber. Ma couldn't afford no metal. You ain't goin' in barefoot, are you?"

She slipped off her Durall boots and out popped the wadded rags she had used for padding. There was an ache where she had wounded her right foot before, and the bandage was filthy.

"No choice," she grunted.

Micah yanked off his boots and tossed them to her.

"Wear 'em," he insisted. "No point in openin' that cut again."

She didn't argue. His boots stank, and they were a few sizes too small, but she was grateful.

"Ready?" she said as she stood.

He nodded.

They exhaled and took their first cautious steps.

The CHAR-blasted ore had a fragile sheen, as if it were the skin of a burn victim. The darker the ground became, the tackier it was, like wet tar. The sulfurous stink made them want to gag.

The metal-threaded diamond pattern of Phoebe's skirt shriveled like leaves, exposing the raw fabric beneath. Micah's coveralls sagged as the metal buttons disintegrated. He quickly tied the straps together to hold them up.

Something at Phoebe's hip grew hot. She reached into her pocket to see what it was.

Her father's spectacles.

The steel frames liquefied in her hands, dripping through

her fingers and spattering the ore. She stared at what was left in her palm—the lenses, cracked and caked with ceremonial rust.

"Phoebe," Micah said, taking her hand in his.

This was the last remnant of her father. Everything else was gone now. There was nothing left to lose.

She closed her fist around the lenses, squeezing until her palm hurt, until she was sure her tears were at bay.

Together Phoebe and Micah marched into Emberhome.

AGLOW

Micah stumbled after Phoebe into the crater.

Looking above, he could barely see the flaming orange sky at the rim. Streaks of white whizzed overhead as stray bullets shot into the blight and dissolved. He hoped that the Aegis could hold off the Foundry. They just had to buy a little time.

After a few minutes of scrambling down the mushy surface, the ground evened out. There were weird bumps and irregular ridges like washed out sandcastles. He reached out to touch one, and the mound collapsed as if it were made of ash.

There was almost no visibility because of the haze, so he

and Phoebe stuck close together. Losing sight of each other down here would be like getting separated in a blizzard.

Micah hated how the CHAR felt under his shoeless feet. Beneath a brittle top crust was a warm sludge that he would sink into if he stopped moving. He glanced back at their footprints and saw them slowly filling in, rising like black dough.

And the smell. Ugh. The metal-mold taste coated his tongue.

But the worst part was definitely the creepy, dreamlike silence. The rumbles of distant explosions were muffled as if they were underwater. The crunch of every footstep seemed to die in the air, half-formed.

"See anything?" he asked.

She shook her head.

"What if it sank? Like hundreds of years ago?" he wondered.

"Then we find it and dig it up."

"Gonna get dark soon," he mumbled, looking at the red ring of dusk that marked the lip of the pit. "We should split up and . . ."

He glanced at Phoebe. Her eyes were closed and her lips moving as if she were lost in a trance. Micah didn't want to interrupt her, but he didn't feel much like wasting time with her mumbo-jumbo stuff either.

There was a rumble up above. Aero-copters would have to fly over the corrosive cloud, but Micah wondered if they might still be able to spot him and Phoebe from up there. He squinted into the murk for a hint of searchlights but didn't see any.

Phoebe began to wander, eyes closed. He caught up and overheard the words she was muttering over and over.

"Guide me, Makina. Illuminate the path."

Micah was getting anxious, but he didn't want to show it. He watched impatiently as Phoebe turned around a couple of times, wandered off again, then stopped.

She opened her eyes.

Somewhere in the hazy distance was a fuzzy pinprick of light. It stood out against the blight, like a lone white star in a foggy, black night. A beacon.

"What the . . ." Micah said, his voice pinched with excitement.

She breathed a noise, something between a sob and a laugh.

They went toward the light.

It was hard going. They had to pull their feet from the clinging muck, and it was exhausting and slow. But the closer they got, the more brightly the light shone.

Micah's feet slowed him down. The splintered CHAR crust scratched his soles with each step. It was hard to tell beneath the tarry glop, but he was pretty sure he was bleeding.

Wearing Micah's work boots, Phoebe was already far ahead. But she saw him lagging behind and trudged back. She grabbed his hand. Not yanking him, not trying to force him to speed up.

Staying together.

The only sounds were their crackling steps and panting breath. Micah forgot his pain. As they approached, they had to cover their eyes, the light was so bright.

There it was—the Occulyth.

It was just a few yards ahead, lying atop the CHAR like a feather floating on a black pond. They fell to their knees before it, and the light dimmed, so that it no longer dazzled them.

As if the Occulyth knew they were there.

It was smaller than they had expected, about the size of a saucer, a star with seven rounded points. A cloud of light danced inside the transparent form, weaving among dark squiggles that looked like veins. Its texture was like jelly, but dry and tough.

And it pulsed.

"It's alive," Micah gasped.

"It's not metal," Phoebe said, reaching out to it carefully. "But it doesn't look like anything from our world either."

"Don't touch it."

She nodded. Using her skirt, Phoebe cautiously picked up the Occulyth. She wrapped it securely, and its light dulled. The kids stood shoulder to shoulder, both of them staring at it in reverent silence as if it were a newborn baby.

"Praise Makina," Phoebe whispered.

Micah looked at her. Her long, filthy face was aglow. She *was* Loaii, he knew that now. The Occulyth was reflected in her golden brown eyes. They looked deeper than he'd ever known, like he had been too stupid to ever really see them before.

The moment stretched out—just her and him, bathed in light. Time was stuck. What the hell was going on? His stomach flopped like a fish. He felt sick. Had the CHAR gotten to him?

Micah licked his lips.

They had done it. They had won.

A horrible thought slapped his brain, as if it wasn't his own.

He should kiss her. Right now. It's what Maddox, hero of his absolute favorite Televiewer show ever, would do.

Micah leaned closer to her.

No, don't be such an idiot!

He hesitated.

A flashlight glinted in the haze.

"Run," Micah barked. He pointed to the fading footprints that the two of them had made. "Follow those back to the Aegis."

"What about you?" she said.

He realized that he had already made a decision. His words came out certain and strong. "Can't run without shoes. I'll hold 'em off. Get that thing to the Ona!"

"But what about you?" she repeated.

A thousand emotions collided in the worlds of her eyes.

"I dunno," Micah admitted.

"We'll come back for you, I swear."

His lips quivered, mind on fire.

Kiss her!

Don't kiss her!

"Run," he croaked.

Phoebe held his eyes for a split second.

Then she fled, clutching the wrapped Occulyth tight, shielding it to hide the light. He watched her receding, climbing through the blight, her shape disappearing into the dark.

"Run!" He screamed it in the opposite direction, hoping his voice would penetrate the muffling CHAR haze and draw the pursuers away from Phoebe. "RUN! RUN!" He jumped up and down, making as much of a racket as he could.

The flashlights found him. Foggy silhouettes appeared, racing men in crinkly, protective suits.

Now it was his turn to flee.

Every step hurt, but he didn't care. He had to save her.

"Phoebe! RUN!" Again, he shouted in the wrong direction. He glanced back—they were falling for it! Some of them branched off on a wild goose chase. More flashlights glimmered.

His feet were screaming agony.

Micah knew he couldn't outrun them, but he pushed on anyway. Every second they worried about him was one more second of head start for Phoebe.

Steps crunched up behind him.

He pivoted, tried to zigzag.

Tackled.

A masked Foundry man in a jumpsuit hurled him to the ground. Micah squirmed, kicked. *Crack!* His bare foot connected with a jaw, knocking the mask aside.

The man's face was exposed. His eyes blazed.

Three other suited Foundry soldiers closed in. Strong hands seized Micah's ankles and pulled him. He dug his fingers into the ground, trying to slow himself.

"Get off!" he screamed.

The Foundry man flipped him onto his back. Micah was momentarily blinded by a flashlight, encased in a sleeve of glass to protect it from the CHAR.

Then his fingers grazed something half-buried in the ground.

A stick.

He seized it, swung with all his might. The blow caught the Foundry man solidly in the face. His nose gushed blood. The man cursed and drove his fist into Micah's belly.

Air whooshed from his body. Vision dimmed.

But not before he glimpsed the stick slipping from his grip.

Its thin, white shape was unmistakable.

Made no sense. Didn't belong here.

Something was wrong.

A human bone.

42
PAYBACK

Mr. Pynch awoke in a place he didn't recognize, and yet it fit his mental state—dank, rotten, and falling to pieces. The walls were coated in moldy gobs of flux scum like congealed fat. Knurlers and pinpods clung to the surface, feasting on the corrosion. Feeble light wavered in from a jagged hatch.

He started to get up, but immediately shriveled back down. At first, he thought it was just too much viscollia, but then a faint memory of getting thumped resurfaced. He felt the back of his bushel of quill hair—yep, matted with his own dried ichor.

That's when he noticed his arms were bound in hoistvyne.

Mr. Pynch tugged on the chain. It was taut and secure.

Footsteps pounded toward his cell. With an unbearable, rusty shriek, the hatch opened to reveal a hulking silhouette.

"Wakey, wakey!" a familiar voice shouted. It was his gohr drinking buddy from the Rathskellar. The brute yanked on his chain, dragging Mr. Pynch across the cell. "Up, scrap!"

Mr. Pynch staggered to his feet while his captor unhooked the hoistvyne and hauled Mr. Pynch out into a cramped hallway.

A rhythmic boom shook the greasy, flux-worn walls.

"Look here, me good mehkie," Mr. Pynch offered. "What do you say you and me arbitrate some manner of agreement? Perchance we could—"

The gohr unleashed a spittle-flecked roar. With a massive, six-clawed clamp hand, he clubbed Mr. Pynch in the back of the head. A fireball of pain blinded him, dropped him to the floor. With another rip of the chain, the gohr had Mr. Pynch on his feet again, sluggishly plodding up a steep stairwell.

Up they went, step after agonizing step.

The booming noise grew louder as Mr. Pynch was pulled through another hatch. What he saw deflated him entirely.

It was a long compartment blazing with humid heat. Rows of gasping mehkans were crowded in the dark, chained together and toiling at crooked axles that ran across the width of the space. They shoved and heaved at giant cranks in unison, the source of that deep, rhythmic sound.

These cranks were attached by slime-coated ducts to a

grisly contraption at the far end of the compartment. It was a mound of exposed viscera, half-submerged in the floor, augmented with rusted rotors and clusters of giant pistons.

A sickening realization dawned on Mr. Pynch. He looked out the oblong windows, hoping that he was wrong.

But he wasn't. Through the translucent membranes of the portholes was churning silver flux. He thought he could make out the dim shadow of a qintriton swimming past.

Although he had never seen one from the inside, he knew with crushing certainty where he was. He was trapped in a submersible vessel on the back of a deep-sea wryl. The rows of laborers were powering this grotesque contraption, which controlled the mind of the massive tusked beast.

And Mr. Pynch knew who commanded such monstrosities.

Marauders—thieves and slayers of the sea.

The gohr led Mr. Pynch through the heaving crowd to a spot between two skeletal jaislids. He chained Mr. Pynch to the floor, grabbed his hands, and slapped them onto the axle handle.

"There must be some mistakement," Mr. Pynch stammered, panicked. "This be unjust. I don't belong here!"

"Oh, but you do," growled a sinister voice.

The gohr stepped aside as a gaunt figure approached. He was mottled brown and red, and though he stood upright on two sinewy legs, his serrated arms were long enough to stab at the ground. The mehkan's head was sickly copper with two pus-white eyes. A ring of oozing snouts and acidic mouthparts dangled beneath his face and down his back.

It was a hiveling—one of the most uncommon and utterly despised races in all of Mehk. And not just any hiveling.

"Tchiock?" Mr. Pynch asked in shock.

"So the fog has lifted," the mehkan spat. "I was so very disappointed when you didn't recognize me in Ghalteiga."

"What be the meaning of this?" Mr. Pynch asked.

"You stole from me, Pynch," Tchiock drooled, snouts twittering. "In Kholghit. An entire shipment of viscollia—gone."

Mr. Pynch attempted a jolly laugh.

"Be that the reason for this whole conflagration?" he chuckled. "Not 'stole,' dear Tchi. A misunderstandimation. I will gladly reimburse any damages me associate and I may have—"

In a flash, Tchiock's saw-toothed arm pierced the front of Mr. Pynch's chusk overcoat and yanked him near.

"You will pay," Tchiock gurgled. He held up a scourge of barbed ivy and dangled it in Mr. Pynch's face. "I will work you. I will starve you. I will make your every cycle a prison of misery until you beg me to end your worthless span. And then . . ." The hiveling's noxious mouth tubes leaked acidic saliva on his lapel. "Once I know you are sincere, I will grant your wish myself."

Tchiock raised his scourge.

"Now pump!" the hiveling bellowed. The whip slashed across Mr. Pynch's shoulders. "Pump!"

Down the barbs came. Again and again.

Whimpering, Mr. Pynch grabbed onto the axle handle and did as he was told. He stared down as he toiled. His green, striped necktie was shredded and splotched with acid. The mismatched stitches that Phoebe had sewn were in ruins.

Selling the poor bleeders at the Gauge Pit had been his idea. It was his fault they had lost all their earnings in a bad toss. His fault that he and his associate had become fugitives of the Foundry, then abducted and used by the Covenant.

His fault that the Marquis was dead.

Oily tears spilled from his swollen eye sacs.

Mr. Pynch had earned this fate. So he pumped and he pumped, knowing that he was cursed to live out his cycles here.

A slave.

The Titan spotted Dollop.

Its battery of cannons lit up in a kaleidoscope of flame. Dollop leapt behind the wreckage of a siege engine as fire rained down.

A fearsome howl drowned out the barrage.

Dollop braved a look.

A team of Covenant warriors was taking advantage of the distraction Dollop had caused. A gohr fended off the Titan's heavy fire with a shield of scavenged debris while a tiulu used his buzzing, bladed forelimbs to hack at the giant's legs. Then an aio dropped down on the machine and enveloped its head with pitch-black folds, stabbing with javelin legs.

The array of lights on the machine flickered. It toppled to the ground with a crunch. The last of the Titans was gone.

But there was no shout of victory. The Covenant had been decimated trying to keep the Titans at bay. Their fleet of salathyls had been wiped out, and so many of Her Children had been lost. Mehkans were scattered across the Depot, taking cover from the screaming turrets and advancing squadrons.

The Foundry was just too big. Too powerful.

The air was choked with so much smoke and fire that Dollop could not see the train tunnel in the distance. That was supposed to be their target. If only they could bring it down.

But it was impossible. This was suicide.

And still, the enemy kept coming. He saw a team of heavily armored Watchmen race into view, each outfitted with a round case on its back, connected by pipes to something bulky in its hands. The way they glided was unnatural. Dollop squinted into the gloom. The Watchmen each stood on a hovering circular platform that emitted that familiar magnetic glow.

Thoom, thoom, thoom—their weapons discharged in rapid succession. There was a swarm of streaking lights like a flock of electric purple birds. The projectiles curved in midair, hooking around barricades, seeking mehkan targets.

BOOM. Death lit up the Depot.

"Retreat!" roared Treth's voice. "All units retreat!"

Dollop and the Covenant ran. Watchman bombers rocketed into the fray. Fist-sized magnetic missiles sought out fleeing warriors and stuck to them. The mehkans flailed to remove the devices, only to detonate in white-hot blasts.

The turrets on the outer walls wailed, shredding the Covenant. So many bodies. Dollop tried not to look as he ran, but his path was paved with blank eyes and broken bodies. So many faces he knew, so many brothers and sisters.

A grenade thumped into place right beside him.

He felt an impact and was driven to the ground.

But it wasn't the explosive.

Treth had tackled him, knocking him to safety behind a dead salathyl. The ground tremored as the missile erupted. The burly gohr picked Dollop up, and together they peered from behind their cover. The explosions had cleared away the train debris from the front gates—the way out. They made a break for it.

Dollop heard a resonant *thunk*. Treth stumbled forward.

Panic split the gohr's broad face. He clawed at his shoulder. Dollop saw the glowing purple grenade stuck to his back. Treth looked at Dollop with a sad but knowing expression.

"Go," the Overguard said, defeated.

Dollop did as he was told. Treth dropped behind the salathyl corpse. Even so, the explosion nearly knocked Dollop off his feet.

On he went, streaming tears.

A Watchman bomber whizzed by behind him, levitating on a magnetic disc. *Thoom, thoom!* A pair of projectiles whistled at Dollop. He separated his body, tossing his parts wide. The missiles shot through the empty space where he had just been. They looped around, trying to hone in, but Dollop kept shuffling his body until he was springing along in a dozen separate parts.

He reassembled and kept on going.

Almost there—only a dozen strides more.

Figures appeared outside the ruined gates of the Depot, blocking the path. More Watchman bombers, armed with those magnetic grenades. They had cut off the Covenant's escape.

They readied their launchers. Aimed.

Dollop didn't even have time to pray.

Thoom, thoom, thoom!

Wavering streaks of purple blurred past his vision.

But it was not the Watchmen who had fired. They stared at purple missiles stuck to their chests. Dollop covered his head.

In a white storm and a rain of debris, they were gone.

The way out was clear again.

Looking back, Dollop saw another Watchman bomber racing toward him on a levitating magnetic disc. He was about to run when he realized that something was off. The awkward figure wobbled, trying to balance on the tilting platform while struggling to keep the heavy grenade launcher in position.

Dollop rubbed his eyes, only half-believing.

The Watchman was gangly and lopsided, and his bulky armor didn't fit right.

"Who a-are you?" Dollop gasped.

The stranger did not speak. Hefting his massive, tube-laden weapon, he managed to lift up the faceplate of his helmet.

It was a face Dollop had hoped to never see again.

A cheery glow flickered down. The flash of an opticle.

Dollop had been saved by the Marquis.

43

LOAII

Phoebe didn't dare slow down.

The last thing she had heard was Micah calling her name, telling her to run. She wanted to race back to his side, but she knew what she had to do.

She prayed that she was still on course. Dusk was darkening so fast that it was hard to make out their dissolving footprints. The Occulyth could light her way, but uncovering it would surely reveal her. She could feel it quiver through the material of her skirt, a living thing buzzing with anticipation.

The slap of bullets against metal grew louder. Slowly, the

Furrows emerged from the haze. The ground sloped more sharply, rising to the crisp edge of the crater above her.

Then a sound so welcome it was like a ray of sunlight—the cry of the ring bird. Even in the dim light, she could make out the buzzing red-and-gold shape. It hovered a safe distance from the blight, like a hummingbird outside a window, waiting for her.

Despite her exhaustion, she pushed harder.

Flashlights behind her. Footsteps crunched through the ore.

She stumbled. Clutched the Occulyth.

It felt like the steep slope would topple her backward, but she kept her eyes fixed on the surface above.

With a snarl, Phoebe fought her way over the crest of the hill. The bird was a spastic blur, its cries shrill. She could tell by how it was moving, dashing away from the edge and then coming back, that it wanted to lead her on.

As the black CHAR faded away underfoot, the air tasted different—lighter, cooler, sweeter. Black tar sloughed off her boots and sizzled into the ore.

Phoebe risked a glance back. She saw flashing beams, heard huffing breath as the Foundry soldiers ascended in pursuit.

The gray texture of the Furrows shifted as the camouflaged Aegis phantoms pressed in. She felt sorry for those men behind her, so certain their success was within reach. They were the enemy, yes, but they were still human beings.

There was no time to consider it.

The ring bird swooped at Phoebe, ruffling her hair with a whack of wind. It ratcheted urgently before disappearing through a secret entrance in the wall. She followed, diving back into the darkening maze. The ground shook with a powerful explosion. The thrum of Aero-copters deepened.

Phoebe clung tighter to the pulsing star. It was the answer. This could end it. *Retrieve the Occulyth, and Mehk will prevail.*

That's what the Ona had said.

The ring bird led her through another series of passages, whirling around sharp turns, plunging through narrow crevices.

Then, abruptly, it stopped and hovered in place.

This was a dead end, a teardrop-shaped alcove within the Furrows. The bowing walls twisted and conjoined to create a vaulted ceiling. The fading magenta light of evening raked through, but otherwise the chamber was dark and still.

Had the ring bird lost its way?

No.

A stir of movement. There was the familiar shimmer of texture that meant the Aegis was near. Many of the camouflaged forms were gathered together.

Slowly they parted.

A figure seemed to materialize behind them. She was shorter than Phoebe and enveloped in billowing veils. Wide, leaflike fins drifted around her and swam before her face as if floating on a languid, dreamy tide. Her skin was the color of weathered ivory, her veils and fins a tarnished gold, yet the figure was somehow luminous, casting a soft glow on the gray walls.

The ring bird let out a bright trill and flew to the figure, whose raised arms ended at long, tapered hands tufted with feathery fingers. The bird nestled into an outstretched palm.

Just like the mosaic in the Housing of the Broken.

Phoebe was awestruck.

"Loaii," sighed the Ona. The word was a kiss of spring, full of sweet music and the promise of renewal.

Phoebe felt a lump rise in her throat. She looked down at her undignified self—bruised and bloodied, clothes in tatters, tracking sizzling CHAR footsteps from Micah's work boots.

"Come" the Ona motioned with a pale hand.

As Phoebe approached, she saw that the Ona was in constant motion, like sea grass beneath the water. Her body was obscured by shifting veils, so there was no way to be sure how many arms and legs the prophet had. She appeared to be weightless and floating, an apparition of grace.

"How I have feared for you, my brave Loaii."

Her voice was different in person, less broken and jagged than it had sounded in the liquid-metal Hearth. It was still difficult to pin down, a mystical mix of childlike and ancient, masculine and feminine—soothing, hypnotic.

"I . . . I . . ." was all Phoebe could muster.

"Please forgive me," the Ona spoke. "I did all I could to find you. The Covenant scoured Mehk. I sent my Emberguard to piece together your trail, but always you were on the move. Yet despite all you have suffered, despite knowing so little of your true function, you have come, dear, sweet Loaii."

A fin parted and Phoebe caught a glimpse of the Ona's face. It was more landscape than skin. The eons had worn deep, pallid crags into her features, which were an intricate lattice of tightly knit, organic gears, locked into place like a jigsaw puzzle crusted over by time. It was a visage of profound love and deep sadness.

Yet the Ona's eyes twinkled with joy. They were like nothing Phoebe had ever seen, shining white orbs flecked with gold and marbleized with copper ribbon. Infinitely wise, unfathomably old.

"Micah," Phoebe insisted. "We have to save him. He's—"

Undulating fronds reached out and caressed Phoebe's cheek.

"Fear not. All shall be made right," the Ona cooed, "for what you have accomplished will realign the gears of fate. No more shall the Foundry slaughter us, Her Children. Because against all odds, Loaii, you are triumphant."

The Ona's feathered fingers twitched eagerly as she reached out and took the Occulyth from Phoebe. It burned so brightly at the prophet's touch that Phoebe had to shield her eyes. The Occulyth knew it was home.

"Please tell me," Phoebe gasped. "What is it?"

"A miracle. Long dreamt, much awaited."

"How will it save Mehk? Why did it survive the CHAR? How . . ." She looked intently at the Ona, a new question bubbling to the surface. "How did you survive it?"

The Ona embraced the Occulyth within her many veils. Its blazing light shone through her fins, revealing a shadowy webbing of bone and musculature before fading to a golden glow.

"I know there is much you wish to ask, Loaii," purred the

Ona. "But your task is not yet complete, and the time is nigh."

"My task?" Phoebe squirmed inside. "There's more?"

The Ona drifted closer, veils waving in a mesmerizing dance.

"Dear child, do you know the tale of Loaii?"

Phoebe shook her head.

The Ona's ethereal eyes smiled.

"In the Word of Makina, Second Accord, the edicts tell of the Primal Age, many epochs after Her Spark brought us all into being: '*Tired was She, but Her work was yet unfinished.*'"

The Ona's voice had changed, a distant song that felt to Phoebe as if it were a mere thought in her own head:

"For although She had hung a wreath of suns upon the heavens to light the day, the night was still imprisoned in the deepest darkness. She did beseech Her Children to help illuminate the night, but they were selfish and slothful, and none was willing.

"At this, She was saddened.

"But there was one who saw the Great Engineer's grief. Loaii was her name, youngest and most pure of the Everseer's Children. And she offered to seek a light worthy of the impermeable night. For she loved her Mother deeply, and longed to reveal the majesty of the sacred machine so all would see and give praise.

"And so did Loaii set forth to search Mehk, traversing it from end to end. Yet no righteous light did she find. So she set forth to search the Mirroring Sea, seeking top to bottom."

Phoebe was captivated. The Ona's veils embraced her.

"And still Loaii found nothing worthy to shed light upon the

darkness. So she set forth to scour the great sky, corner to corner. Still was no light deserving of the honor.

"And Loaii saw then the rise, that wreath of suns made by her Mother's loving hand to kiss Her creation every day. And Loaii did cherish their light, for they were perfect in their glory.

"And thus spoke Loaii:

" 'For Thee, beloved Mother of Ore, for Thee I give of myself, that Your light may forever shine upon us, Your Wayward Children.' "

Phoebe was lost in the depths of the Ona's eyes.

"And Loaii did cast herself into the suns and set herself ablaze. 'Take the sacrifice of my body, O Great Engineer,' Loaii declared as the golden flames consumed her, 'and with it, chase away the darkness and illuminate the night forevermore.'

"And Makina did rise from Her slumber, and lo, She was overcome, for Her daughter, youngest and most pure of Her Children, did love Her beyond measure. And Makina did raise Her mighty hands, and She did clap thunderously. Loaii, blanketed in flame, was exploded into the million stars of the night sky."

Phoebe's eyes were heavy with tears of bliss.

By the time she noticed the Ona's veils tightening around her throat, it was too late.

PROMISES

I have waited all day.

Red suns are dying on the horizon, but I dare not venture from this spot. I will wait. Mr. Goodwin will come.

He promised.

Been laying in this crevice for hours, feeling the metal soften beneath me, listening to the distant music of war. The Depot is far away, but I feel the anguish through the ground, taste the blood on the air. I yearn to be there—to kill.

No. Must wait.

Feel the pulse of the Aero-copter long before I hear it.

Joy floods me. My not-skin burns with it.

A searchlight dances across the mesas. I leap from my shelter. Wave my arms, shout, "Here I am!" in bubbling sounds that no one but I can understand. The light bathes me. Blinds me.

I raise my arms to the sky.

The chime of a targeting system. The whisper of the Aero-copter's Dervish turrets pivoting into place.

Sounds no man can hear. But I do.

And I know what they mean.

I dive for cover, crawl back into my crevice before the gun erupts. The world lights in explosive flashes. The mesas shudder.

But I am not hit. Not this time.

Why? Why are they shooting?

The confusion is a blip. Survival smothers it.

Men coming. I taste them on the wind. Hear the scrape of steel clasps as they descend the cables. Six of them. No, eight.

I know this maneuver. When I was a man, I led strikes like this. They come from two sides to pin me in. If I run into the open, the Aero-copter will cut me down. Must be a sniper nearby too.

The crevice is not deep. Nowhere to hide within. The walls on either side are sheer. Dig my fingers in, feel the ore soften to my touch. Climb up like a lizard.

I wait.

They think they are silent. Cannot hide their heartbeats.

The assassins press in, edging along the walls, guns ready. Their commander signals. They spin into view, ready to kill me.

But I am not there. Delicious panic.

I drop.

A storm of hot blood.

Bullets punch the wall. A round enters my armpit. I breathe pain. It flows through my blistered veins. I do not fear it.

Charge.

They are well trained, but not for me. I pulp one against the wall. Another empties his rifle at me. Peel him like an orange. The last knows there is no point in fighting.

He is right.

Spotlight of the Aero-copter finds me. Opens fire.

I dash across the open plain. Hot rounds tear into me. I leap, grab one of the cables the soldiers used to rappel down. It gums in my hands, my weight stretches it. Must go quick.

A shot. Shell bursts through my leg. Incandescent pain, beyond solar. I roar. Cling to my rage. Climb.

They wait for me inside.

I smash, I maim. I hurl a soldier out the side. The pilot is helpless. Squeeze his helmet until it flattens under my touch.

Grab the controls. Find the sniper.

In a nest, a divot at the top of the mesa. He sees what I am doing. He has nowhere to run. I steer the Aero-copter at him.

Plummets from the sky.

I jump.

The night comes alive with flame.

I hit the ground hard, roll off the cliff and fall. Hit the ground again. Lay still. Stare up at the fire tasting the sky.

I do not want to believe. But I know it's true.

They knew I was here. Must have been ordered to come to this place and kill me. Ordered by the man who sent me here.

Mr. Goodwin.

But he promised me.

Confusion is drowned by sorrow.

Feel it digging into me like the Greencoats' needles. Drawing my life from me, replacing it with stinging ice.

Why? Why would he do this?

I am the Dyad. His creation. He gave birth to me. In return, I gave my life to him. He knows I am his to command. Knows I would carry out his every order without a second thought.

Like the directors, slaughtered them at his request.

Perhaps that is why . . .

I see it now.

Mr. Goodwin turned me into a monster. Used me to rid himself of his enemies. Now I am inconvenient. Needs to dispose of me.

So he has named me an enemy of the Foundry.

I pound at the ore, carve into it with my jutting bones.

Sorrow is burned away by rage.

I make a promise of my own.

Mr. Goodwin.

I promise I will taste your blood.

FINISHED

Evening had fallen, and the place was packed with Foundry.

Micah tried to yank his hands out of the digital manacles as a team of paper-suited men marched him around the edge of the blight. He knew it was pointless—even if he could slip out and split, he wouldn't get far. Micah dragged his feet, figuring every second of delay improved Phoebe's odds, but they were having none of it. The men shoved him forward, hurrying him toward a spot marked by red flares blazing on the ground.

A ton of Watchmen were standing sentry at the edge of

the Furrows. Micah knew they were just stupid brainworm robots, but he wished they felt fear—he wanted them to be terrified that the Aegis might pop out any second and waste them.

He saw a bunch of footprints, irregular dents in the ash-gray ore, running from the lip of the crater into the winding maze. Micah instantly knew what it meant. Phoebe had made it out of the blight, and the Foundry had followed her.

Had she reached the Ona? Had she gotten away?

Then he saw the body bags.

Four, five, six of them. And blood. The Aegis must have taken down the men that were pursuing Phoebe.

A spark of hope.

A curtain of camouflage cloth was pulled aside, revealing a passage. Foundry workers examined the mehkan fabric, cutting samples and inspecting it. Micah was prodded through.

More Foundry workers and Watchmen lined the winding, flare-lit channels. Footprints twisted this way and that. He kept his eyes fixed on the smallest ones, recognizing the tread of his boots—the ones Phoebe was wearing.

Micah was led around corners winding into the Furrows.

He froze.

Even before the man turned around, Micah knew him. His broad back, impeccable suit, and bone-white hair were unmistakable. Goodwin filled the passage, a pin-striped mountain blocking the way. The crimson flares glittered in his eyes. Behind the Chairman, Micah could see a small alcove, a dead end.

"It is done," Goodwin stated, his voice black and brittle as the CHAR. He towered over Micah, looking down his nose at him. The corners of the Chairman's mouth were upturned, not in joy, but with some hint of self-satisfaction.

"Where's Phoebe?" Micah said, his body hot with alarm.

Goodwin's shadowy smile vanished. He considered the boy for a long moment, then stepped aside to reveal the alcove.

She was on the ground, crumpled like a discarded sack of laundry. One hand was flung out, as if reaching for Micah. The rest of the alcove was empty.

No.

Micah mouthed the word, but no sound came out. He stepped toward her, and no one stopped him.

Her eyes were half open, staring up, seeing nothing. Her lips were parted, tongue slightly protruding between her teeth, lips curled back in a blank expression of disbelief.

"No." This time it came out as a feeble rasp.

There was a dark bruise wrapping her neck.

Micah fell to his knees and grabbed her shoulders to rouse her. Her skin was loose and cold. He tried to speak a third time.

All that came out was an incoherent howl.

She was not unconscious.

She was not breathing.

Phoebe Plumm was dead.

GLOSSARY

accord one of several sacred texts that form the scriptures of the Way.

Aegis, aka "Emberguard" the group of deadly and mysterious mehkans that serve as the Ona's personal guard. It is said that they are silent and able to vanish into thin air.

Ahm'ral one of the oldest mehkan cities, considered sacred by the Waybound.

aio a secretive mehkan species with a sinister reputation as hired assassins. The aios are distinguished by the black, membranous folds of their bodies, which obscure their features.

Albright City capital of the nation of Meridian, Albright City is the wealthiest and most resplendent metropolis in the world.

Albright, Creighton (1597–1646) creator of the Foundry, and widely considered the father of the modern age. Centuries ago, he was the owner of a struggling mining company, when he stumbled upon the portal that leads to Mehk. He kept this discovery a secret and transformed his company into the Foundry, using it to reap tremendous profit and usher in a new era of technology.

Alloy War a global conflict that lasted from 1630 to 1646. Many nations united against Meridian, afraid that the Foundry's technological advantage was becoming insurmountable. More than thirty million people died during the long and bloody war.

Amalgam, aka "the amalgami" an isolated, idyllic community of cave-dwelling mehkans.

arch-axial exclusive title for a mehkan high priestess of the Way.

The Arcs a vast mehkan geological formation of stair-step ravines and natural land bridges, carved by the elements over the millennia.

augurweed a mehkan grain that is fermented to produce viscollia.

axial a mehkan priestess of the Way.

balvoor (e.g. "Mr. Pynch") a boisterous mehkan species with a highly developed sense of smell. Balvoors are known for their expressive emotions and colorful way of life. Their talent for languages makes them uniquely suited as diplomats and politicians.

Bearing holy mehkan vestments worn by the ancient Waybound.

Bhorquvaat a mehkan port city whose name roughly translates to "The Grand Mark," the ancient landmark around which the city was built.

bleeder the mehkan term for a human.

blight one of a number of quarantined zones in Mehk that has been rendered useless due to the lingering effects of CHAR.

Bloodword mehkan term for human language.

The Board the ultimate authority within the Foundry, elite and anonymous overseers known only by their voices.

bonding round white chemical bullets designed by the Foundry to incapacitate and kill mehkans, striking their target in a semi-liquid state and hardening upon impact.

Callendon a wealthy southern state in Meridian, known for its luxury beach resorts.

CHAR, aka "Colloidal Hypo-Amaroid Retroacid" a Foundry-made chemical weapon that dissolves metal, invented specifically to assault Mehk. The Foundry has banned the use of CHAR due to its permanent and cumulative corrosive effects.

Children of Ore a term used by the Way to refer to all mehkans, who they believe were created by Makina.

Chokarai a dense mehkan forest of pipework trees that is home to the chraida.

chraida (e.g. "The Ascetic") arboreal mehkan species with a fierce tribal culture. They are hostile toward humans due to the Foundry's incursions on their land.

chusk knobby mehkan vegetation eaten by grundrulls and used by langyls to create metallic textiles.

Citadel an ancient mehkan palace, once home to the dreaded emperor Kallorax, now occupied by the Foundry. It is widely reviled for its façade, which is covered in melted mehkan corpses.

click a mehkan unit of time, roughly equivalent to an hour.

Coiling Furrows a natural mehkan maze formed by tectonic pressure that forced rippled sheets of ore to the surface.

Com-Pak a small, versatile communications device made by the Foundry.

Control Core a massive tower in the Depot that serves as the new center of operations for the Foundry in Mehk.

Council of Nations an international cooperative organization to promote diplomacy, founded in response to the Alloy War.

Covenant secret rebel army of the Way, an underground network of mehkan freedom fighters sworn to defend their world from the Foundry.

Crest of Dawn the towering, sculpted arch in the shape of a sunburst that looms over the bridge leading to Foundry Central. A depiction of this landmark serves as the company's logo.

cycle a mehkan unit of time, roughly equivalent to a day.

Cyclewynder sleek Foundry racing vehicle with a flexible body atop a row of sharp wheels, used in Mehk to navigate difficult terrain.

cyndrl tumorous growths that are cultivated on the backs of freylani. These organic weapons can be harvested and used as grenades.

The Depot the Foundry's central transportation hub in Mehk, located at the mouth of the tunnel that leads back to Albright City.

Dervish rifle a silent Foundry-made firearm with four rapidly spinning barrels and an internal solenoid that heats bonding rounds to the melting point.

Dialset a Foundry-made telephone.

directors Foundry supervisors and representatives of the Board. They have immense power in overseeing day-to-day operations, especially in Mehk, but answer directly to the Board.

Divine Dynamo a holy name for Makina.

Durall a durable metallic fabric of many uses, derived by the Foundry from the mehkan textile known as chusk.

Dyad Project a top-secret Foundry project focused on creating a human-mehkan hybrid. Kaspar is the sole surviving experimental test subject.

dynamo symbol of the Way, a circle bisected by a jagged line like the teeth of a gear.

Dyrunya a mehkan river city of meticulous pipework architecture that extends both above and below the river surface. Home to the lumilow.

edict one of many verses in the sacred accords of the Way.

ember according to the traditions of the Way, embers are the sparks of life in every living thing. When a mehkan dies, its ember travels beyond the Shroud to be judged by Makina.

Emberguard a term for the revered Aegis.

Emberhome secret sanctuary of the Ona, thought to have been destroyed long ago.

ember-reaper a term for the feared Uaxtu.

Ephrian Mountains a massive range of living mountains on the eastern continent that disappears into the Shroud.

Ephrian plains a wild mehkan province on the eastern continent that remains undeveloped by the Foundry. It is said to be home to many species of mehkan that are otherwise considered extinct.

Erghan an ancient mehkan language.

ettik a brusque mehkan species that typically dwells in arctic regions, recognizable by their stout, tripod legs and their dense, bristle-haired carapaces.

Everseer a holy name for Makina.

The Expanse a term used by the Way to refer to the course of all time, as created by Makina.

ferro-crotic pertaining to the liquefaction and decomposition of metal, especially as resulting from exposure to CHAR.

Ferro-nomic Treaty the trade agreement that ended the Alloy War. It permitted, for the first time, international distribution of Foundry products. The terms were favorable to Meridian, imposing strict guidelines on the kind, quality, and price of materials that could be sold to other nations.

firkin pipework dwellings of the lumilow.

flux a toxic liquid metal that makes up mehkan oceans. In its solid state, flux falls from the clouds as bullet rain.

The Forge a celestial furnace in the afterlife, which Makina uses to judge the embers of the dead, according to the Way. They claim She *douses* the wicked, *stirs* the imperfect to be reborn, and *blazes* the righteous to live in harmony with Her for eternity.

The Foundry the world's largest and most profitable corporation, established centuries ago by Creighton Albright. Due to its clandestine operations in Mehk, it is the foremost manufacturer of metal and technology.

Foundry Central an extensive complex located on an island in Albright Bay, home to the Foundry's primary research, manufacturing, and distribution hubs.

freylani (e.g. "The Mercanteer") a physically ponderous mehkan species that has a talent for commerce and trade. Their hunchbacks are fertile biomes used to grow a staggering variety of goods, from which they always seek to profit.

function mehkans who adhere to the Way believe this to be their spiritual purpose in life, a unique reason for every individual's existence that, if discovered and pursued, will lead to enlightenment.

Fuselage a langyl settlement in the Chusk Bowl that has been destroyed by the Foundry.

fusion mehkan term for midday, when the ring of rising suns coalesces in a singular zenith.

gauge mehkan currency of metallic rings. The worth of individual units, or "tinklets," is indicated by the size and color of the ring.

Gauge Pit a black market in the mehkan city of Sen Ta'rine, featuring an auction house that specializes in slave trade.

gears of fate a term used in the Way, referring to the aspect of Makina's plan that influences the lives of all sentient beings and how they impact one another.

Ghalteiga a squalid mehkan settlement on the Inro Coast with a reputation for lawlessness.

gha-tullei a mehkan word for "sanctuary."

gohr a physically imposing mehkan species with crane-claw hands that honors warriors above all else. Known for their brute strength.

The Grand Mark a prominent landmark in the mehkan city of Bhorquvaat, from which the city derives its name. It is a massive crater surrounded by concentric rings of white, petrified waves of ore. The Waybound claim this is an impact crater formed when Makina smote the wicked mehkans who once lived there.

The Great Decay an era that began with the appearance of humans in Mehk. The Waybound claim that the Great Decay

is a result of mehkans losing faith in Makina, which led to the decline of the Way, widespread enmity among mehkan species, the dissolution of mehkan society, and the rise of the Foundry's power.

The Great Engineer a holy name for Makina.

Greinadoren a human nation that is a prominent member of the Quorum with a sophisticated military and an agency known for espionage.

Haizor a prominent mehkan language.

The Heap a mehkan ghetto in the city of Sen Ta'rine, home to refugees displaced by the Foundry's incursions.

Hearth a secretive method of communication used by the Covenant, in which remote individuals can speak and be seen through surfaces of specialized molten metal.

hiveling (e.g. "Tchiock") a rare and reviled mehkan species that is said to have been bred as slaves for the ancient megalarchs. These amphibious monstrosities are cruel and fearsome, almost never seen outside the lagoons of dead lands.

hohksyk (e.g. "Korluth") a gentle race of mehkans that can eject a self-propelled liquid metal, which acts as a remote sensory organ. This ability makes them experts of surveillance.

hoistvyne a sturdy mehkan ivy that functions like an organic block-and-tackle pulley system, used in lifts and elevators.

Housing a temple of the Way.

Housing of the Broken temple of the Way that serves as a sanctuary and hospital to mehkans with handicaps or deformities.

Hy'rekshi jungle a lush and expansive region of Mehk known for its staggering biodiversity.

ichor the viscous, dark brown life essence of many mehkans.

indruli a trained, nocturnal mehkan beast, known for its aggression if roused from sleep.

Inro Coast the craggy western shoreline of the Mirroring Sea in Mehk.

interval mehkan term for "season."

jaislid (e.g. Axial Phy) members of a populous species of mehkan that commonly work as drones and laborers, often considered second-class citizens.

jelyp oceanic mehkan critters with tubular shells that emit jets of pressure for locomotion.

kailiak (e.g. Orei) a harsh and solitary mehkan species, whose bodies are precise instruments of measurement, allowing them near-psychic mathematical insight. They are averse to emotion, which can inhibit their ability to measure, thereby putting them at risk of physical harm.

Kallorax an ancient mehkan megalarch, notorious for his sadism and delusions of being a sun god.

Kappermane a northern state in the nation of Meridian, home to Albright City and famous for its natural beauty.

kav'o living mehkan weapons rumored to be bonded to and wielded by the Aegis.

Kholghit a mehkan city that has banned the consumption of viscollia, leading to a ruthless black market in illicit liquor.

Kijyo Republic a human nation in the Far East that is a founding member of the Quorum, openly hostile toward Meridian.

knurler a small oceanic mehkan scavenger known for its impervious grip when it clings to surfaces.

kulha a peaceful mehkan species with a nomadic tribal culture.

lacepetal frilly mehkan vegetation used for decoration and tribute.

langyl, aka "lang" an industrious mehkan species notable for their bizarre sheet-metal appearance. They tend grundrulls and harvest chusk fiber from their excrement to make textiles.

Lateral Provinces the larger, western mehkan continent and its various principalities.

liodim giant mehkan beasts with segmented shells and tank tread feet. They live in herds and are routinely hunted by the Foundry.

Loaii honorific term for a Waybound who is chosen to serve Makina for a specific purpose. Named for a mythical mehkan saint.

Lodestar XC-8 non-lethal Foundry weapon, a baton topped by a powerful magnetic coil that can repel and attract.

lumilow, aka "lumie" (e.g. The Marquis) an advanced race of mehkans who have bodies of prehensile tubing and communicate using a visual language of light. Their insular culture is renowned for discoveries in science and engineering and has a reputation for arrogance.

"Maddox" popular Televiewer show about a heroic soldier from Meridian. "No guts, no glory" is the title character's catchphrase.

Makina a mehkan god worshipped by the Waybound, believed to have created the universe and said to have abandoned Mehk because Her followers strayed from the righteous path.

megalarch title for ancient mehkan emperors.

Mehk a mysterious realm of living metal and organic machines. It is connected to our world by an underground portal, which is hidden and controlled by the Foundry.

mehkans, aka "mehkie" term for all the creatures of Mehk, both sentient and non-sentient.

Meridian the most prosperous nation in the human world, due entirely to the wealth and success of the Foundry.

Mirroring Sea a vast ocean of flux that surrounds the two main continents of Mehk.

Moalao a third-world nation of the human world, active member of the Quorum.

Mother of Ore a holy name for Makina.

Multi-Edge a Foundry-made survival knife with a versatile blade that can transform into multiple practical tools with the turn of a dial.

NET system a lattice of magnetic cables and tubes suspended over the Depot to prevent aerial attacks.

Nhel K'taphen mine a mehkan ore quarry on the eastern continent, now under the control of the Foundry.

nozzle the spinning, cylindrical organ that gives balvoors their advanced sense of smell.

Occulyth a mysterious object sought by the Ona to save Mehk.

ohneshalo a mehkan device that emits a distinctive moan, used during the funeral ceremonies of the Waybound.

Olyrian Isle an opulent and isolated community where Foundry employees who were stationed in Mehk retire. Though they live their remaining years in luxury, communication with the outside world is strictly prohibited to protect company secrets.

The Ona fabled prophet of the Way, she was Makina's messenger and the living interpreter of the sacred accords. The Ona was renowned for her wisdom and strength as leader of Mehk until she was supposedly killed by the Foundry in a surprise CHAR attack.

opticle versatile sensory organ of the lumilow that can both receive visual information as well as project various wavelengths of light.

ore the primal mehkan substance that all living metal comes from. It is thought by the Waybound to originate from the physical body of Makina.

Overguard military commanders in the Covenant.

Panzamine medication for managing motion sickness and nausea.

phase a mehkan unit of time, roughly equivalent to a year.

pinpod small mehkan critters that burrow into surfaces and pucker to take in air.

Primal Age a mythical era the Waybound consider the beginning of time.

puddlemudge a mehkan expletive.

quadrit a mehkan unit of measurement, roughly equivalent to two meters.

The Quorum an alliance among several nations of the human world that feel threatened by Meridian's supremacy and vehemently oppose its trade policies.

ragleaf a common mehkan weed that is highly reflective, though it degrades rapidly when trimmed or plucked.

Rathskellar an ill-reputed tavern in the seaside settlement of Ghalteiga.

Rattletrap the most common language in Mehk.

Rekindling a mehkan astronomical event involving swirls of colored starlight. This spectacle has religious significance to the Waybound.

rot-pox a gruesome, degenerative mehkan disease that causes premature decomposition among tchurbs.

rust the mehkan term for "death."

Rust Risen fabled home of the ancient and dreaded Uaxtu.

rustgut a mehkan ailment caused by the consumption of water.

rusting rites funeral ceremony for the Waybound.

sacred machine all of Makina's creation, the entirety of the universe, according to the Waybound.

salathyl a peaceable, sentient mehkan species that is subterranean and massive in size, used by the Covenant as a secretive method of travel.

salathyl prong a mehkan device shaped like a spike that emits a signal when planted in the ground in order to summon a nearby salathyl.

Scrollbar a handheld tablet Computator made by the Foundry.

Sea Bullet a high-powered Foundry speedboat that can be retrofitted with a magnetic operating system for use in flux.

Sen Ta'rine, aka "The Living City" one of several mehkan metropolises constructed out of the towering sendrite growths that give these cities their "Sen" prefix.

sendrite a gigantic species of mehkan vegetation, cultivated as living architecture in major cities.

The Shroud the afterlife, according to the Way. It is a physical place in Mehk, a wall of dense, obscuring fog where Makina is said to reside and judge the embers of the dead. It remains unexplored by both humans and mehkans.

silver steppes a mehkan region of barren plains that conduct heat in such a way as to be impassable during the day.

Sliverytik a mehkan gambling game. Players assemble a set of curved rods marked with symbols into a formation that rearranges itself as new rods are added.

span mehkan term for "lifetime."

sungold a brilliant, extraordinarily reflective mehkan material, so rare it is thought to no longer exist. It was once used to create religious artifacts for the Way.

tahnik bulbous mehkan vegetation with branching tendrils, capable of growing to tremendous size.

The Talons a harrowing, spiky reef in the Mirroring Sea that is infamous for destroying ships.

tchurb a pathetic species of diminutive mehkan, regarded as the untouchable bottom-feeders of society. The arrival of humans in Mehk introduced rot-pox, a contagious genetic scourge that afflicts only tchurbs.

thiaphysi a sophisticated, highly empathetic race of mehkans who prize artistic expression above all else. By touching their hands to the moving, helical bands that surround their sprocketed bodies, thiaphysi can create both speech and music.

tick a mehkan unit of time, roughly equivalent to a minute.

tinklet an individual unit of mehkan currency.

Titan giant military automaton made by the Foundry with advanced intelligence and powerful cannons.

tiulu an intimidating mehkan race with chainsaw forelimbs on bodies reminiscent of praying mantises. Although they are farmers and vegetarians, they are fiercely competitive and known to subjugate jaislids for slave labor.

torch bloom colloquial term for a carnivorous mehkan plant with flowers that burst into flame when their stamens are touched.

Trel slang for a person from Trelaine.

Trelaine proud human nation that is a founding member of the Quorum and has been in protracted peace talks with Meridian for years.

Uaxtu, aka "ember-reaper" a mythical cult of ancient mehkans, rumored to have conducted unspeakable rituals to resurrect the dead. It is said their spirits were cursed to wander for eternity like ravenous ghosts, devouring life to feed their empty souls.

vaptoryx a flying mehkan predator that snares its prey with musical tripwire.

vesper an oily, orange liquid found in streams, rivers, and lakes throughout Mehk, as vital to mehkans as water is to humans.

viscollia a popular mehkan liquor distilled from augurweed.

vital component a term used in the Way to refer to those who have pursued their function to the fullest and have become enlightened.

volmerid, aka "vol" a gruff mehkan species covered with shaggy steel wool, distinguished by their oversized right arms and prehensile chain fingers. This species has earned a reputation of being grunts and thugs.

VooToo, aka "Vesper to H_2O Conversion Unit" a Foundry-made device used to convert vesper to water.

Vo-Pykaron Mountains a prominent range of living mountains in the Lateral Provinces of Mehk.

V-Stalker a Foundry surveillance automaton with powerful olfactory sensors, highly adept at tracking.

Ward of Broken lighthouse beacon of the Housing of the Broken. Its precious sungold reflector was stolen long ago.

Watchmen Foundry-made automatons with advanced intelligence that serve a variety of functions from menial labor to foot soldier, capable of complex multitasking.

The Way an ancient and nearly extinct religion that worships a deity named Makina. The fundamental tenets of the faith have to do with living a compassionate life, finding one's spiritual function, and serving the rest of creation.

Waybound a term for those devoted to the ancient religion of the Way.

Waypoint ancient altars of the Way scattered across Mehk, where travelers once made devotional offerings in exchange for blessings from Makina.

whist a ceremonial shawl that has the remarkable ability to mute all sound, bestowed by the Waybound to the loved one of a martyr.

wryl a gargantuan, oceanic mehkan creature with a dangerous array of tusks. Because they have simple brains that can be mechanically modified to make the creatures docile, pirates and marauders often use wryls as a deadly means of conveyance.

Wycik a remote mehkan hamlet built amid the Arcs, considered primitive.

For a complete glossary with illustrations, go to booksofore.com.